LILITH'S BABY

Dar Kerr

BLACK FLAG
ANARCHO-PUBLISHING

Lilith's Baby

We nearly lost you to Lilith, Gabe. Love you loads and loads.

BOOK ONE

'Kerr's writerly gifts are impressive'
JOYCE CAROL OATES

THE
DAO OF THE
WITCH

DAR KERR

If you do not open the gates for me to come in,
I shall smash the door and shatter the bolt,
I shall smash the door-post and overturn the doors,
I shall raise up the dead, and they shall eat the living,
And the dead shall outnumber the living.

THE DESCENT OF ISHTAR

What is now in preparation and will quite definitely come to
pass on Earth in a none too distant future is an actual
incarnation of Ahriman.

RUDOLF STEINER, *The Influences of Lucifer and Ahriman*

EVA'S PREGNANCY

Eva was perched on the toilet seat. Her hands trembling as she tore open the plastic wrapper.

She'd felt it in her breasts, which had been heavy, tender to touch these last two weeks. And in her belly, a strange pulling-down.

That metallic tang in her mouth, like her gums were bleeding. Tell-tale sign, too.

All the going to the loo-ing, sitting there reading The Tattooist of Auschwitz, but nothing was happening.

Classic symptom. Constipation. Known to midwives. Taught to nurses like Sister Eva Kadmon. Her body was telling her in its own language: You are going to have a baby. Your baby might be the size of a poppy seed in your womb, but in eight months you will be giving birth.

But, thing was, her body was a joker. Her body had pranked her twice before. So, it was time to take a test. Get confirmation.

With her blue scrubs and frilly red knickers round her ankles, she was just about to pee on a stick to find out, yay or nay. So tense, it was hard to pee on that stick. Because if the test was positive, it would change everything.

Talk about Freak-out Central. This was what a pregnancy test could do to an Englishwoman in the Hebrew Year 5778 (what the Goy insisted was 2018 A.D.); even a married Englishwoman, who aged 26, should really know her own mind.

It was three days after she should have had her period. Two days after doctors, midwives, fertility experts, instructed women to use the test. Clearblue claimed you could use it four days before your period, but that was a bit silly, given that hCG levels could only be detected in 53% of women at that stage.

hCG stood for Human Chorionic Gonadotrophin. That was what the pregnancy test detected in the urine—if it was there. Please be there.

Testing, testing, the tingle of excitement, swelling in her belly. Was this an hCG high, or the result of holding it all in, literally, for three hours, no beverages?

She held the strip in position and then peed. All over the strip. And, her fingers. For way longer than the five seconds needed.

Messy cow.

Sister Eva Kadmon intended to be more clinical. She pulled the stick out from between her legs, and shook the warm wee off, into the wash basin.

She held the stick out like a magic wand.

The Law of Attraction. They would have a beautiful, healthy, baby boy. His name would be Abel. Abel would grow up big and strong, wise and wonderful, save the world from evil, and live happily ever after.

Eva and Adamo joked about Genesis.

Enjoyed revising Genesis.

The Temptation.

The Fall. It all never really happened. She was a thoroughly Modern Jew, with a few Buddhist tendencies, and Adamo was certainly no Evangelical Goy. Their mockery of holy scripture wasn't blasphemy.

Genesis was not literally the word of God. Genesis was just a bunch of myths, full of metaphors, like the serpent, and the woman, and the tree, to explain the miracle of human life, and the beginnings of consciousness, being in time, and the no-thingness of infinity.

It should take two minutes for lines to appear in the oval window of the stick.

Two minutes...

Bang goes the Sauv Blanc—if this is positive. For nine months.

When was the last time you got wasted?

Jesus. Last Saturday.

What if the baby is already brain-damaged...? Too much responsibility. Too much everything.

What if she got hyperemensis gravidarium and was vomming every morning, baby bulimia?

Okay, Eva. Stop thinking. Just breathe. Mindfulness.

Mindfulness. "I am whole," she said. "I am creative. I am capable of change."

A horizontal line manifested in the oval window. "I am enough. I have enough. I am doing enough. I accept myself and my life fully right now. It's always now. It's always now. It's always now."

A vertical line appeared in the oval window, intersecting the horizontal, forming a cross.

A cross—the sign of the cross, meant she was going to have a baby. She laughed. "I am going to have a baby. We are going to have a baby." After 12 months of I.V.F. Fertility cycle mapping.

Ovulation timing. Fucking, to fucking exhaustion. Propping her ass up in the air with pillows afterwards. Fail. Fail again.

Despair. Fail better.

Fail worse. Fail completely to conceive naturally. Endure a cycle of I.V. egg harvesting.

Ex vivo fertilization with Adamo's squigglers. A viable embryo! Implantation into the wall of the uterus finally connected her baby to her.

All worth it in the end, every bit. Smiling, beaming actually, she held the stick up again—to be sure. The cross on the stick darkened from light blue to navy blue, rapidly turning black.

The cross got darker and then, like the ink was running, black started to ooze out of the window of the stick. So, she dropped it.

Vile blackness spattered on the white tiles. More, trickled out of the stick like it was a pen, a fountain pen spurting ink.

Ink flowing, into the runnels of the grouting. Spreading into the cracks of a fractured tile. Sketching out the outstretched talon of a bird of prey.

Small. Like an owl's...? As if in a trance, she stared at the clawing, broken white floor tile, scared to blink again, until her eyes dried out. *Why an owl, though?*

She blinked, involuntarily, several times in rapid succession. The blackness disappeared.

She was unable to believe her eyes. She leaned forward and snatched up the stick.

The cross on the strip. The cross. No ink.

Did she just imagine the ink running? She heard Adamo's voice telling her:

It's just a projection of your fear.

The fear of being pregnant.

The terror of impregnation, which every woman nursed.

Pregnancy, and giving birth, having been the death of millions of women. Anything could go wrong. The littlest thing, and you might lose the baby, or your whole life. To be pregnant is to be at your most vulnerable.

She would repeat the test. *To be sure, to be sure, begorrah,* as her dad would sometimes quip. Ever the Irish Jew, not English, even after decades of exile in North Leeds. Her late dad would have been so chuffed. It broke her heart that he would never play the role of Zaydee, that her child would never know him.

Testing, testing... Peeing, take-two.

The resurrection of the cross in the window of the stick.

No repeat of the horrible blackness.

She was pregnant. For sure. Which meant: she absolutely-positively would not tell Adamo about her hallucination.

There would be no talk of evil omens. No. That would spoil his joy. A lie of omission was called for.

THE LAWRENCE HOUSE

N ed stank, meaty and salty. Ripe as a corpse. The blaze of the midday sun popped beads of sweat from his brow, yet here in Syria, he was shivering, shaking, in his cricket blazer, as if it were winter in Oxford.

Drink, Aurens! he heard Saleem say, clear as day.

Saleem was not at the table, nowhere to be seen, actually. Still, he would obey, cupping his hands around the glass of bitter tea. Wormwood. Warmth radiated through his palms. A star named Wormwood. Heating his bones, the marrow. The third angel blew his trumpet and a great star fell from the heavens.

Drink, Saleem would nag.

So, he sipped at his tea. Rancid. So bitter, the hot sourness rushed to his stomach, he gagged, nearly retched, but he held his gorge from rising.

Wormwood did nothing to stop the quake of chills. The vile heat within seemed rather to accentuate the cold without, and he quivered, simply couldn't stop quivering. Dancing St. Vitus' Dance.

Which meant the fever was surely breaking...? The heavy malarial fug giving way to anarchic jitters. Chitter-chatter of teeth. *Dear God, make it stop.* It was as if he was in the grip of terror. A deep, deep dread, all the symptoms of dread.

I must get back to work. The excavation of the foundations of the round town house was due to be complete by the end of November 1913. Or Shawwal, 1331, reckoning by the Islamic Calendar.

The round house would, in time, become known as 'The Lawrence House', but Ned himself referred to it as 'The Black Lodge' because the earth was scorched inside the walls.

The black tell had been sifted, stratum by stratum. Whatever they found in the dark entrails of the earth had been examined, tagged, and shipped to the British Museum. The ephemera of the material world. Small matters, like a spill of a rich woman's ivory and ebony beads. Glyptics.

Phalli.

Saleem unearthed some nice Hittite bronze pendants.

A burnished clay pot, Assyrian. The bones of a bird, likely a chicken, flattened into a mud-pie.

The strata of History. Thousands of years sieved in these last two years.

It had been a lot of work for little reward, and yet something told him to keep digging. Nothing really exceptional had been discovered here, until the crystal.

He had happened across it, in the wall of an exploratory trench in the left-hand corner, buried in the black dirt.

A blue crystal.

Dusting ever so gently with the brush, disclosing the gleaming point. Bright. So clear, despite the flaws, the clouds locked within the azure.

The way it reflected the sunlight seared his eyes. He had to work on it whilst looking away, or go blind.

Chipping away at the black dirt using a specially sharpened teaspoon. With much care, he was able to remove it from the encrusting earth, to remove all of it from the dirt. Longer than the span of his hand, nine inches possibly, it was heavy for its size. Dense.

Holding it up to the heavens. Revealing a polished, cut exterior. Squinting at it, with wonder. Six facets, he counted, hexagonal, cut with such precision, sheering down from the pommel, to the sharpest point. Like a dagger. His fingers thrummed with the palpable energy emanating from it. Power, raw power.

No Assyrian made this. It was terrifically out of place. Surely not Babylonian? Nor was it Sumerian. It didn't look at all Egyptian. How could they have carved it so precisely? The technique was otherworldly, he felt.

He showed the crystal to Saleem first. In the privacy of their tent.

A sudden terror crossed the boy's face. He shook his head, wincing as if in pain. Shrank away. "This is evil, Aurens."

"It's lapis lazuli, actually."

Saleem ran from their tent.

The Druse were a superstitious lot. Ned put it down to that, and took the blasted thing to Hogarth, the Oxford Don who knew everything.

Except, Hogarth didn't know. "It doesn't look at all Semitic, Neddy-Boy. Might be Ur, or Earlier. We shall send it back to London, see what they say."

A sharp toot-toot of steam, dusted his thoughts back to the present.

He shifted his legs under the table. He located the sound—over on the far shore of the Euphrates. A steam train. Hauling a long line of freight boxcars. About to cross the Baghdad Railway bridge that spanned what The Bible referred to as 'The River'.

This was why he was really here.

Amongst the ruins of Karkemish. In the sprawl of mud-brick buildings situated on the southern shore of the Euphrates, what the Arabs called 'Jerablus'. To keep an eye on the Germans, as they built the line for the Turks.

To spy.

The archaeology was a cover story. Because the British wanted to smash the Ottoman Empire before it became too Modern, and thus able to compete.

Hogarth was ex-Naval Intelligence, and recruited Ned at Oxford because of his background in Medieval Archaeology, and his extraordinary fluency in Arabic, French, and German.

This amazing desert double-life was the gift of the Arab Bureau, and what a gift it had been. Three years of bliss, the happiest sojourn, even as the storm clouds of a great war stacked, black and foreboding, on the horizon.

The reason was Saleem.

Or, more precisely, the man Saleem made him. Master and manservant. They could be much more open here than back home. Live together.

In sin, but also, innocently. Hogarth turned a blind eye. The Arab diggers tolerated their relationship with a scandalised acceptance.

The crystal, though.

It had changed things between them, somehow. Nothing would ever be the same again. Saleem was very disturbed, having bad dreams, calling out in his sleep.

When questioned, the boy claimed he knew the bright stone was of the djinn. "The Druze know. My father was a Knower. I am a Knower. The Knower's dreams are full of the Dark-Haired Woman, *Am klu amshayitan.*"

He had to look this phrase up, after the fact. It translated from Arabic as: 'the Mother of All Demons.'

He wanted to tell Hogarth this revelation, but it was too late. The crystal had been sent home to Blighty, and the malarial parasites infecting his blood, those blighters, had other ideas. The fever came on so strong it had him bed- and chair-ridden for five long days.

Dark dreams of a toadstool giving birth to a man-dragon. A theriomorphic sense he was become the Dragon, incinerating first London, then the whole world. Ashes to ashes.

Dust to dust.

Salim stayed by Ned's side, day and night, through Arthurian hallucinations, in which Nimue, the Lady of the Lake, promised to make his boyhood dreams of becoming the most famous, chivalrous knight ever come true—if only he would return Excalibur to her. Excalibur, and the Grail.

Back in the ruins, Saleem nursed him into the acceptable degree of madness known as 'sanity', with the bark of the cinchona tree, bitter with quinine, and gallons of the ghastly, gastric tea.

Wormwood: the mind-altering source of the Bohemian's 'Green

Fairy', absinthe, that 'Devil in a Bottle.' He would not be sitting here right now, overlooking the Euphrates, without that damned tea.

"More tea, Aurens?" Saleem emerged from their tent, carrying a pewter pot of tea, nimbly scaling the slope, kicking up dust in Russian-made shoes he wore like slippers.

The dark of Saleem's shadow slipped over the table. "Thank you, Saleem, for taking such good care of me."

Saleem nodded. Placed the new pot of revolting concoction on the table. Removed the old.

"Tell Hogarth. He must bury it. She make you sick, this woman. I see it, what is in the stone. Fire. It is the end of the world."

Ned sighed. "Do try not to be so melodramatic, Salim. I will be perfectly all right. Right as rain by tomorrow. You will see."

DADDYDOM

Zionism: How the Future determines the Present, and the Past. The premise of Dr. Adamo Kadmon's late afternoon lecture at Birkbeck University. After the performance of this exercise in retro-causality, he rushed home. Bloomsbury to Kilburn Park, on the Tube.

He couldn't wait to see Eva. To tell her what he'd discovered that day, and to listen to her news. The shifts she worked in the I.C.U. generally got in the way of this connection, and it became a speed-download sometimes.

This would likely be one of those days, so he wouldn't get his hopes up. She'd been on nights this week. Graveyard Shift. Maybe he'd get 10 minutes of quality time before she had to leave for U.C.H.

Missing her—in between every single heartbeat, that need to be with her. Absence did not make the heart grow fonder. It pissed him off.

Thoroughly. But, it couldn't be helped.

Critical Care was Intensive. Sometimes, he dreamt the most vivid dreams, that he was a crash victim, a long-time coma patient, whose only life was in dreams, dreams of getting back into the I.C.U. Returning to consciousness just to be with her, Sister Eva.

The bright-red front door of No. 235 Kilburn Park: he would enter, and slam it shut behind him. Sifting through the spray of junk-mail and utility bills on the hallway floor.

Stuffing two for him, and one for her, under his arm—along with *The Daily Mail* he'd stolen out of a university café because the front-page headline made him absolutely, totally livid: *ANTI-SEMITISM DEFILES THE LABOUR PARTY*.

Adamo took the stairs, two-at-a-time. Long, strong legs, making short work of the two flights. Up to their second-floor flat. Flat 3. And flat, it was. Original Kilburn. Non-gentrified. Non-chic. Non-glam. Not big enough to be deemed an apartment. A turn of the key in the front door and click!, it unlocked. "Eva..? I'm home!"

She ran out of the bedroom in blue scrubs, beaming as she hugged him. A big kiss on the lips.

"Well now. Looks like somebody's had a good day being Mrs. Couch Potato?"

"I really did. I've got news for you."

"Look at this for news." He held up The Daily Mail, pointed at the headline. "The icing on top of the Brexit bulldog."

"Time for us to move to Israel."

"No shit!" He nodded. "What's your news?"

"Doesn't matter... I have to go to work."

"Come on. Tell me!"

"It'll keep." She turned, went to the door. Lifted her coat, then her handbag off the hooks. "Don't want to be late."

"Hey." He squeezed her from behind, wrapping her up in a big bear-hug. "I'm sorry that I upset you with that fascist crap."

"It's not that."

She tried to wriggle out of his arms.

"I'm not letting go until you fess-up."

"I'm. Pregnant."

He looked down, deep into her eyes. "You sure?"

"Couldn't be later."

"Wow." He could not help smiling. "That is news!"

"Yeah. And, for my next trick—work!"

She broke out of the bear hug.

"No way... You can't go in after that. Cry off!"

She slipped her arms into her coat.

"You know I can't cry off."

"Okay! Go save some lives! If that's so bloody important to you."

"Hey! I am off for three-days-straight after this shift. Thank the Lord for small mercies.'

Looping her handbag over her shoulder, she opened the door.

A kiss, blown.

"Love you."

"Love you too, Woman. I'm bunking-off tomorrow. We'll go out to lunch, yeah?"

"Yeah. Fatten me up."

She blew him another kiss as she left.

He sighed, gazed up at the full-size print of the Queen of Modern Art, Tamara de Lempicka's 'Adamo ed Eva' that hung pride-of-place over the fireplace. Art Deco ass cheeks and post-Cubist cone-titty. So spiky. Distorted. Fractal. He didn't know why Eva liked it so much, for the life of him.

For dinner, he microwaved up a sad-singleton's singed-at-the-edges Red Thai curry. He would binge on it, and a hefty serving of *Twin Peaks: The Return*.

Episode 4 was a total head-melt—it was like he'd fallen asleep and was dreaming—but he was really rooting for Good Coop to escape from the Black Lodge and replace the infuriating Dougie. He had to hope David Lynch (F.B.I. Agent Gordon Cole) could nail Bad Coop, the Other, the doppëlganger, the 'tulpa', locked up in prison.

After the episode ended, he was left wondering: What the hell is 'Blue Rose'? He felt compelled to watch on, find out whether Blue Rose was connected to Project Blue Book, and the alien presence.

After Episode 5 started, son-of-a-bitch, the wonder of real, actual life, hit home. *Dada!* That sense that things were meant to happen the way they did, swelled in his chest. An almost religious feeling for an atheist, well, agnostic.

Adamo Kadmon, Historian with a capital 'H', had been suspending disbelief in Life, capital 'L'. And not just since his wife told him her good news tonight. But for a long time.

Maybe his whole adult life?

Certainly, since the accident, age 20.

The Crash.

Not daring to believe fully in the goodness of life. The hope.

The love at the heart of it all.

The oneness.

There was so much joy in him, he simply had to phone his mum, the woman who brought him into the world, Helena Kadmon, and tell her the good news: "Eva is preggers. You're going to be a granny."

"That's wonderful news... Oh, Adamo! It's so... I'm so pleased for you both."

Nadine, her wife, started sobbing.

"I'm going to be a dad," he said. *A dad. Daddy!* That title seemed so downright odd because he didn't get to call his dad, 'Daddy', because the man left. Left home. And, never came back.

"You guys must come over tomorrow. We'll celebrate, yes?"

"Offer accepted."

"Say one-thirty?"

"We'll be there."

VISCOUNT
ARMAGEDDON

The sun, low on the horizon, like Mars visiting with Earth. The last pink-purpled embers of Day dying, dying away. Night, an army of shadows, pungent with jasmine, slipped into the city of Cairo.

This forever war of Dark on Light, was observed from atop the Semiramis Hotel, in the roof-garden, by the blue-eyed, modern-day crusader known across the world by 1921 as 'Lawrence of Arabia.' T. E. Lawrence. T for Thomas. E for Edward. 'Lawrence' for bastard.

"I would happily kill her," someone yelled from the bar.

Churchill. Tongue at full tilt. Outlandishly drunk. Railing to any boozers who would listen about his hideous monster mother, 'Lady Randy' and her latest scandalizing outrage.

The Air Marshall and Air Vice Marshall were his unlucky audience tonight; these new Lords of the Power of the Air, given dominion over King Feisal's Iraq.

Churchill might have been a great statesman, but he really was a bore in the late evenings. A mama's bore. Better to abstain, tea-totally, than to rant like an idiot.

Or a madman.

Ned, the man the Arabs named 'Aurens', detached from that alias;

positioning himself off-side in the roof garden. He needed space, not to think, to simply be.

Churchill's '40 Thieves' had gorged themselves at the banquet—an Imperial ceremonial feast at which he alone ate raw lotus root. The Blue Lotus. Nymphaea Caerulea. The flower of the gods of Egypt.

His fellow conference delegates found that frightfully odd.

Lawrence the Lotus-eater, hahaha. It is almost impossible to excuse the ignorance of the wilfully ignorant.

Field Marshal Allenby, Viscount of Armageddon, was the first Thief to track him down. In fine fettle he was, after his promotion to High Commissioner, circling the Hine brandy in his snifter as he searched for the right words. "As this is your last night in Cairo, I wanted to thank you Lawrence, for your help with Egypt."

He nodded, said nothing, staring out at the Nile, 'the Father of Rivers', as a felucca glided under the Kasr El-Nil bridge in the falling dark. At half-sail to catch the last of the breeze. Timeless.

Allenby added: "I think this model of democratic government might work a tad better than well, other more favoured propositions."

He smiled, broadly, fondly, knowing that Allenby would appreciate this rare gift from him. "You will make it work, sir."

"Alas, I'm not sure old generals make very good governors as a rule. Certainly not ones with nicknames like 'Bloody Bull'." Allenby raised his glass. "Still, I'll do my damnedest to keep their canal open for business."

"Yes, indeed. Mustn't aggravate John Company." The least and most that could be said about Allenby was that he was a good soldier. The 'good' was something that could be understood by a child or a savage or a soldier, any simpleminded person. It was just a feeling that man and boy got from him. A fatherly feeling. His legendary fury was always tempered by his paternalism, a knightly sense of honour.

"Hail, Great Pharaoh Hynman-Allenby!" A shadowman appeared out of the palm trees behind them.

Allenby laughed. "Hail, Vizier Mein."

'Vizier Mein' was Lt. Colonel Richard Meinertzhagen. The Field Marshal's 'Left-hand-man'. Head of Military Intelligence, Middle East Department.

6'4" of unadulterated menace. The absolute best one could say of Meinertzhagen was that he was a bad man, but one who would in no way deny this charge. In fact, with every anecdote, every boast, he gleefully handed more evidence to the prosecution.

It was Meinertzhagen who had air-dropped opium-laced tobacco pouches on the Turkish Lines before the third battle of Gaza, Geneva Convention be damned.

It was Meinertzhagen who conceived and executed the 'Haversack Ruse', in which false battle plans for the push to Jerusalem were allowed to fall into enemy hands. Malice positively radiated off the fellow. Waves. Of pure contempt. Directed at the Darkies. The Chinks. The Camel Jockeys. Everyone else in the whole world.

Perhaps Meinertzhagen had a point—a greater sense of humanity seemed a forlorn hope these days. That oneness one felt sometimes, when say gazing up at the stars at night.

Whatever happened to that cosmic consciousness? Modern mass-and-massacring man being so very out of touch with what the ancients valued. The Primordial Man. The Great Man. The Anthropos. 'Adam Kadmon', as the Jewish mystics called him.

"Hail to the Kingmaker of the day," Meinertzhagen said, lifting his whiskey tumbler. "I hate to butt-in as the Yanks would say, but I need a word with you, Chapman, before you bring fire and sword to the Holy Land."

An affront.

To mention 'Chapman'. His secret shame. For 'Lawrence' was not his real surname. His father, Sir Thomas Robert Tighe Chapman, Baronet of Killua Castle, had assumed the name 'Lawrence' after he deserted his first wife, to live in sin with the nanny. Do not rise to Meinertzhagen, he told himself, Best to deny a fire the air it requires to breathe.

"You two gentlemen-adventurers will excuse me." Allenby downed the dregs of his brandy and set the glass down on a nearby table. "I don't envy you your task in Palestine, Lawrence, but I wish you every success. And, if I can be of any assistance in biffing the French, do not hesitate to ask."

"That's very kind of you, sir."

"We'll march north. The Frogs really do deserve a proper biffing over Syria."

"Yes, sir."

"Goodnight." With a nod, Allenby retired.

He stared over to the bar where Churchill was still holding court with the squadron of R.A.F. Staff, giving his stock-in-trade soapbox-speech about the struggle for the soul of the Jewish people: "Zionism simply must triumph over the evil of Communism."

"Winnie is steamboats," Meinertzhagen said. "I can't believe he fell off his camel today, can you?"

He ignored this. It occurred to him: The R.A.F. uniform is simply a cut above the other military orders. Soon, he'd be wearing that grey-blue hue, monkishly. Once this last crusade was over, the character of the Arabesque hero would quietly die-off, and be resurrected as Aircraftsman John Hume Ross— a man obsessed by machines. Planes. Tanks.

Power-boats. Most particularly, high-power motorcycles made by Brough, each of which in turn he would right-royally name 'George': George I, II, III, IV, V, VI, and the one he would die riding, George VII.

Meinertzhagen was chuckling away, at his own wit. "Blotto at noon, in front of the pyramids, witnessed by the world's press. I nearly split my sides. 'We are making History', indeed."

"And the Sphinx didn't even bat an eyebrow..."

Meinertzhagen sipped his whiskey. "Winnie did recover well. I'll give him that. Turned the remount and ride back here into a show of Great British resilience. You, most famed of the Camel Jockeys, at his side, offering advice."

"This feels like a creeping barrage, Meinertzhagen. Skip forwards to Zero Hour. I have a book to read."

"Oh, Aurens. Such a spoilsport. It was quite the softening-up I had in mind."

There was a steamer puffing down-river, trailing smoke behind her. He watched the crew of stickmen on deck being directed by their stick-captain.

Meinerzhagen did not like to be disregarded. "Didn't your mother ever tell you that strong, silent, little men are even more insufferable than strong, silent, big men?"

Silence, sharp as Excalibur.

"I am in receipt of intelligence reports sent today that state — regardless of the terms agreed at the conference—Abdullah is attacking the French, to restore his brother's honour."

"Your reports come from Zionist sources, of course?"

Meinertzhagen was doggedly Zionist, having run Aaron Aaronson's Nili cell until the carrier pigeons came home to roost—with the Turks hot on their tail-feathers.

"On the contrary, they come from a very anti-Semitic little birdy within the French 4th Division."

"With you being such a keen ornithologist—he would tweet-tweet that, wouldn't he?"

"My little birdy says that the French will invade Palestine, drive to Jerusalem, if they are attacked once more by Abdullah's bedu. They are mobilising forces to the Golan Heights with that plan in mind, right at this juncture."

"They would not dare."

"Ah. That's what you said before the French took Syria."

He sighed. "Here is what will happen, Meinertzhagen. Abdullah will meet Churchill in Jerusalem, and gratefully accept his new emirate of Transjordania, which he will rule as a British Mandate. Mark my words, that will keep the peace."

"If not, the Last Days, eh." Meinertzhagen's smile was grim.

"Armageddon, Mark II."

Meinertzhagen made a tactical withdrawal.

Left alone, he found himself smiling. There was something in him that appreciated chastisement, the way it deflated his sense of being the Lawrence of Arabia. He left the roof terrace lighter. Let the Forty Thieves go on with their backslapping, thinking they are going to kill Ali Baba. They haven't read The Book of a Thousand Nights and a Night, how Ali Baba has Morgiana, the slave-girl, to protect him. Her dance of the swords is yet to come.

Spiralling down, taking flights of the red-carpeted stairs, two at a time, to the lobby, which was decked out in bronze and marble, with knock-off ebony statues of Isis and Osiris for the tourists.

Such ostentation made him positively Bolshevik!

This was largely why he stayed at the Grand Continental. An altogether more elegant hotel. Run by an old Swiss family. Touch of class did it; that, and the Botanical Gardens, for his morning constitutional.

When he got into his room, he laid his weary body down on a comfortable bed and opened the pages of his latest copy of *La Morte d'Arthur*. Therein, a commoner boy, a bastard, drew a sword from a stone and became king. Mallory's Romance was his one true travelling companion, his oldest and best-loved friend, whose story he would always suspend disbelief in.

GOOD NEWS
GRANDMAS

The Bakerloo Line. A reedy, young Chinese wouldn't stop eyeing-up Eva in the carriage. His eyes, eating her alive. The intensity of his gaze. Super-uncomfortable. She glared back. Let her defiance show.

But he kept looking. Would not stop.

Adamo picked up on her discomfort, and with a single, hard glance pinned the Chinese's gaze to the floor.

She loved that her husband was a big, big man. 6'6" tall. Adamo's father was German, of all things...German. She would not bring herself to use the tainted, Nazified word, Aryan, but she liked it that other men cowed in the presence of his sheer physical power, or fawned, acknowledging him as 'Big Man'.

No one would ever suspect him of being a History lecturer at U.C.L., even when he dressed all tweedy like an academic. Dandified Harris-checks could not disguise his alpha-ness.

They changed at Piccadilly Circus for Knightsbridge.

Eva would rather be spending the afternoon with Adamo. But thanks to Mr. Big-blabbermouth-flobbychops, the cat was out of the bag. Helena and Nadine would have taken massive offence if they'd refused the offer of family lunch.

Which was a kind offer.

From two amazingly generous souls. One of whom was the nicest narcissist with bipolar disorder a person would ever meet.

The Great Nadine Nadiri would have been insufferable, but for Seroquel, Lithium, and the fact that she had been in Transpersonal Therapy for 20 years. She was a super-successful Brit Artist, up there with Damien Hirst, Tracey Emin, Grayson Perry, the Chapman Bros, whose early works sold for six-figures these days, thanks mainly to the hoarding instinct of Saatchi.

Small doses of medicated Nadine were fine. Entertaining. But, she had this power to drain people. To suck the life right out of the room.

Adamo had bundles of energy, and was by nature a giver, so he annoyingly didn't mind the vampire's bite, the kiss of the lamia. Quite the opposite, he enjoyed Nadine's batty stories about the world of high darlink, sweetie-luvvie culture. Laughable, in his view.

But, Eva Kadmon...

Hmm, not so keen on being drained of lifeblood, thank you. She believed there are two types of people, uppers and downers. Uppers inspire, ennit. Downers, nah.

It wasn't all bad. Nadine's narcissistic tendencies, and reflections on them, in the form of art, had purchased the dream house Adamo and Eva would be eating their celebratory lunch in. The five-bedroom Georgian end-terrace, worth £15.5 million.

£15.5 million! Nurses and lecturers like them, had zero chance of living in West London. Fat chance. It was full of the 0.01% who do nothing for a living, and proud of it. May as well be another dimension, she thought. And like aliens, they walked hand-in-hand from the Tube, into Knightsbridge: the most desirable, and expensive district in West London.

He sighed, deeply. "I even love the shitty parts of this neighbourhood."

"It's called homesickness. You're supposed to get over it as part of growing up."

"I know. I know. A man can dream, okay?"

She walked on, gazing up at the shabby-less-than-chic Georgian terraces, in contempt, more than in envy. They didn't even look like billionaires' mansions, sleb rezs. But, they were. The great and the good bought all the property here. Second homes. Third. Fourth. Sickening.

Final destination: Trevor Place. The couple turned into the tiny driveway of No 9 and walked up past the hers-n-hers Teslas, personalised reg plates SYZYGY 1 and SYZYGY 2, to the big, lurid pink door, shocking between the mock-Doric columns. A testament to Pink Power. The arty-fartyness of the Creative Industries.

She pulled the chain beside the pink door. The doorbell rang loudly.

Helena took a moment to get to the front door and open it. "Hello-hello-hello." She threw her arms up over her head, like a grey-haired kid, and stepped out to embrace her daughter-in-law. "Oh, Eva. I'm so thrilled."

Mwah-mwah-mwah.

"Congrats, son." Big-big-hugs over, Helena herded them inside.

In the hallway, Eva and Adamo automatically removed their shoes and slid on Japanese silk slippers. A house rule, amongst many a Nadine-enforced house rule.

"Nadine is prepping for a show,' said Helena. "So, it's like an artquake has struck in there."

Pink-haired Nadine was propping several black-framed black-and-white photos up against the wall. A big smile flashed. "Congrats, you two."

"Thanks, Nadine," she said.

"You're to call him Nadine—if it's a boy. I want my grandson to be all Trans-n-peculiar."

"Maybe," she replied, "if they're a girl."

"It's a ze, for sure." Nadine laughed, but her features hardly moved, paralysed by Botox.

As if, she thought. Staring down at a photo on the floor.

The top of an iPhone protruded from solid rock. The label: *The Jurassic iPhone*. Puzzlement.

"I'm calling the show 'Oops-arts' based on the idea of Ooparts. Out-of-place objects—to non-crypto-zoologists."

Helena tutted. "Speak English, dear."

"I'm trying to wind up the Young Earth Creationists by debunking their 'Christian Science', their ridiculous claims that there was a human presence long before humans evolved."

Helena looked very proud. "The clever thing has sold a shedload even before the show. Richard Dawkins bought three in a show of solidarity."

Nadine basked in her partner's admiration. "What can I say, Empiricists love me. Materialists want to have my Skeptical babies."

"That's amazing." She played her part in fluffing The Great Nadine Nadiri's ego with a couple more questions about the exhibition but, lacking the years of practice, she was nowhere near as good at ass-kissing as Helena or Adamo.

Nadine had hired an ethnic caterer for the celebration, and dinner was served on the sun terrace. Dinner was always lavish. Today was no let-down: a Kashmiri dish, Nadroo Yakhni, steamed lotus stems in a spicy yoghurt gravy. Everybody was really enjoying it, until Nadine brought up the subject of Kilburn. "You can't live in North London with a baby!"

"We'll have to," Eva said. "We don't really have a choice."

"Come West," Helena said. "Allow us Grannies to nanny."

Adamo laughed. "You know only Russkis, oil-sheiks and wanker-bankers can afford to live here now."

"Break into that empty house around the corner," Nadine said. "Squat. Occupy. That's what we did in the '70s. When we were punks."

"Yeah." Adamo tried not to sound bitter. "We could live the dream."

"Until the bailiffs, and the cops, arrive to crack heads," she said, trying not to be resentful. "Not exactly the ideal nursery, a squat."

"Oh, where's your inner punk, Eva?" Nadine was not going to let her off the hook.

"Okay-okay, Anarchy in the U.K.," she said. "We'll go view the dream house after dinner. What's the address?"

"8 Blackcross Crescent."

Adamo was beaming. Altogether lit up. "This is going to be completely ace."

GETHSEMANE

C hurchill was sitting out in the garden of Government House, behind an easel, daubing a view of Jerusalem onto a canvas.

Painting was Churchill's second favourite pastime. The first being—the making of History; not just the writing; the doing. All the devilment that it entailed.

Ned had no wish to talk about Impressionism or Imperialism and so avoided the garden, making his escape via a side door. Objective: The Garden of Gethsemane. Quick march, past the sentries' picket at the gates, down the Mount of Olives, into the grounds of the Church of All Nations.

Without escort, he went.

Unarmed.

Expressly against orders, given the current state of unrest amongst the Palestinian Arabs.

To the very grove where Christ prayed three times. "Father, if it be possible, let this cup pass from me, nevertheless not as I will, but as Thou wilt."

His temples were slick with chilling sweat; his imagination in a feverish state. 'The King of Diseases' had him in its grip again. Malaria.

Countless returns of it since he contracted it in France aged 16. He had taken triple the recommended dose of quinine to get through the day without his brains being boiled.

In this altered state, there was a yawning gap between the different parts of the mind, the thinking, and the doing. It was as if he was both the writer of his story and the character within it, and sometimes even the actor playing that character.

The gnarled olive trees in the Garden of Gethsemane were reputedly two millennia old. Biblical by 1921. The trunks, near-petrified.

He drifted around the well-trodden stone path prepared for pilgrims. Stifled a yawn with the back of his hand; had not slept a bloody wink because of the chill-sweats. Nerves bring it on.

Abdullah was coming to meet Churchill today. Finally, the 28th. And 'the Sharifian Solution' was unravelling. The Gordian Knot—it was not.

He stepped over the rock verge. Kicked a scrabble of stones away. Cleared a space to kneel-down.

Looked up, to the heavens.

It was hereabouts, under these branches, that Christ sat and sweated blood.

Here, Yeshua wept. *Flevit Super Illam.*

Here, he rebuked his disciples for falling asleep on watch. The spirit was willing, but the flesh was weak.

Here, he was betrayed. By his disciple, Judas. And taken by the Jews to be judged. Thenceforth, delivered to Pontius Pilate, to be sentenced: Death, by crucifixion.

A sacrifice, to expunge Adam and Eve's Original Sin.

To expiate humanity.

The Historical Christ. Was He real? This Yeshua. Never Jesus, for that was not His name. Did it really matter if the gospels were not the gospel truth? The story of the Christ burned so brightly in his childhood imagination.

Fired by Father James. A Jesuit priest, at the school in Dinard. Sweating blood was an actual condition, caused by extreme stress, called 'Hematadrosis'. That fascinated boy never dreamt that as a man he would someday kneel down here. Neddy-boy could pray to his Christ like a Templar.

Ned, the man, would not.

Not even for the miracle required to bring a lasting and just peace to Arabia. For Meinertzhagen was right, in all his wrongness, bang-on. The latest dispatches from Syria confirmed that Abdullah was rashly attacking French forces, using all of the petit warfare tactics his mentor Aurens employed against the Turks: ambushes, sabotage, hit-and-run raids.

But there was much graver news than that. Intelligence reports from Bedu sources in Emir Auda's Howietat, confirmed that Abdullah was employing agent provocateurs within Palestine to cause havoc while Churchill was in Jerusalem.

Events on the ground seemed to confirm this: right from the moment the Colonial Secretary alighted from the train onto the Holy Land, there was an ugly demonstration at the station in Gaza, with Arabs screaming: "Death to the Jews!"

"Palestine is ours!"

"Go home Jew Samuel!"

Of course, Churchill handled the fracas marvellously, waving over, smiling his most political smile, as if the mob was a welcoming commit-tee. Agreeing to meet the Palestine Arab Congress, which issued him with a list of demands, that were not in any way pro-British, or philo-Semitic. A list, His Majesty's Government would, of course, privately ignore, because the Palestinians had sided with the Turks in the Great War.

All of Abdullah's skullduggery was sedition, the very highest trea-son. He secretly cursed the Prince. He found his patience with the Arabs as dry as a wadi in high summer.

Their medieval machinations. He was fed up to the back teeth with them. Never wanted to utter another word of Arabic in his life. He sensed, kneeling in the shade of the olives, that he was going to be betrayed by his former followers, his former friends. Betrayed today. By two Judases, of his own making.

Abdullah.

Feisal.

For the Hashemite Brothers were not content with their lot. It was an open secret that in time, they wanted to rule all of Arabia. This was their destiny. Arabia, the Garden of Allah.

Their father, Hussein ibn Ali al-Hashimi, ruled in Mecca as Sharif. Feisal would accept the throne of Iraq from the hands of Churchill. Abdullah would accept the emirate of Eastern Palestine, what would become known as 'Transjordania', but that would never be enough for the prideful princeling.

'King Abdullah' would push for control over the whole British Mandate of Palestine. East and West. Forcing the issue in the negotiations. 'Because what is Transjordania anyway, Aurens, but lines drawn on a map?'

True. Too true. Transjordania. Stupid name, even when clipped to Transjordan. It would become known in the circles of those in-the-know as 'Churchill's Hiccup' or 'Churchill's Sneeze'. Largely because of the story Churchill told about it in his after-dinner speakings.

Après copious quantities of champagne-wine-brandy, and a couple of his favourite cocktails, Highballs, he boasted that he had drawn the borders in a few minutes. How he synthesised the thorny problem of the McMahon-Hussein correspondence and the Balfour Declaration. How he pleased both the Arabs and the Jews. "It was a political paroxysm," he joked. "Divinely inspired, of course."

All this hot air was to cover up the fact that this new country had been a product of his very own imagination. His every suggestion— barring the name he gave it, 'Jordan'—had been approved by Churchill, in London, before Christmas last. The map of the Modern Near East reflected his states of mind, the borderlines sketched by his pencil. With a little help from old Gerty Bell.

Churchill took all the credit, had to—given his close relationship with the Zionist leader, Chaim Weizmann and 'the Manchester Jews'. The Cairo Conference was simply a public relations exercise to give the impression that the British listened to Orientals before commanding them to fall-in-line.

Transjordania was to be a modern-day Crusader State, akin to the

County of Tripoli, the Principality of Antioch, the Kingdom of Jerusalem, and deep down, he feared it would share their fate, unable to stand the test of time, because the reasons for its existence were entirely Imperial.

Tribal lands. Trade routes. Water, the disputed ownership of wells. The religious divide between Sunni or Shia Muslims. The history of the desert nomads, long-running blood feuds. Low population, subsistence poverty, and thus a poor tax yield. All these were secondary considerations to the requirements of Empire.

Churchill argued: "If the state fails in two or three decades, then it fails. The failure will be Abdullah's or his son's. The Hashemite dynasty will have had their day in the sun and the Empire Upon Which The Sun Never Sets will deal with their fall, as and when."

The sun was almost gone from the Garden of Gethsemane. Night was falling fast, crude as oil.

The Christ in him rose from his knees. Dusted his trousers off. The time for praying, all meditative contemplation, was over.

He would confront Abdullah before the talks. Have it all out. There would be no renegotiation. Abdullah would sign on the dotted line, accept his prize, and then Aurens could go home to Old Blighty.

The track on the way back up the Mount of Olives was dusty. Filled his nostrils, hot pepper in the back of his throat.

His attempts to hack it back up, rather unceremoniously, were witnessed by a man, stepping out of the shadow of an olive tree up ahead.

His hand reached for his Colt M1911. Damn and blast: it was holstered, hanging off the back of a chair in his room.

The man was dressed in the uniform of an officer of Churchill's newly formed British Palestine Police, 'the Gendarmerie'.

He wiped his mouth. When a man had lived with a price on his head, he saw his death in every stranger, well- or ill-met.

The officer saluted. "Captain Montgomery, sir."

The captain was joined by three other gendarmes, one lugging a Lewis gun, two with sniper rifles.

He nodded. They had been shadowing him. And he hadn't noticed. Either he was getting rusty or they were very stealthy.

"I do hope we're walking back to Government House together, sir?"

"Indeed."

"That is a relief. We wouldn't want an Arab sniper shooting the famous Lawrence of Arabia by mistake, would we sir?"

"Quite." He always appreciated the Irish gallows humour.

Captain Montgomery fell into step beside him, flanked by his men, in formation. "I remember reading in the papers that your family hail from Meath, sir?"

"Planted as charged, Captain."

"There lot of us Proddy Paddies out here now that Ireland has gone to hell. Former R.I.C. Auxiliaries. A few Black and Tans. We are having a riotous oul time with the Grand Mufti's fedayeen."

"It does seem a tad lively for this time of year."

"Like a little Jewish Ulster, it is. Let us hope we don't get pogromed like back home. There are not enough of us to stop that bloodlust, if it starts. And, we certainly are not being paid enough to weigh-in. We only get half our R.I.C. salary here."

He tutted sympathetically and let Captain Montgomery sound-off the rest of short way up to Government House. Soldiers must gripe about their pay. It's the law.

Delivered directly to the front gate of Government House, he repeated the old infantry saying—"Keep the head down, lads"—as he struggled to keep the chin up.

Venus was twinkling blue-white, high in the sky above. Venus, the Morning and Evening Star. Also known as 'Shalem'. This was the god whom the Holy City was named after.

He made a mental note to include this in his memoirs, whether it was Shalem or Shalim. 'Lucifer', in other words. And, he must outline how 'Lucifer's Crown', a five-pointed star, spinning within another five-pointed star, would be created by the orbital conjunctions of Venus and Earth every eight years, and how this astronomical meta-alignment might grant the enlightened man forbidden knowledge of the smallest of the Golden Numbers, phi, the 'Golden Ratio'.

The quinine was not ameliorating the symptoms. He was sweating through his shirt. *Whichever it is, the root of the Jewish 'shalom' is peace.* That seemed pertinent. *Peace. Is peace the product of one force over-*

whelming all others? His mind, racing. Empire. *Shalom. Pax Britannia.*

The deep-seated fear of passing out. Swooning like a lady in an over-tight corset. Thankfully, before this unmanning could happen—he would never live it down—he staggered to his own quarters. He would absolutely have to bathe before bed. He had sweated through everything. *Dolphins were drier.*

HOUSE HUNTING

Wine, red and giddy as spilt blood, had gone to Adamo's head. He could not resist the temptation, and after dinner, arm-in-arm, he walked Eva round to view the Knightsbridge mansion that once belonged to Arthur Koestler.

8 Blackcross Crescent.

The wine in his stomach flared hot at first sight of it. The lotus he'd eaten earlier seemed to reanimate, attempt to flower in there.

8 Blackcross Crescent was three-stories tall. The wisteria plants either side of the grand Corinthian columns of the Georgian portico, had scaled the rough cream stucco façade, twisting all the way up to the huge windows on the third floor, shrouding the whole frontage in leaves. "It certainly has kerb appeal," he said.

"Crazy to think it's been empty for ages."

"Must be a haunted house."

She feigned a look of terror. "Woooo."

He looked at his watch. "Tsk-tsk. Where is this bloody estate agent?"

"The Slacker."

"We should start the viewing without them, no?" He opened the gate, led her up the garden path.

Under the portico, was a mahogany front door, encarved with three winged men, wielding flaming swords, fighting against a serpent, an owl, a woman. "Are those angels?" she asked.

Who knows? He reeled away from the door. Why he was to walk the path that snaked perversely around the side of the house, into the back garden, was a mystery to him.

And why she would dare shadow him, through that bed of stones, raked into concentric ripples around three jutting rocks, and under the branches of a weeping willow, was more mysterious than Zen to her.

He peered into a window pane set in the back door—hands shaped like a pair of binoculars to block the glare. "Look."

She pressed the heel of her hand to the glass, spying into the breakfast area in there, a huge oval table, surrounded by built-into-the-wall pews and chairs, was like a set from a magazine.

"Kitchen heaven," she said.

"You betcha." Before he could stop it, his hand gripped the doorhandle. The hiss of the seal breaking. The door, swinging open. He looked back at her.

"Dude?" she said.

He expected an alarm. In silence, his heart accelerated its way to 180 B.P.M. But, there was no beep-beep countdown to an alarm. Nothing.

"Dude!" She grabbed him by the arm, but he had crossed the threshold, was already two steps onto the herringbone floor of the kitchen. "There must be a silent alarm, or something...?"

"Nah."

"This is breaking and entering."

"We're prospective buyers, viewing the property, remember?"

"No. This is trespassing!"

He advanced, running his fingers along the huge rectangular island that dominated the room. Turning on one of three taps. A stream of silver whooshed into the sink.

"Wow!"

She was being sarky.

He turned one of the dials on the industrial-sized hob. Click-spark. A blue ring of fire. "Imagine cooking here. I'm getting agoraphobia. You could fit our whole flat in here."

She turned off the dials, snuffing out the ring of flames, pointed at the doorway. "Come on—let's go, Adamo! This isn't funny anymore."

"I dare you."

"You're drunk."

"I double dare you."

"I'm going to kill you."

"Triple dare you." He took her hand, which was shaking with excitement, and walked her into the adjoining room.

It was a huge room. With blood red walls. The long wooden dining table in the centre would have seated 12 comfortably. Five on each side. Plus Mummy and Daddy on the ends. The entire left wall was covered with a single giant painting of a red dragon breathing fire onto screaming, fleeing, people.

The far end of this room was a living space with a sofa facing a bookcase shaped like an Arab gate: a bab. It was over in that spot, decades before the million-pound refurb, that Arthur Koestler and his wife, Cynthia, jointly committed suicide.

"How many bedrooms do you think we have?" He pointed at the door to the hallway.

"I don't want to see the rest." She was pouting.

"What?"

"It's just going to depress us later. Like the hangover you're going to have from the red wine."

He put his hand on her tummy. "I think the pre-bump would like to see their nursery, no?"

"I don't want to spoil the pre-bump."

"Where's your spirit of adventure?"

"It's in jail already, reflecting on its stupidity."

"Aw. Come on. Nest with me." He kissed her.

She who kisses back seems to assent, so he led her on. The hallway was dominated by four huge Phoenician amphoras. They had a choice of a glass-stairwell or a glass-sided lift to take them up onto the glass-floored landing of the next level. They took the stairs.

The entire first floor was a health suite. A fully kitted-out gym, free weights, two running machines. A stepper. Peleton bikes, the lot. Partitioned off from the gym, there was a wooden sprung-floor for Yoga and

Pilates. Through an Islamic pointed archway, lay the jumbo-sized spa. Sauna. Steam-room. Showers. Massage table.

Stupified by luxury, they ascended another flight of stairs to the third floor. Up there, they toured six-seven-eight-nine Neo-Venetian bedrooms, each with a super-kingsize bed, walk-in wardrobes, and en suite bathroom, kitted out with either a free-standing bath or wet-room shower. "You could have his 'n' hers, 'n' pre-bump's bedrooms, couldn't you?" he said.

"Separate bedrooms, eh," she said. "What are we—50?"

He stopped to seriously admire the tenth bedroom, the Master. The bed was enormous, with a bookcase for the bedhead. "I begsy this one," he said.

"So, you really don't want sex anymore?"

"I do. I do. I do."

"Well, I want the pre-bump to sleep with us, in a cot in our room when he or she is born. None of this seven-degrees-of-separation."

"Awwww. Of course, we will all sleep together. Speaking of sleeping together...? We could try out the bed right now..."

"—No."

"No Nurses-n-Doctors?"

"No, ya filthy animal. Let's go. You've had your fun."

"O-kay. But..."

"—We're leaving."

The thought of leaving all this luxury, provoked a stabbing pain in his temples, or maybe that was just him sobering up?

She led the way down the flights of stairs, through into the kitchen, and out the back door. "Say buh-bye to the Mustapha Mansion."

"Buh-bye, Mustapha Mansion," he said.

She closed the door, firmly. "Home we go."

THE BANKS OF THE JORDAN

O bjective: To rendezvous with Prince Abdullah at the Allenby Bridge at ten o'clock, sharp, and escort his convoy to Government House, Jerusalem.

To achieve this objective he had made himself Commander (Acting) of a Rolls Royce Silver Ghost armoured car.

This marvellous machine was simply made for desert warfare. He loved the Ghost. What man would not love the Ghost. The deep throaty vroom of that 16-cylinder engine. Top speed: 45 miles per hour.

That rata-tat-tat-tat of the water-cooled Vickers 303 in action, tracer streaking off into the desert heat-swirls, cutting the enemy down in swathes like wheat at harvest time. Fighting in the final battle. The Battle of Armageddon. Rata-tat-tat-tat: the reek of cordite, the stink of blood and shit, exploded onto the wind. Victory. Philonikia. With only nine Ghosts, they had beaten the Turks back!

Goggles-down. Full speed ahead, they roared up the road, past the crumbled walls of Jericho and on, on through a lushness of Zionist fruit plantations to Allenby Bridge. *Bolshie Jews really are making this wind-blasted desert a garden once more, Eden reborn.*

He tapped the thermometer on the inside of the turret. 94 degrees Fahrenheit, in the shade. The poor driver and gunner were being roasted alive down there, while he was standing up in the turret, washed by the breeze.

Like water it was, sluicing over his face, rippling through his hair, flowing down the neck of his linen shirt. Dear God. So much cooler than last night. His fever had broken after midnight, and he had been granted the unexpected boon of a good night's sleep.

The Ghost reached the Allenby Bridge, parked up. He pulled out 'Kairos', rubbed his forefinger and thumb on the worn copper fob of the watch.

On his very first solo expedition to Syria, to explore the Templar castles, he had been cracked on the noggin, nearly killed for it, robbed while he lay bleeding on the ground. But he survived, to retrieve Kairos from the thief. He flipped this little reminder of his own mortality open, and read the time. 10 minutes to spare.

He dismounted. "At ease, men." The crew got out for a smoke in the fresh air. Puffing away, they all watched an egret hunting on the far bank of the River Jordan, dead-still over the waters, poised to spear a fish. At ease.

Prince Abdullah's convoy of three cars approached the far side of the bridge. Two black Daimlers and a white Mercedes Benz 1914 28/30 S. Ten o'clock. On the dot. First ever time Abdullah had been punctual.

The convoy crossed over, and he raised two arms over his head. It was pure theatre, a gesture he made his own en tour as Feisal's 'Aurens'. Whilst going native. Donning the white robes of the Bedu. All of it, a most Machiavellian ploy, for Prince Feisal knew his warriors would respond to 'technical advice' from a British officer if he did not look like the infidel, the White Devil.

The cars stopped. Prince Abdullah was in the middle car, an open-topped Daimler with his coterie of Syrian Druse.

He walked up, bowed stiffly from the neck. "*As-salaam alaikam.*"

"*Wa-alaikum-salaam,* Aurens." Prince Abdullah was in the habit of swishing about a horse-tail fly-swat.

"I need a word with you. Here. Now. Privately."

Prince Abdullah alighted nimbly from his car. He had very cleverly chosen to wear a British military dress uniform and *keffiyah* patterned with his family colours, held in place at his brow with a golden agal, so that he would seem kingly, Occidentally-oriented, yet thoroughly blend-in with the British officers at the talks.

"Churchill has been fully briefed about the raids you have been conducting against the French in Syria."

Prince Abdullah did not bat an eyelid. "Statecraft. It is nothing you yourself would not have advised—to improve our position."

"I would expressly not have advised this."

"Aurens. The French did not fight for Syria. We took Damascus. Damascus is ours. They know this, and yet they invade, and depose my brother."

"The French are threatening to invade Palestine if you do not disengage. They have mobilized their 4th Armée to Golan."

"Risk war with the British Empire and all Arabia?" Prince Abdullah shook his head, sneered.

"All raids against the French are to cease." He sighed deeply. "I want your word of honour."

"—It shall be so, when Churchill makes me Emir of all Palestine, West and East of the Jordan."

"Abdullah. You will be Emir of the East. Transjordania. There will be no renegotiation of the terms of our agreement this day."

"It was revealed to me in a dream that my destiny is to be King of Greater Syria, reunited with Palestine and Jordan."

"It has been revealed to me whilst wide awake—that you have been fomenting the Palestinian Arabs. I have not informed Churchill about your betrayal. But if you do not cease politicking and accept Transjordania, I will be forced to."

"I am not responsible for these riots." Prince Abdullah shrugged. "The Palestinians are angry at the numbers of Jew immigrants, and the appointment of a Zionist High Commissioner, this Samuel."

"If Churchill learns of your treachery, he may make Ibn Saud Emir of Transjordania."

"Do not speak of that dog. I forbid you to speak to me of that dog."

"Then I take it, when we get to Government House—you will sign the agreement as it stands."

Prince Abdullah frowned heavily, was about to reply. Instead, he gritted his teeth, mounted the Mercedes Benz 1914 28/30 S, barking at his driver: "*Yallah.*"

He returned to his Ghost, and led the way to Government House, sticking to the back roads they came out on. The safety of Jewish settlements. Skirting the limits of the Holy City, in case news of Abdullah's presence sparked fresh trouble in the Arab quarters. They made it back to Government House in one piece. At the entrance, he dismounted the Ghost, removed his goggles, smoothed down his hair.

He motioned for Prince Abdullah and the Druse to mount the steps, as if they were his honoured guests, and not the lackeys of the British Empire.

A Sikh orderly, with a wooden arm, escorted them perfunctorily along the long hallways to the vast room the negotiations were being conducted in.

He took the empty place on the British side of the table, at Churchill's right hand.

"A sight for sore eyes indeed, Lawrence," Churchill chuckled. "It looks as if you are still wearing your goggles."

He traced the imprints around his eyes. Smiled. "Spectercles. Ha!"

Prince Abdullah signed the agreement—after 30 minutes of protesting the appointment of the Zionist Herbert Samuel, and demanding written guarantees limiting the rate of Zionist immigration into Palestine. He would be Emir for the first six months of a trial period and, at the pleasure of His Imperial Majesty, George V, called King thereafter.

Tetelestai. The Greek for 'It is finished'. This was what he would scribble later in his notes: aide de memoire. Although nothing was finished, strictly speaking. There would be much more shuttle diplomacy, months of work to get the Sharif of Mecca, and Prince Ali onside. But 'it is finished' was the exoteric, not the esoteric, meaning of *tetelestai* for him.

Yeshua cried out, "It is finished," bowed his head and gave up his spirit. John 19 v 30. What he meant was much more complicated because *tetelestai* was the present perfect tense. One could say: It was finished in the past, it is still finished in the present, it will remain finished in the future. More accurately rendered in English as: I have done my work.

Lawrence of Arabia was finished.

The wretched fellow had finally done right by the Arabs. All those young warriors who rode into the Turkish guns, scimitars flashing in the sun, spurred on by his promises of freedom, and were cut to pieces. He had undone their cruel betrayal at Versailles in 1919.

In truth, he had kept his word. Publicly restored his own sense of knightly honour. The same sense of knightly honour that had prompted him to decline a knighthood, offered by King George V, in 1918.

Lawrence of Arabia was finished.

The movie-star persona that captured the public imagination after Lowell Thomas' exhibitions in London. It was still hard to believe that crowds numbering in tens, and hundreds, of thousands, flocked to see an American journalist's collection of war photographs, a lecture, some Arab music, all entitled: 'With Allenby in Palestine and Lawrence of Arabia'.

Military Intelligence had promoted his legend vigorously in 1920. The powers-that-be felt that after the industrial slaughter of the Western Front, people wished to see something of the nobler, romantic qualities of men at war: honour, gallantry, courage.

Their mythic Lawrence of Arabia conveniently embodied this: one noble man could make a difference, war could be civilising. All of it was jingoistic poppycock. Their caricature bore so little resemblance to him he was revolted by it. Revolted in the desert. Their adulation was a form of ritual humiliation.

If the prudish British and American publics only knew why he fought for Arab freedom.

The God's-honest truth.

Then, he would be imprisoned. Like Wilde. These poor judges would not see the romance in his promise to free one Arab in particular. The boy who revealed to him so many, many splendid things, all the pleasures of this world, and more.

The Gnostic Ismaili secrets of his Druse faith, their Seven Pillars.

These poor judges would never truly know why his opus The Seven

Pillars of Wisdom, more novel than autobiography, was dedicated for all time: *To S. A.*

Salim Ali.

Sometimes known as Selim Ahmed.

Nicknamed 'Dahoum' by the Arab diggers at Karkemish.

Meaning 'the Little Dark One'. The boy who died of typhus long before his Aurens could liberate Damascus, and deliver freedom, self-determination, dignity, to the Arabs.

These poor judges would never know this small tragedy of man, and boy.

After God created Adam, He said, 'It is not good for man to be alone.' He then created a woman for Adam, and called her Lilith. Adam and Lilith immediately began to fight. She said, 'I will not lie below,' and he said, 'I will not lie beneath you, but only on top. For you are fit only to be in the bottom position, while I am to be the superior one.' Lilith responded, 'We are equal as we were both created from the earth.'

THE ALPHABET OF BEN SIRACH

The born adepts of Atlantis blindly followed the insinuations of the great and invisible dragon, King Thevetat.

HELENA BLAVATSY, *Isis Unveiled*

El Harrag

Muhend started awake. Peeled his face, slick with drool, off Boudris' neck.

"Open up! This the Garda!"

Police! He de-spooned from Boudris.

Thunderbolts nearly rattled the door off its hinges. "Open up."

In his stomach, instant intifada, last night's red wine rising up, having to be re-swallowed, kept down.

"If yis don't open the door now, it'll go worse on yis."

He sat bolt upright. "Wake up!"

Boudris moaned. "*Putain.*"

"*Les gendarmes.*"

Boudris' pillow-face cracked-up, into glacial crevasses.

"I am coming," Muhend called out. He leapt out of the bed, pulled on a pair of trousers. Too fast. Head-spins, to the door.

There were two Guards looming in the corridor. An old one. A young one. And standing along with them, Mr. O'Brien, the Manager of The Atlantic Hotel, looking very angry. "Are you Mohammed Mrabet?" asked the old Guard.

"I am," he lied. Mohammed Mrabet was a famous Moroccan story-teller. A friend of the American writer and spy, Paul Bowles, who lived in Tangiers for many years. The driver of Paul Bowles. Allegedly, the lover of Paul Bowles. He chose the name because he liked Mohammed Mrabet's style. His ghost stories. *The Big Mirror. Love With a Few Hairs.*

He'd read them in English, many times, because Paul Bowles translated them. He used them to improve his English. Just like he used Paul Bowles' novels, *The Sheltering Sky* and *The Spider House* to improve his understanding of English. He had always been a reader, in Arabic, in French, and latterly in English. He'd even read Salman Rushdie's *The Satanic Verses.*

"Is Hassan Saib in there?" the young Guard asked.

Boudris reported to the door in Calvin Kleins. "I am Hassan."

"I'm arresting you two for Assault," the old Guard said.

"The fight was not our fault," Muhend stated.

"Yis are not obliged to say anything unless you wish to do so, but anything you do say will be taken down in writing and may be given in evidence. Now-so, that's your caution done. I'll be needing you lads to come down the station with us right away. We need to interview you. Do yis understand me?"

He had to say: "We do."

Boudris burped, beer degraded to sulphur.

"Better get dressed then, eh, quick-smart?" The old Guard pointed into the interior of the room.

Muhend followed the finger. Pulled on a T-shirt, socks, trainers, his coat.

The Gardai waited at the open door with Mr. O'Brien. "Cowardly fuggin sand-nigger bin Laden," said the young Guard.

"Saudis need a good nuking, I tell ya," Mr O'Brien said.

Their talk was all about the terrorist attack on the Twin Towers last Tuesday. 9/11 was all anyone in the world was talking about.

He told Boudris softly, in Berber, to go to the bathroom.

In there, they pulled the door closed. There was a window, which led out onto the fire escape. It was kept open to get rid of the eye-watering reek from the toilet that would not flush properly.

They slipped out of this window.

Quietly, *tip-tap-tip-tap*, descending the metal staircase.

Nobody was coming after them. Nobody had noticed they had gone. At the bottom of the fire escape, they started running.

Running for their lives. Heading up the road, Boudris in the lead.

Darting through wide-open iron gates, into some rich person's big garden.

The Lodge. He was a forward thinker, the brains of this pair. *We have to make it to The Lodge.* He knew from listening to A-K that the owner, Crazy Danica, was in Dublin. So, they could hide there. Wait for A-K and Lilit to come around. They were friends. They would help.

Dublin, 'The Fair City'. Where refugees could get the jobs Irish people didn't want. There, people could be anonymous.

They would be in Dublin now—if the Customs men had not stopped the lorry, opened the container and discovered the cargo was not Proline televisions, but 32 half-suffocated men, women, and children, scared and hungry, using a single bucket in the corner of the container as a toilet. For two days.

Yes, perhaps A-K and Lilit could smuggle them to Dublin? And then, they could forget about their claim for asylum. This false claim, under false names, that they had been forced to lodge that cold, rainy night Customs caught them.

They did not need a translator that night. They had prepared their story in English. They knew what to say—thanks to their conversation with Boudris' second cousin, Nourredine Belaid, in Le Café Paris, where Jack Kerouac, Alan Ginsberg, and the other Beats, used to hang out.

It was Nourredine who had been a student leader in the Kabyle rebellion in the 1990s.

Nourredine, who had been forced to flee for his life—across the border into Morocco, to Boudris' relatives in the Rif.

Nourredine was a good storyteller, in the tradition of The Book of a Thousand Nights and a Night, and he spared no detail. For the price of two mint teas, they took the story of Nourredine's life and made it theirs.

Like Shahrazad, fighting to stay alive by reinvention, they told this story every night for six nights; rehearsing in the 32-dirhams-per-night Pension Miami, at the bottom of Rue Salah Eddine El Ayoubi, until they both believed it.

Mohammed Mrabet and Hassan Saib were involved in student agitation in Tizi-Ouzou, the capital of the Kabilye region, where Berbers were killed every day, like the singer Matoub Loounes—for the right to speak their own language and have a sense of their own cultural identity.

The paramilitary *Gendarmerie Nationale* caught them on the street and beat them with batons.

They were taken to the *Sécurité Militaire*, who stubbed cigarettes out on their hands and feet, and warned them that next time they would be killed. Their families would never find the bodies. Their souls would roam, ghosts lost until the Last Day.

This was the hard part. He had to stub cigarettes out on his own hands and feet to make the story seem real, so people would believe, because people had to see to believe. It was human nature.

Nobody willingly stubs cigarettes out on their own hands and feet. The scars, the evidence of torture, were the most important parts of their lies. Especially on the feet, the little toe. What sort of animal, what kind of monster, burns someone's little toe?

Only the Algerian military dictatorship—under the fat puppet of the Generals, President Abdelaziz Bouteflika—would do such an inhuman thing, because it was a recorded fact that torture was routinely used there, in interrogations.

Many, many Moroccan prisoners captured in the forgotten war in the Western Sahara, and imprisoned for 20 years in desert concentration camps, testified to such inhumane treatment—that is, after their release.

After lighting the first menthol cigarette, Boudris refused to mutilate himself: not drunk enough on local vodka, un-numbed by the painkillers. *"Asif*, Muhend."

So, it was up to him to put his best foot forward: an English idiom he liked, up until that glowing point.

The orange end of the cigarette fizzled out on his skin. He hissed through his teeth.

Ash flaked off to reveal a red-raw circle.

Spit bubbled on his lips.

He licked it off, lit another Marquise. Ten in the sadistic pack.

He was floating by number 10. High on vodka, paracetamol, and hurt. The smell of burnt chicken kebabs, and the aluminium taint of bad tobacco, filling the small room. Mint—only the overpowering pure scent of mint, stopped him from being sick.

Boudris was weeping.

"*Maalesh*, it will be okay, Boudris. The wounds will heal."

Boudris was ashamed of his weakness, and this when he was so strong.

"*Sahfee.*" It had been a terrible ordeal, but the relief, the pride he felt. *Sahfee, if I can do this, I am capable of anything.*

His feet did not heal up for three weeks. It was hard to walk, hard to work. The puckered hole in the little toe kept weeping.

He learned to take the pain. Limping down from Rue de la Liberté to the seafront, to work in Club 696 every night, dusk till dawn, without fail. They needed the money to put in the bank, to save for the journey. If he didn't go to work, they would give the job to somebody else, and then he would lose the wage, tips, and the skim he and the Fassi barman, Ahmed, made from serving cheap local vodka, whiskey, and *chiba*, as Smirnoff, Glenfiddich, and La Fee Absinthe.

He made 1,000 dirhams per weeknight at Club 696 and 2,000-plus dirhams on a Friday and Saturday night. This was a good wage in Tangiers, better than Boudris' wage as security for the belly-dancers at the Morocco Palace, but not as much as the teenage Tanjawi prostitutes who frequented the bar, or the glue-sniffing muggers operating along Avenue D'Espagne.

Hans Smidt, the Danish bar owner, hired him on the spot: "You are a good-looking boy, educated, speaking many languages."

Hans, known as 'the Great Dane' in the homosexual community, would often say: "Soon, I will connect you with a smuggler."

He knew Hans' promises were like *m'hencha*, sweet almond pastries, gone rotten, worm-ridden, but he had to flirt, act like they were the very bread of heaven or the Great Dane would replace him with somebody new.

There were so many good-looking boys in the city, working, saving, awaiting their opportunity to get away to Europe.

Awaiting *el harrag*. The Burner. To become *harraga*. The burners. The nameless ones. Destroyers of the souls that Allah gave them.

Trespass Against Us

Back at Number 235 Kilburn Park, Flat 3, Eva inserted the key into their lock.

It didn't catch. So, she would jiggle the key, trying to push up and stab in: the knack of the lock. But, no joy. "Bloody useless thing."

"Fingers like courgettes." He stepped in, took over. "Let the safe-cracker at it."

The lock did not open. "Hah!" She folded her arms.

"It feels like there's another key in the door...?"

"Don't be silly. Let me have another go." She took a hold of the key, pulled it out, and thrust it in. Jiggling it, wiggling it, forcing all the pressure she could into that jagged little hole. Infuriating how it resisted her. "Fuckballs!"

He laughed. "Total fuckballs!'

"Mega-fuckballs." She loved delivering that topper.

Their frustrations seemed to chuckle away, to nothing.

"Go away!" said a male voice...from behind the locked door.

She looked at Adamo, eyes widening. Whispered, "What the fuck?"

"Go away—or I will call the police." The voice within had a foreign accent.

"This is our fucking flat!" Adamo bellowed. "You go away!"

"I am the legal tenant. You are trying to break into my flat. I'm calling the police."

Adamo stared at her in bewilderment. "You do that," he replied. "Phone 999, Eva!"

"What do I tell them?" She reached into her bag for her mobile phone, pulled it out. She dialled 999. No dial-tone.

Redialled.

Nothing. It wouldn't work.

"We will see whose police arrive first," the voice said.

"What?" Adamo snorted. Laughed a little. "That's bonkers."

No emergency service. She was confused. *That's not possible. Is it? In London?*

Adamo's face began to redden. "If you don't open this door right now, I'm going to kick it in."

Silence.

"Do it," she said. "I'm right behind you." She fumbled in her handbag for that hairspray can. *I will fucking frazz this guy!*

Adamo lined himself up to launch a front-kick, and booted the door as hard as he could.

The jamb by the lock splintered. Surface cracks split the paint, but it stayed shut.

Another power-kick from the hip, and the door crashed in, Adamo lurching forwards, parrying the door with his right arm as it bounced back on the hinges.

A kitchen knife flashed through an arc, like white flame. "*Kahwoud!*"

"Jesus." Adamo backed off.

She followed suit. This is crazy. The knife-wielder was an Arab.

"Out, *shakhs majnoon.*"

"—This is our flat," she said. She expected her husband , the Big Man, to do something, but there he stood, simply stood, and stared. A weird paralysis.

She found that perplexing. It was as if he'd recognised this home-invader, this squatter. *How could that be so?*

The Squatter had a phone pressed to his left ear. "Yes, Police? My address is...."

"Get out," she screamed.

The Squatter thrust the knife out. "Please, Police—they are inside my home—come quickly!"

"This is not your home," Adamo yelled.

The Squatter held up the phone like a trophy. "The police are on their way."

She peered past Adamo's shoulder. This was when she noticed: The layout is different. The T.V. The couch. All our stuff. Gone. She glared at the Squatter. "What have you done with our stuff? My Lempicka?"

"This is my flat, *majnoon*! I have lived here for one and a half years."

The disorientation of it, the dislocation, a disaster, the sheer Dis of it. She stared at the Squatter in utter disbelief. They had been joking about squatters, being squatters, and here, was a squatter. A squatter, in their place. *How had he gotten in?* It must have been in the afternoon. He could have moved their belongings out, the furniture, in that time. Maybe. If he had help. All gone!

"If you do not leave now, you will be arrested," the Squatter said.

"Arrested?" She pointed to the number on the door. "Number 3. We live here. We were just out for the afternoon, and now we've come back."

"Hah." The Squatter pointed the knife at the door. "Are you going to pay for my door? You have broken it."

Adamo looked down at the pile of mail on the table by the door. He bent over, snatched a letter up.

"I live here! Mohammed Mrabet!"

"Mohammed Mrabet." Adamo read it out, like the name of an old friend. All of the rage, in fact any red, drained from his face into the small hole that was his mouth.

She took hold of a letter. The name was typed out: *MOHAMMED MRABET.*

"Read the date, Eva," Adamo said. "The 12th."

She read the frank-stamp, the date in the red circle was indeed the 12th. "That's not possible. How can you have stolen our address?"

The Squatter advanced, stabbing the air wildly. "I am no thief. You break into my house, you destroy my door, and you dare call me a thief. *Kahwoud.*"

"Whoa. Take it easy. We're out of here." Hands-up, arms wide, Adamo backed off into the hallway. "Go. Down the stairs, Eva."

Adamo is terrified, she realised. Flitting down the stairs sideways, hand on the banister. "Come on!"

The Squatter occupied the landing. "Yes! You go, *djinn*! Back to hell!"

Adamo stopped at the threshold of the front door. "You cannot be Mohammed! Mohammed is dead!"

"I am Mohammed Mrabet." The Squatter ran downstairs. Slammed the front door in their faces. "Curse you! Curse all you *kafir!*"

THE MUSLIM
BROTHERHOOD

A siren, wailing.

Crouching in some rich person's driveway, Muhend strained to hear which way the Guards would go in their car.

Only when he was sure they were heading the other direction, did he dare speak: "The Lodge. We will go to the Lodge."

"*Wakha.*" Boudris sprinted off.

He would lag behind, three years younger, but less fit.

They made the Lodge gates without being seen. The Lodge was Crazy Danica's holiday-hideaway. They'd been to a legendary party there. But now, summer was over, and Crazy Danica was back partying in Dublin. The rusted iron gates were closed. They crossed a mat, soaked in pine-scented disinfectant.

The Foot-and-Mouth outbreak had caused everybody to take quarantine measures. There was a faded green sign hanging off the gatepost to the right, red capital letters: *PRIVATE ROAD, NO TRESPASSING.*

Boudris lifted the gate, slipped through. "*Yallah, andak.*"

They ran along the rutted track; slowing to a jog, panting through the trees. Fugitives. On the run.

The Lodge had a boathouse. There was a boat in there. It was foremost in his mind that if all else failed, they could use this boat to escape.

All they would have to do was hug the coast, keep turning left, pilot a course to Cork, maybe even Dublin.

On their last boat-trip, across the Straits of Gibraltar—called the Pillars of Hercules in the Ancient world—they had simply been passengers. Two souls amongst 35, crammed into the powerboat.

Their traffickers were Riffi Berbers, lapis-eyed, very Germanic looking. People were product, like blocks of hashish, being transported from A-to-B.

35 people at $3000 per head equals $115,000. This was what the traffickers make on that run alone. And they did runs many times when the moon was right.

The two 500cc motors kept their boat powering along. The roar of the engines made speaking impossible. Up near the prow, salt spray off the bow, caused the face to tingle, the eyes blur. The lights of Spain, the city of Tarifa, flaring bright.

It should take half an hour to get over there, *inshallah*, but of course it did not. Life was never so straightforward. The traffickers could not head straight across the Straits. They had to zig and zag to take advantage of the currents in and out, the powerful tidal surges of the Atlantic bullying the Mediterranean.

It took 45 minutes to get to Spain. Landing on a deserted beach in darkness. Thousands of people drowned here every year, trying to make this treacherous journey: Third to First World, so everyone was glad to be alive.

He hugged Boudris, wanted to kiss him, but could not. Instead, he scooped up a handful of wet sand. *The stuff of new life.*

The traffickers marched them into a container truck they had waiting. "*Viajes seguros,*" they wished the driver.

Espagñe: that great country, once a colony of the Moors, now the occupier of Ceuta and Melilla, was a dark dream that passed in the night and the day to follow.

The doors opened and they stepped down onto the concrete floor of a warehouse, in Marseilles, France. This was where another life as an *illegal* immigrant began. The driver directed everyone over to a smoking, rusted steel drum, and said: "*Quemar todo.*"

Burn everything. He emptied his wallet of his identity, his history.

Driving licence. Passport. Student card. His Union of Moroccan Workers membership card. His Justice and Development Party (P.J.D.) card. Membership of the Muslim Brotherhood in *Maroc*. All his I.D.s would melt away in the fire of other peoples' identities.

From here on, he would be Mohammed Mrabet. That alias, the lie arising from the ashes was worth a lot, potentially—if he could just get a job. Any job. Waiting tables. Washing dishes, pots and pans. Cleaning hotel toilets. Labouring. The sort of working-class jobs his poor father Abdullah had to do as a young man, and he would go mad if he knew his spoilt youngest son was wasting himself on these things.

From the beginning, Father pushed and channeled *his* Muhend to utilise his intelligence to become a lawyer. Because Abdullah had such a great respect for the rule of law, which he regarded as the cornerstone of a civilised society, he ignored his son's love of studying and reading English.

Father would not entertain his son's desire to study abroad. "I did not save up every *cent*, every *franc*, every *dirham*, for this!"

So, Muhend would attend Mohammed V University, struggle through Constitutional Law, Islamic Jurisprudence, International Relations, History of Institutions, Legal Terminology, Political Economy, grappling with the subject like a blind man, for the first year.

In Year Two, when he was supposed to be studying Civil Law, Criminal Law, Administrative Law and Major International Events, Father was killed outright in a car accident on the coast road.

A lorry crashed into Father's car head-on, and the gendarmes claim he died: *Like—that.* The *snap* of thumb and forefinger. In that instant, Father was reduced to a statistic, and everything that he could have been was gone.

Absurdly gone. Like Albert Camus, writer of *L'Étranger* and the anti-Nazi *La Peste*, whom Muhend loved so much as a teenager.

The driver of the lorry, a local from Mohammedia, was unhurt; he received not a single bruise or scratch. The crushing irony was that although *les gendarmes* knew the driver to be a heavy drinker, they did not have the equipment to test him at the scene.

The killer of Abdullah Aatabou was therefore *not* charged with Dangerous Driving either, or Reckless Driving. *Pas de confiance.* The

Law proved to be as senseless and full of holes as Muhend had always told Father it was. It occurred to him that fateful night: *Les gendarmes might have been lying. Father might not have died instantly. He might have been in pain. He might have been fighting to live for his family, fading away to his god, his blood staining the asphalt.*

You will not think this, Muhend!

The next day—in keeping with tradition, the funeral of Father was staged without paid mourners, because to know him was to respect him.

After it was done, and all those familiar faces were gone, in the quiet of the evening, he found himself sitting at odds to the television, telling Mother, and his youngest sister, Aisha, that he was going to drop out of university, the family would not be able to afford the fees anymore.

Mother told him: "I will gladly commit some of the money we will receive from Father's life insurance to your education."

"*Barakalaufik, Yamasse.* You are generous to a fault, as always, Mother. But, no. That would be a waste of the money and time. I do not want to be a lawyer in Morocco. The corruption. The injustice. We protest against it every Thursday. At the parliament building in Rabat, every Thursday. The *Compagnie Mobile d'Intervention* beat us, drive us back up Avenue Mohammed V to the sanctuary of the Grand Mosque. Nothing changes."

"We? Who is this *we*?" Mother asked.

"The Brotherhood."

"Muhend—I do not care about your ideas of *jihad* or social justice at all. I have suffered enough today. I have no more tears to cry." Mother began wailing into Aisha's chest, like she did at the graveside.

Aisha, the baby of the family at 14, quietly, humbly, asked: "If you do not study Law, Muhend, what are you going to do?"

"Maybe I will help run one of Father's shops?"

Mother sobbed. "Your brothers run the businesses. They already have help—their wives help."

"Then I don't know," he said. But, he did! He would not be some shopkeeper selling furniture like his devout elder brothers, Lhadj and Hussein. He had dreamt of what he would do for a long time.

He and Boudris—Brothers, active members of the P.J.D. and the Union of Moroccan Workers—would get on the train north, to Tangiers, and leave the parochial, conservative, stuffy stupidity of Rabat behind.

Azrael, Angel of Death, had been and gone. Azrael, the Liberator.

Muhend would leave Father's idea of his future behind, the law, his second cousin Najma from the town of Berrechid, whom Father wanted him to marry and have his grandchildren with. Najma, his wife-to-be, had a beautiful smile and a glowing personality. Najma was truly lovely, wonderful. But, he did not want a truly lovely, wonderful wife from the lunatic asylum.

It was an old joke in Morocco. Go to Settat—go mad. Go to Berrechid, for the cure.

Muhend and Boudris would go to Tangiers, 'the International City' for the cure to Morocco. He would find a job as a barman, save the money needed to get to Europe. He would work hard, and over the years become wealthy, and have enough money to send home to Aisha for university. *Amiyn. This is the best way, for everybody.*

No Room At The Inn

Talk about seeing a ghost! Adamo was shaking. Adrenalin jittered through him, fight-flight body-shocks.

He squinted up at the crescent moon in the sky. An Arab moon. A scimitar. A blade slicing down from heaven. He could have been stabbed. Eva could have been stabbed. Their baby could have been stabbed. *Curse you! Curse all you kafir!*

"We'll say we've been squatted." Eva was pacing up and down the driveway, waiting for the police. "Squatted-out. Is that what they call it?"

"I don't know what they call this." The jitters really had him, in his hamstrings. He tried to suppress the jigging. Pace about, expend the electricity. Look manly. In control. Alpha.

"Mohammed Mar...?" she said. "What was his name?"

"Mrabet." *It's not the same Mohammed*, he told himself. *Mohammed is dead, dead as Lilit.*

"I can't believe this is happening," she said. "We've lost our home. We're homeless. At knifepoint. That isn't even possible."

"We're not homeless, Eva." He hugged her, attempting to comfort himself as much as her. Mohammed had died in the car crash. "We'll sort all this out."

She pushed him away. "How are we going to sort this out?"

"I'll phone Mum. If all else fails, we can stay there."

"Mr. Practical."

"That's me." He smiled. Tried the number. There was a problem. Christ. No signal. A siren wailed, less than a mile away, by his reckoning.

"They're coming," she said.

"Don't bet on it. This is London. One knife-crime every 14 minutes."

"They're coming. We'll tell them that he has stolen our flat. That he threatened us with a deadly weapon. They'll arrest him."

"Or—they'll arrest us. Arrest us all."

"They wouldn't do that. Why would they do that?"

"That's generally what the cops do. Arrest first. Ask questions later."

"We are in the right. All they have to do is talk to the neighbours, the landlord."

"Eva. We broke in."

"Because it's our flat."

"He'll say it's his. Then, the police will probably arrest all three of us, take us to the station, charge us, throw us in cells."

She shook her head. "They wouldn't do that."

"That's their job."

"I can't have a criminal record. I'm a nurse."

"Uh-huh. Yeah. So, let's do the fuckoffski, get an Uber to my mums', and we can phone the letting agent in the morning to set it straight. No police."

"No police."

"Yeah, fuck da police." He took her by the hand, walked her out of the driveway, and up the pavement. The wailing siren got louder. They looked back and saw blue flashes, spectral, through the trees.

They got off the main road, ducking down a side street. Pelting the whole way down the side street. And, out-of-breath, they stopped in an alley before the junction with the next main road.

There, in the shadows, they worked as a team, two-having-truly-become-one: she set about ordering an Uber, and he redialled his mum's number, left a voicemail: "Mum. Give us a call. Bit of an emergency. Can you put us up tonight?"

Four minutes later, a Toyota Prius glided up.

The Uber driver's name was: Hassan.

They got in.

"Did you see the dark moon tonight?" Hassan asked, his sad eyes looming large in the rear-view mirror.

"No. We didn't see anything," she said.

"They said it would be there, on the radio. I waited for the dark moon. But it did not come."

She gave that look, wide-eyed telepathy: *This—Arab—is—nutso.*

He fired right back at her: *No diggity, no doubt!*

It only took 15 minutes to get to the Double-Mum's, though it seemed much longer because they didn't talk. Not in front of Dark-Moon-Hassan.

"Thanks, mate," he said, as they bailed out of the Uber. He waited for the Toyota Prius to silently slip away, before adding:

"Another total mega Arab nutso!"

"No diggity," she replied. "Check your phone."

"No calls." The good news was there were two Smart cars parked in the driveway. So, Helena and Nadine had to be home. He strode up. Rang the bell.

No security light clicked on. Nobody answered the door. The house remained still, in the darkness.

She banged on the front window. "Hello? Helena! Nadine!"

"They must be out," he said.

She tried the side gate, to get around back. It was locked up.

He picked up a stone, with the idea of smashing a window, but stopped himself because Nadine had installed a Star Wars alarm system to protect her art.

"Plan B." She sat down on the front steps, set about looking for cheap hotels on her phone. "B for Booking.com."

He took his best shot at the 5-stars, boutiques, phoning the Chesterfield Mayfair, the Langham, The Lost Poet.

All the receptionists were very nice, but there were apparently a lot of conventions in town. The receptionists were very sorry. "It's official," he said. "There are no rooms available at any inn. Maybe we could try to walk-in somewhere?"

"Seriously?" she said. "What are we going to do, Adamo?"

"Let's go around to Blackcross Crescent."

"You're kidding, right."

"We got squatted out of our place—why the hell not squat there, in style?"

"The back door will be locked."

"You want to sleep on the street?"

She seemed too tired to argue, so he led the way, around the corner, to 8 Blackcross Crescent.

SODUM WAEAMURA

Wrapping his arm in his coat, Muhend used his elbow to shatter a pane of glass in the back door.

No alarm. Only the sound of waves folding on the beach. So, he reached in, turned the key and yanked the handle down.

With a push, the door slid wide open and he entered the kitchen, scrunch-crunch on glass shards.

Boudris followed him into The Lodge, closing the door behind them.

He flipped his phone open, and called A K. Because A K is a good friend. *Good friends, friends who do not let you down, are rare creatures in this world, rarer than angels.*

A number of bleeps, then A K answered sleepily: "Yep?"

"It is Mohammed."

"Mohammed—what's up?"

"The Guards try to arrest us for assault..."

"You're shitting me?"

The people of Glenshee, had never shown the Berbers Irish hospitality. They were 'Feckin illegal ignorants!' or 'Asylum-sneakers!' Outsiders before Nine-Eleven. The attack on the Twin Towers changed notional tolerance to open hostility.

Boudris had only defended himself from the young men of the village. The Irish had started the fight to exorcise two demons from their midst. "Yis cunts are al-Qaeda," the toughest guy said. "Fuck off back where yis came from."

"Where are you guys?" A K would ask.

"Hiding in The Lodge."

"I'll get Lilit. We'll be there as soon as we can."

The sirens wailed up on the road, coming and going, foreboding tautening every muscle and sinew in his body. Half an hour choked by. Don't let the Guards search here...? Then, the sound of an engine. A car, coming down the track. *Be A K. Be A K. Be A K.*

Boudris went to the window. "*C'est* A K."

He unlocked the front door, opened it.

Three people got out of a grey Fiat: white Rasta Robin, A K, and Lilit, an Anglo-Armenian yoga instructor who was inhumanly beautiful, caramel-skinned, dark-haired, her every feature a feast for the eyes. No wonder A-K was so bewitched by her, so helplessly in love.

"The Guards are looking for you, up on the road!"

The Guards would catch them. A shudder of dread shook Muhend, colder than a mountain night. The Guards would deport them. And it would not be to Morocco. It would be to Algeria, because this was the story they told the authorities. Even if they told the truth now, the immigration officials would not believe it.

"I can't believe this fascist shit is happening," Lilit said. "When did they come for you?"

"Not long ago," he replied.

"Bastards," she said.

"We want to go to Dublin," Boudris told A K. "Can you help us?"

Robin shook his dreadlocks. "Don't know that running away is going to help your case."

"Our case is lost," he said. "It was over before this. They will deport us. Back to Algeria. The *Sécurité Militaire* are used to breaking the bones of G.I.A. and M.I.A. terrorists. They will torture us, beat our faces into granite. They will accuse us of being human-bombs."

"I'm pretty sure the Republic would never deport people to dictatorships," Robin said.

"Look, Robin. We have to get them out of here—drive them to Dub."

Lilit agreed: "Yes, let's get them out of here."

"In my car?' Robin said.

"Come on, Robin! What are you, a man or a mouse?"

"I'm a law-abiding citizen, A K, you know. Apart from dealing weed —which should be feckin legal!"

"Mouse," A K said.

"Shut up," Lilit said, "Let me talk to Robin."

A K walked off.

Muhend would let them talk. They needed to talk to make this decision. It was a big decision. Lilit took Robin aside and spoke to him quietly.

The wail of the siren, being strangled by distance.

Lilit was using all her charm and beauty, but Robin was shaking his head a lot. Words like 'insurance' and 'licence' were mentioned repeatedly.

Boudris' eyes were so fierce with love.

Be strong! He would use this love to keep his composure. Do not give in to fear.

Lilit took the keys off Robin and threw them at A K, who missed the catch, fumbled. "You're driving. I'm navigator."

"Fairnuffski." A K picked the keys up off the stone floor. 'Okay. Road-trip to Dub!'

Robin asked: "Do you have enough money for petrol? The tank is half full."

Lilit slapped her jeans on the back-pockets. "I don't have a penny on me."

'Here!' Robin produced three crisp £20 notes from his wallet. Handed them to her.

"This is really good of you Robin." Lilit kissed him on the cheek.

"Merci beaucoup, Robin," he said.

"Let's go-go-go," A K said.

They hustled outside, to the car.

A K opened the passenger door, flipped the seat forward, before going around to the driver's side.

He would get in the back seat and slide over, so Boudris could get in beside him.

Lilit locked the passenger seat back into its position, plonked in. "Enough legroom back there?"

Boudris said, "Yes-yes."

A K got into the driving seat.

Lilit smiled at A K, patted him on the knee. "You guys had better keep your heads down—at least till we get out of Glenshee."

They shrank down like scared children in the back seat.

A K started the engine. The fan belt, missing a few teeth, shrieked.

Lilit waved bye to Robin.

Muhend sighed. Their destiny lay in the hands of others. He knew he should relax because of this, but somehow, total reliance made him more distressed.

They had relied completely on Quinn & Son, their appointed lawyer in Dublin to present their case to the Immigration tribunals and look what had happened.

Tribunal after tribunal, conducted in their absence. Appeal after appeal. Verdict: case dismissed: asylum denied.

Legal advice dispensed by Mr. Quinn, a small voice on the end of a telephone: "Behave yourselves Lads, they're watching you. Don't give them any excuses to send you back. They will, given half a chance, you know."

The Fiat jolted him and Boudris together, and apart again. The track was so full of holes, and bumps. It was like having butterflies in the stomach, like the sickness of love.

Mashallah: the first time they made love on the beach after leaving the Tahiti disco in Ain Dab. He was very drunk and took Boudris in his mouth, sucking him to ecstasy, swallowing his salty-sweet *baraka*.

Boudris had taken him to Casa for the weekend. He had been taking trips down there, and to Marrakech, for two years, ever since he admitted he liked men.

They were in love, but very discreet, shy, walking the streets during the daytime, as the muezzins called the faithful to Asar prayers: *Allahu akhbar, Allahu akhbar.* Not even holding hands, even though this was okay for men to do in *Maroc*.

They were aware of Article 489 of the Moroccan penal code—which prohibited any 'shameless or unnatural act' with a person of the same sex: maximum penalty, three year's imprisonment and, a fine.

They could recite word-for-word 'The Destruction of Sodom and Gomorrah', a soura from The Holy Quran never to be forgotten: *We sent upon them a storm of stones. Taste my punishment and warning.*

Boudris gave himself over, completely, in the hotel room; hotels and their attitude to the segregation of the sexes were a salvation. Sinking into him from behind, bucking and kneading his buttocks; perversely the world had never seemed so right.

After the *moussem*, this festival of the flesh, was over, and they were spent, he wanted to open the window and sing out the words of 'The Table', with the powerful voice of the murdered political activist and singer, Boujemma Hajour: *Where are they now? My friends who sat at my table?*

Why was it the lyrics of this particular Nass el Ghiwane song sprang to life? Friendship can be bitter, but it is was also sweet to sit at my table... A mystery. Like the mystery of his adoration of Boudris, this saint to worship. *Sidi* Boudris, slouched down in the back seat of the car, grinning at him madly.

A K stopped the Fiat up at the top of rutted track, where it met the main road, and got out to open the gates.

Dublin. He dared to imagine Dublin. Going to a bar, the one with the statue of James Joyce outside it. To sit in that pub with Dubliners. Pretending to be Spanish. To be treated like a tourist. It should happen like this.

HOME AWAY

Morning had broken, like the first morning, blackbird had spoken, like the first bird, when Eva awoke with a start. In a strange bed.

In a strange bedroom.

In a strange house. But, to the familiar face of Adamo, still fast asleep on the other side of the ginormous emperor-sized bed.

Desire stirred within her, hot in her belly—to mount him while he's asleep, to take him without permission, to possess him like some demon lover.

It made her throb, great surges of heat, to think of the power of that, and she sidled over to him. He had always been a heavy sleeper, and a hard riser. Not a morning person. Especially not after a week of her night shifts.

She kissed him gently on the lips.

He stirred, without opening his eyes.

She rolled him over on his back, climbed on top, lay on him. He moaned.

She wrapped him up in her arms and legs. He loved to be wrapped up tight, to fall asleep in her arms, with her right hand cupped over his left pec', and his heart. Like a big baby, the biggest. She waited, until his breathing fell away into a deep rhythmic pattern of sleep, and then she reached for him, gripped his cock.

His mouth opened in a moan, an ancient sound from somewhere else, not belonging to him. A mantra from another world.

Watching him all the while, slyly, the side of his face, she played with him, until he was stiff in her fingers.

He drew quick breaths. His eyelids fluttered, but remained shut.

She mounted him. The thought that he would fully waken up inside her increased the thrill.

His eyes flickered open as she took him inside.

Engulfment. That exquisite friction made her gasp.

"Rapist," he groaned.

She loved it when he said dirty things like that. *Say more bad things.*

"Rape me harder."

"I love raping you." She fucked him. Hard and fast. That popping noise of her butt-cheeks slamming down on his thighs. The ferocity overtook her, and she fucked him until she was sweating, panting. Slowing the tempo, to gather her breath. "Get on top! Fuck me. Hard."

He turned her, took on the rhythm, thrusting up, deep into her: hard-long, short-fast.

The way she loved.

All shook up, like being electrocuted. When she could feel he was right on the edge...teetering on the brink...she told him: "I want you to come deep inside me, come in me."

That command. He heeded her. Was hers, as she was his, energy rising within, surging, merging with his. Their thrusts quickening, into a ripping away, a tearing apart of the veil that separated man from woman, hurtling into lights, blue and purple spin. Feeling his cock spurting inside, she came with him, and it was blinding, all the heaving, dark joy of love. And in the breathless hereafter: "I fucking love you, Adamo."

"Tell it to the judge," he gasped. "You're going down, big-time, for rape."

"No, you are. Down. Down. Now."

He kissed his way down her body. "I think my testimony at your trial is going to sound...depraved."

"Do you solemnly swear to tell the truth, the whole truth, and nothing but the..."

His tongue entered her. Falling away from who she believed she was in the world. His fingers slipping inside. All truth ceasing to matter as little sparks of energy thrilled the nerves all over her body.

He could make her come again, so quickly, if he wanted to—but he played it out, laying off at the moments of high anxiety.

Waves rising and falling; three crests, before he increased the intensity all the way, to draw out a shuddering orgasm, shrinking her into a foetal ball, a ball fringed with extreme sensitivity.

He tortured her a little bit, for fun. Caresses. Nips. Licks.

"No!" She ordered him: "Stop it."

"Okay." He got up, pulled his boxers on. Got fully dressed. "It's breakfast time. I could literally kill for some crispy, streaky-bacon sandwiches."

"Trespasser breakfast?"

"Yeah. Forgive us our trespasses..."

"—As we forgive those who breakfast against us."

"And deliver us from sausages..."

"—For thine is the bacon and the butty, forever and ever..."

"—Amen."

DJINN

P RIVATE ROAD, NO TRESPASSING: Muhend read the sign.
They were at the end of The Lodge's driveway.

"Heads down, folks. Right down," A K said, and pulled out
onto the main road.

Muhend slipped down into the footwell of the back seat, groped for
Boudris' hand. Squeezed bones.

A K accelerated up through the gears. "Dublin, here we come!"

Lilit laughed. High. Nervously.

They stayed down in the back, holding hands, for a mile, until A K
said, "Say buh-bye to Glenshee folks, you can get up now."

Muhend sat up. Looking out the window, to see what was going on.

It was a stupid thing to do, the stupidest thing on a long list of
stupid things he had done, because the Guards were in a car pulling up
at a T-junction on the right.

Scything blue lights, the blare of a siren.

He cowered down, trying to disappear in between blinks of blue,
but it was too late. *Praise be to God, Lord of the Worlds, the Compassionate, the Merciful, King of the Day of Judgement. We worship you and seek
your aid. Guide us on the straight path, the path of those whom you have*

bestowed your grace, not the path of those who incur your anger nor of those gone astray.

The Guards had spotted them in the Fiat and were giving chase, powering up the road, until they were tailgating.

"Pull over!" Lilit was scared.

The siren wail was loud and shrill.

The blare of reality: Muhend looked up at A K. Blue lights flashed over his face, the seats, off the windows. Blue. Blinking in his eyes. Everything. Blue.

"We can give them the slip up a side road. Make our getaway."

"In this rust-bucket?" she sneered.

A K kept driving, was not going to give up so easy. "We'll be all right."

Muhend was compelled to sit up, look out. Forgive us Lord. Do not punish us like the people of the Prophet Lut in Sodom and Gomorrah. Forgive us the sins of *al fahisha, al kabair, al munkar*, and *as sayyi'att.*

There was the back end of a camper van looming up ahead. What the Americans call a motorhome or an R.V. This particular R.V. came all the way from the 1950s, and had a nickname—'the Lobotomobile'.

"Oh, Jesus fucking Christ," Lilit said.

A-K tried to overtake the R.V., without anticipating the sharp corner ahead.

A motorcycle, a Brough Superior SS100 with the name George VII, was overtaking a white Mercedes Benz convertible on the apex of the bend, cornering at high speed, heading straight for the Fiat.

Lilit screamed.

The motorcycle jinked left onto the hard shoulder, averting a head-on collision.

The Mercedes kept coming.

A K wrenched the steering wheel to the left. The wing of the Fiat clipped into the front wheel of the motorhome. Shrieking metal. Whipping one way, then entirely another.

Boudris was yelling for the mercy of Allah. Crunch, a blizzard of glass as the passenger window smashed.

The Fiat glanced off the motorhome, out of control, slewing across the road, the hard shoulder, and smashing through the crash barrier. Catapulting into space, into thin air.

Inside, Lilit was screeching, until everything crumpled into the rocks and sand of the beach. Rolling over, and over, heads clashing in the back of the car, banging off the roof, the seats, the floor, battering each other.

It was all over quickly.

All still, and upside-down, heavy, fuzzed. Lying there, somehow sprawled on top of Boudris. He is not moving. Not making a sound. *What of the others?* The wailing of the siren had stopped. *Is Boudris breathing?* The body, numbness, limbs buzzing like they were swarms of bees in smoke. *Breathe, breathe.*

Mais, il est très difficile. In a smashed-up world of black-and-white flicker, seen through narrow slits, melting in tears, he turned to see the lovely, soft hair on the back of Boudris' head. In his heart, he knew his love was gone. *And A K?* He could not see.

Lilit's eyes were open, but there was no one looking back at him.

Why am I the only one left? The reek of petrol, choking. The smell of burning. Fire. The terror that he would be burned alive, burned alone, drove the need to move.

Except, he could not. Not a muscle. The susurration of waves folding onto the beach. Death rolling in.

He knew he was dying. Not at all instantly. Unlike the account of Father's accident. Slowly. Suffering. Awaiting Azrael. But it was not the Angel of Death who took him to the place beyond Time, it was her.

Lilit.

And yet, not her. For she was now someone else, or more properly, something else, an entity known as 'Am klu amshayitan', whom he would now serve. *If you do not help me birth my baby,* she warned, *the army of the dead will devour you.*

I am the first and the last
I am the honoured one and the scorned one
I am the whore and the holy one
I am the wife and the virgin
I am the mother and the daughter
I am the members of my mother
I am the barren one, and many are her sons
I am the silence that is incomprehensible
And the idea whose remembrance is frequent
And the word whose appearance is multiple
I am the utterance of my name.

THE THUNDER, PERFECT MIND

A person who cannot escape from his own separateness goes into
Avitchi. All these Avitchi men will eventually become
inhabitants of the Eighth Sphere.

RUDOLF STEINER, *The Foundations of Esotericism*

LUZIFER'S CROWN

O tto unclipped the Walther PPK in his shoulder-holster. They had come to the Ritz for cocktails, but he was being hunted. He knew, the way all animals know when they are being hunted. This seventh sense, *einfühlung*, he had developed it to the maximum. The German term for what he was—*ein Hellseher*.

The bartender, Hans, delivered a tray to their table, with considerable effort, and placed a French 75 and a *Kommando* correctly, in front of his patrons. "Enjoy your drinks!"

"The best *Kommando* cocktail in Madrid," Otto declared. The young couple at the bar. At first glance, a handsome businessman and his young mistress.

Hans smiled, and removed their empty glasses. He'd served in the Condor Legion in the Civil War, somewhat carelessly lost a leg below the knee in the second Battle of Toledo, so as he stood up straight, he overbalanced. A small stagger backwards.

Otto helped the man steady himself. "The drunken bartender is a terrible cliché, *Oberfeldwebel*."

Hans smiled, then looked back at the bar, deadly sober. "I hate to say this, Herr Steinbauer, but those two at the bar are staring at you."

"A very attractive couple," Ilse said, lifting her French 75.

"*Zehntausend dankeschön*, Hans." He tucked a folded 10,000 peseta note into Hans' top pocket. He always gave whopping great gratuities for introductions and information on the Madrid social scene. It paid to have friends in the battalion of mâitre d's and bartenders.

"Why don't we invite them over?" Ilse said, and winked.

"You are *blau, Liebchen*. The bubbles go to your head, and stay there."

Ilse giggled. "Oh, finish your story then."

Before Hans' interruption, he had been telling the story of how Otto Rahn's Crusade Against the Grail led him up to a cave, near the Cathar stronghold of Montsegur, where he changed the course of History by finding what some called 'Luzifer's Crown', and others referred to as 'The Holy Grail', but what was in truth, the largest of the seven Firestones of the drowned Atlantean Empire: 'The Amilius Firestone'.

"Tell me again, my brave Scar, how you sent the fateful telegram to Adolf!" Ilse patted his arm, play-acting the fawning wife who doted on her husband's every word.

Such a ballbreaker, as the Yanks would say. "The moment has passed, *Schatzi*. You will excuse 'Scar'—who must venture to the bar, to find out who the attractive couple are."

He got up. Adjusted his jacket, making sure to cover the shoulder-holster. Then, he made his approach. The woman was all curves. Pure sexuality. Who would not love to overpower her, tear off that mini-skirt, take her in the moment? What red-blooded man could resist? Those breasts, alpine, the cleft vertiginous.

The man was resting against the counter. He was holding a bloody napkin over his left arm.

"*Was ist los?*" Otto asked.

The man removed the napkin, held his arm up. A blade had slashed through his jacket and shirt, jagging a bloody line on the muscles there. "We were mugged."

With horrified look on her face the woman told the tall tale of an attempted robbery. By two muggers.

He would nod in all the right places. Muggings were commonplace in Madrid, even in 1962. Despite Franco's crackdowns on the lower orders.

The woman was very convincing, a natural storyteller, could make her feet and hands tell lies in near-perfect German. "They took it all," she said, "money, passports, travellers' cheques, they even took Kurt's work briefcase."

"*Drecksack,*" was his response. He would not hesitate to shoot a mugger, or two, fatal shots, no witnesses, no Guardia Civil. He had an extreme aversion to justice since the travesty of Nuremberg. Justice was merely vengeance. *The only law in this life is: Whatever you do, do not get caught.*

Otto nodded to Hans for counter service, then said to the couple: "Cocktails will steady your nerves. Name your medication?"

"*Vielen danke.'* Kurt looked suitably embarrassed. "A Sidecar, if you please."

"Ah. A wrecking drink."

"And I will have a—Roman Punch," she said.

"You are clearly a professional."

She frowned at the implications of this, then laughed.

Otto pointed to the table where Ilse was sitting, smiling. "Please. Join us?"

They were pleased to, and he led them across, presented Ilse as Ilse. Normally, he introduced her as Alice, but she was drunk, and would make a mistake. He did use the cover, Steinbauer. Von Finkenstein was just too Prussian, too big a name, proud as Luzifer.

"*Guten abend,* Ilse." Kurt took her hand and kissed it. "*Sehr schön.*"

The name the beautiful liar gave herself was 'Anke'.

They talked, small talk. Anke spoke German like a Bavarian, but she was not a native, no, too much High German. Kurt spoke colloquial German with an Austrian accent, and claimed to be from *Wien*, born in Sudbahn. The truest part of his cover.

To be *Wienese*. To speak *Wienese* German. He always had a weakness for his fellow countrymen. They knew that. How he loved his city. The Imperial City. *Wien*. They were using that against him. The enemy.

But, he could not help himself. He was sentimental. Not to mention nostalgic. And so very homesick. He wished nothing more than to return to the *Vaterland* of his youth, in spite of the hardships of defeat. The Traitors' Treaty of Versailles. The separation of Austria from Hungary. Crushing reparations. Rampant inflation. Food shortages.

It could not be helped, this lost love. It was part of his condition. The condition of all true Germans these days. A strange vagabondage, which he sometimes thought mirrored the wanderings of the Jews through the centuries after their exile from their Promised Land, but considering Delitzsch's *Die Grosse Tauschung,* he corrected himself. Judaeo-Christian history, as recorded in The Bible, was the vilest lie ever told! He should be thinking of the Aryans, the Master Race of Atlantis, and see his journey as a reflection of their glorious voyages of conquest across the globe, tens of thousands of years ago.

The enemy laughed, and flirted. Otto noted Kurt focusing his attention on Ilse, while Anke distracted her mark, and was so very-very distracting. The rush of blood to the head! Like he was 20 again. In the spring. A stag bellowing in the rut. Her heavy scent in his nostrils. Overpowering pheromones. He wanted this female.

Ilse looked over, saw lust in his eyes, smiled. He smiled back. The game of seduction played out a little more before an incredible coincidence happened, except that it was no coincidence at all. In games like these, there were no coincidences, as in fiction.

Because it was fiction, and the dots must connect. Kurt was also a pilot. He flew a Messerschmitt Bf-109 in the Battle of Britain. He was shot down in 1941, over the South Downs, taken prisoner, and spent the rest of the war learning English and, gardening.

"I always wanted to join the Luftwaffe and fly fighters. I was told I was too old. They would not accept a man of 30, so I had to join the blasted artillery."

"That probably saved your life." Kurt laughed. "Us pilots had very short lifespans once the Spitfires appeared. I should know. One bagged me. And later, I hear the P-51 American Mustang was unbeatable, in the right hands. Unless, of course, you were lucky enough to fly the Jet."

The Jet, the Messerschmitt 262. Ah yes indeed, to fly that in combat...

Otto wished for more of Kurt's tales of derring-do dogfighting, his clever lies. He put the pilot to the test to see if he knew the inside of the

109, and he did, every last detail, and kinetically. No doubt he had flown one, but not for Sacred Germany. *How did that come to pass? An intelligence operation? So intriguing.*

"You must stay with us," Ilse told them. "At our villa, *Die Wolfsschanze.*"

He coughed, more of a squawk. Why would Ilse say that? She will be the death of us someday!

They flatly ignored the reference to the Führer's H.Q., looked to him for assent.

"Ya. You absolutely must stay," Otto said.

"You can go to the embassy tomorrow to sort things out," Ilse said. "Otto will drive you."

Otto!

Not Rolf!

Not the agreed cover!

Ilse had used his real name. He shot her the dark look which, given all his scars, terrified most men under his command, but she laughed it off.

"That is such a kind offer to make! So generous of you, Otto!"

Otto! Not even a glint of surprise in Anke's eyes.

They knew his name, of course: Otto Skorzeny!

Agent for the B.N.D. and the C.I.A.

Head of *Die Spinne.*

The question being: Will they try to assassinate or kidnap you, spirit you to Zion for trial, like Eichmann?

"We gratefully accept your hospitality," Kurt said.

"I have a car downstairs," he said. "Follow me."

They will not take me! Whatever their plans! The old saying he was apt to use when talking to his boys of the vagaries of war bubbled up in his mind: *The soup is never eaten as hot as it is cooked.*

DREAMHOUSE

Bacon-bacon, streaky-bacon! Foraging in the kitchen of a vacant mansion. Probably a tad idiotic, but Adamo opened the fridge with great expectations.

Zippo food. Nevermind bacon!

He pressed the fridge door shut, click. That was when he heard it. A pounding noise emanating from the floor. Bang! Bang! Bang! Shuddering up through the floor into his bare feet.

The cellar?

Was there a cellar?

A basement?

Somebody down there? He would follow the rhythmic vibrations, locate the basement door in the hall, and open it. Sure enough—found, the source of the sounds. He stared down the steps into a very grey area. The steps, the walls, the floor. Grey as fog.

What if there was someone down there?

Reason would dictate that in this situation he should retreat, withdraw before being discovered, and punished for his transgressions. Reason being however, a relatively late invention of the human species. Emotion was führer. The heuristics of the heart. It was the heart that drove him to descend the stairs. As if he was being bidden, had to heed the call.

Halfway down, a powerful engine sparked into life, time seemed to speed up on the lower steps, and in the no-time that he found himself in at the bottom, where he would witness a big, broad-shouldered man, bending over the engine of a car, a sports car, a white Mercedes Benz.

The man was not dressed in mechanic's overalls, but in a sports jacket, and trousers. The clothes of middle age, fatherhood. Could this be the owner of the house?

The engine revved into a scream, then dropped into an entrancing thrumming.

"Morgen," the German said, without turning.

He was struck dumb as a shy boy. *Morgen?*

The German turned. Twin scars sliced deep down the right cheek. Sharp eyes were set in more scars. "You must be surprised to see me here, ya?"

"Yes." This way of speaking. *Your father's voice...?*

"You will be staying here with Oasis Collections, ya?"

"Yeah," he lied.

Oasis Collections was advertised on the Tube ads as a posh Airbnb. He had always wanted to go somewhere hot-hot-hot and stay in a grand villa, sip champagne by the pool, live like a king.

The German sighed. "She didn't tell me. The owner. Very remiss of her. I apologise for invading your privacy. You will accept my apology?"

What else was there to say? "Yes."

"Sehr gut. I am your neighbour, on the extreme right. Otto is my name." The German offered his oil-stained hand.

He shook the hand. 'Adamo.'

"I maintain the Mercedes for the owner while she is away, which seems to be always. Do you know your classic cars at all?"

Adamo so wanted to be able to say, Yes! But—"No."

"This is a 1957 300 SL Convertible. A beautiful piece of German engineering."

"Yeah. It's incredible."

"I have to take her out for a spin round the neighbourhood, turn the engine over. Why don't you get dressed and come with me? We can stop at El Pirata and brunch. I need some bacon."

'How can I refuse an offer like that?' Adamo had never been in a classic convertible before. And, bacon! so he rushed back upstairs, and blitz-dressed, taking care not to waken Eva, who was still lost in Dreamworld.

Otto drove the wonderful Mercedes Benz, out into Knightsbridge, accelerating around the sun-dappled Hyde Park, going up and down through the gears, giving the vintage engine a good workout. Time seemed to slip into a different gear. The car as time machine. It was hard to explain, but that was how it felt.

As a historian, he'd lived his life in the past, the past tense had come to dominate his cast of mind, but now, he shifted into the futuristic state of becoming. A life lived in the prophetic will be, not the ever-so-limited is or was. The heat on his face made him beam, as the light breeze tousled through his hair. He never would want this drive to end.

But it ended, with Otto parking on Down Street, in front of the Sheraton. After purchasing a parking ticket from the meter, they walked to El Pirata, and sat down at an outside table.

A waitress came straight over.

"*Zwei grosse biere, bitte.*" Otto ordered six tapas dishes and politely dismissed the girl. He talked of Spain, Madrid, where he lived for many years; his abiding love of their deconstructed cuisine.

The beers arrived, pints.

"Cheers!" He raised his glass.

Clink!

"*Prost.* You know for me, nothing in this dimension beats an ice-cold beer with peasant tapas. I love the way you may mix the dishes to your own taste."

Otto talked about a crystal, a blue crystal, he had misplaced in the house, how he must find it, until the tapas was served, and they began to eat.

Only then did he ask, "Tell me. What is it you do for a living, Adamo?"

"I am a historian. Twentieth century."

"Ah. History is a subject that is close to my own heart. What is your, how do you say—specialism?"

"These days, International Jewish History."

"Zionism." Otto nodded. "Zion was so nearly Madagascar, you know. The Jews would probably have been so much happier there."

"I think the Jews are happy in their ancestral homeland."

"The Exilarchs would never accept any other territorial solution to the Jewish Problem, but Palestine was never truly theirs. It belonged to the Anakites. They merely conquered it by force of arms, David versus Goliath."

"They would argue that it was given to them by the Lord."

"The Enlil giveth and the Enlil taketh away."

"He doth indeed."

"Hah. He has certainly given you lots of material for a book. Tell me —are you a Jew?"

"No."

"A mere Judaeo-Christian then. Would you say you are a Zionist?"

"No."

There was a silence in which Otto seemed to be contemplating saying more. "You can drive back, my boy."

"Really?"

The car keys slid across the table. "Of course."

He bolted the rest of his food.

Drove back to Blackcross Crescent. Wonderful. Flow-state. He did not want it to ever end. But it would end, down in the basement. With the car parked. A handshake, and the word, "*Wiedersehen.*"

HITLER'S KOMMANDO

K*rieg*, thought Otto. But not *Blitzkrieg, nein*. A snail-slow war. A phoney war. A cold war, to be waged back at *Die Wolfss-chanze*. So, on the back terrace of the old villa, he would go to war most munificently.

Magik fingers, the foil ripped, the wire uncoiled, the weapon primed —the cork exploded away from his thumbs.

The *sekt* spumed forth.

The ladies gasped, laughed, and Anke looked at him with naked desire as he poured the bubbles into the glasses. He would love to spit the *sekt* into her open lips.

"*Prost!*" he offered the toast with his left hand. It felt unnatural, but his right hand must be free to draw the Walther at any moment.

"*Prost!*"

Raised glasses, clink-clink-clink, customary nods, and then sipping at their drinks.

"What a spectacular house you have, Ilse," Anke said.

"We live the life of a King of France," said Ilse.

"This is such excellent champagne," Kurt said, ogling Ilse. "So full-bodied."

"It is not mere champagne, Kurt. It is *Winzersekt*."

"I stand corrected, Otto."

"*Reichsrat von Bruhl*, no less."

"You must forgive my husband," Ilse said, blithely. "He is such a snob about wine these days."

"I am not a snob," he declared. He could not tell Ilse of the violence to come. It would remain *hintergedanken*. "To have taste, *Schatzi*, is not a crime."

Laughing, Anke reached for her purse.

"I must apologise," He drew the Walther, pointed it at her chest. "Remove your hand from the bag, slowly."

Anke looked stunned, hurt. "My cigarettes."

"Set it down on the floor."

"What are you doing?" Kurt played horrified. "Otto?"

Ilse, though completely *blau*, was a former Abwehr agent, and stepped clear of the couple. She knew her 'Scar' weighed everything up, did nothing lightly.

"The charade is over," he said. "I know who you are. I know you are here to kill me."

"We are here to make love to you," Anke said, desperately trying to stay in-character.

"You are Mossad," he said.

"Mossad?" Ilse gasped.

"The Mossad," Kurt said. A wry grin. "If we were here to kill you, you would already be dead."

"That is a gross overestimation of your capabilities," he countered, "and a most stupid underestimation of mine, which I'm afraid has cost you your lives."

"If you kill us, the next agents won't be sent to have drinks with you. Think carefully, *Obersturmbannführer* Skorzeny. The world is a small place, and it's getting smaller all the time for war criminals, no? Adolf Eichmann will not be the last Nazi to stand trial in Israel."

He nodded. Too true. It was 1962. Even the Amazon jungle was not safe anymore. He was on Wiesenthal's stupid list. The Mossad, with their ethic of total retaliation, would hunt him down, even though he had never been ordered to kill a Jew, or given an order for his men to kill a Jew. Perhaps he killed Jews in Russian or American uniforms, but he served in the S.S. artillery as an engineer officer, and after being wounded, as a *kommando*. War is war.

He was on the list of war criminals because of his infamy as 'Hitler's *Kommando*', leader of the feared *Jagdkommando*, propaganda which Goebbels manufactured to strike terror into Allied, and Axis, leaders alike: *Der Teufel Skorzeny* is coming for you.

The Devil Himself's wartime hit-list included: Admiral Horthy, whom he deposed in Hungary; Winston Churchill, Marshal Tito; Supreme Allied Commander, General Dwight D. Eisenhower—who went on to become the 34th President of the United States.

'Old Ike' was sufficiently terrorised to declare Otto Skorzeny 'Public Enemy Number One', and 'the Most Dangerous Man in Europe' in 1945. Such infamy, such global notoriety, was worth a fortune as a soldier of fortune, but it had its downside.

It had always been his darkest fear that The Mossad would come for him. That the C.I.A. would sell him out, despite his usefulness. And, in the third part of the night, they would come to spirit him away.

"We have a proposition for you that we think you will find intriguing," Anke said. "We need your help."

"You need my help?"

Kurt smiled, most disarmingly. "We need to halt the Egyptian missile programme. All the German rocket scientists must leave. We will pay you handsomely for it."

"I have no need of money," he said, to cover up the shock offer of employment. "Money-schmoney."

"You worked for Nasser for pay. Is our money not good enough for you?"

"It is not that." Surely The Mossad had intelligence enough to know that Ilse was Ilse von Finkenstein, 'the niece' of Hjalmar Schacht, Hitler's finance minister, and that they both had access to the vast, hidden, Nazi financial reserves...

Aktion Alderflüg, aka 'Operation Eagle Flight', funnelled all the loot of war—$900 billion—off through Swiss banks into big commercial beasts like Chase Morgan, and smaller 'front' banks, thence into holding corporations to fund 750 newly set up corporations in the sympathetic states of Spain, Portugal, Switzerland, Sweden, Turkey and Argentina.

This treasure hoard was to be used for the eternal glory of the Fourth
Reich, the International Reich, and the Fifth Reich to come, the Extra-
dimensional Reich.

"Listen," Kurt said. "We know you work for the C.I.A. in Egypt. We
know that they helped you become 'the man behind Nasser', his military advisor, training his men in commando tactics. If you contact your
handler, ex-Director Dulles will inform you that we are of one mind on
this."

"I will ask Allen, personally," he said. But of course, Dulles was not
the führer of 'The Eighth Sphere'. Only a select few knew it was King
Thevetat of Atlantis, Codename: 'Belial'. Also Known As: 'Ahriman'.

"Do. The Yanks don't want the Reds getting into Egypt, not with
missiles primed, and aimed at Israel."

"The stinking Reds!" Ilse almost spat the words.

"We must all do what we can to stop the spread of Communism,"
Anke said.

His trigger finger stiffened. His hatred of the Russians, the Communists, far exceeded any racial concerns about the Jews. He was a man of
political conviction. But it was Jews who created Marxism to destroy the
real socialism, National Socialism. A fact—that there would be no Reds,
no Lenin, no Trotsky, no Stalin, no Khrushchev, without the Black
Nobility of Venice and their little drummer-boys, the Rothschilds, the
Warburgs, the Rockefellers. Still...

"The enemy of one's enemy can be a friend," Kurt said.

An alliance of convenience with The Mossad. It was like déjà vu
with the O.S.S.: acting as a double agent would enable him to identify
their most senior intelligence officers, and...influence them.

The thrill of the great game of power tingled deep in his brain, it
almost made him quiver, but he channeled it: "If the C.I.A. were to
authorise my involvement, my name must be struck off Wiesenthal's list.
It should never have been included. I was no *Totenkopfverbände*. I was
an officer in the Weapons S.S. A *kommando*. This is a matter of
honour."

"Okay," Kurt nodded. "I'm sure we can do that."

"Then, as the Yanks say—we have a deal." He took his finger off the
trigger and sheathed the Walther.

"Deal!" Kurt stepped forward, offering his hand.

Otto's grip had not lost any of its iron since his fencing days, and he applied extra pressure in the shake. "Wiesenthal must write to me, personally."

"Understood. Wiesenthal's letter will be the sign of our good faith."

THE CRIB

E va was sleepwalking again.

    She'd had this tendency to sleep-walk and sleep-talk since childhood. For a child, this condition could be terribly frightening. The idea that something else—be it demon, ghost, dybbuk—could be inhabiting, and animating, the sleeping body. To snap-to, discover that the body had decided to go somewhere else from where the owner left it, this was the stuff of nightmares.

For Sister Eva Kadmon though, after the umpteenth time, Sleep Behaviour Disorder had ceased to be that big a deal. All nurses were in reality somnambulists.

'Dream-walkers' as she called it.

The shift-work did it. The nights on the ward. Not ever being fully awake or fully asleep. Existing in an altered mode of being was a professional hazard she had to accept.

Zav maveth. There was a silver Three Angels' mezuzah nailed to the door jamb. Three angels. Like on the door. The front door of the house. Zav maveth was Hebrew, meant: 'Death remove thyself'.

She kissed her fingers, brushed the mezuzah with the tips, then drifted past, into what was undoubtedly the most magical nursery she had ever seen.

All the original 22 letters of the Hebrew flame Aleph bet had been painted in shining gold on the wall, over a four-poster cot. The walls were baby blue—because she was convinced she would have a boy, Seth.

Seth. Potent as the flaming letters shin and tav.

On the floor: the Tree of Life felled, flattened. The Sephiroth as rug. She crossed over this one-dimensional representation of the Kabbala. Stepped on the owl perched on one of its highest branches. She could almost hear its hooting.

What does the owl-birdie do, Seth?

Ta-wit-ta-wooooooo. Her hand rested on the top rail of the crib. A cot fit for a king. The loveliest little prison bars. With one side of the rails lowered, so she would be able to lift, and lay, her precious baby son.

Over the crib, hung a sparkly mobile, lots of psychedelic hands with eyes in them. *Hamsas.* To ward off the evil eye. To chase the *mazikin* away.

There was a huge blue nursing armchair—more sofa than chair—over by the window so she could feed Seth there in the afternoon sun.

She went over and sat in it. Could almost feel her boy's lips and gums suckling on her nipples, the strange intensity of that sensation, being milked, a tiny hand squeezing her breast, wanting more.

She brushed the wisps of blonde hair into silly little tufts, chuckled as he suckled, and smoothed them out again. The cutest little murmur. His eyes opened, cornflower blue orbs, tiny pupils, and then, content that she was there, the archetypal Great Mother, all-he-would-ever-need, closed again.

It was the strangest thing to be a mother-to-be. After all this time. After all the effort. Two cycles of I.V.F. Ovulation production. Egg retrieval. Fertilisation. Embryo transfer, and implantation. Times-two. To finally conceive.

After the swollen fallopian tube, on the left. Half the chance of a normal woman. Her family doctor told her when she was 16, that she would have more, and more, difficulty conceiving, the older she got. That she should get pregnant young, before the age of 19. If she didn't, she might be barren.

But, 19...? Who gets pregnant at that age, post-Feminism? Silly girls, who never dreamed of being anything, of having a life of their own, before giving their life to their child. *Nope. No, sirree.* Way too much F.O.M.O., Fear Of Missing Out, tempered her mothering instincts. Sublimated them. Her caring nature drove her to become a nurse, even though, her mum and dad thought this to be beneath her, a waste of her talents.

Nursing was somehow seen as un-Jewish. Not intellectual enough. Un-abstract. De-evolved. Her late father actually went so far as to say: "You are so smart. Why not become a doctor? Doctors make good money."

Her mother, Laima, the only daughter of two Lithuanian emigres, chance-survivors of the *Einsatzgruppen* 'Special Action' in Vilnius, 'the Jerusalem of the North', actually said: "You are throwing your life away. Go to university."

Neither understood—Nursing is a calling.

She did not need to reflect on her vocation. She'd found a purpose to her life, early. Which was rare. And precious. She went to nursing college straight from school. This was the path for her. The Royal College of Nursing, in the heart of London.

That nurse, standing in this nursery, laughed at herself nursing, and she woke up, to find she was lying in a strange bed, a strange bedroom. Seth? The loveliness of her new son, Seth. A dream. The nursery. A dream. The crib. All a crazy dream.

She got up, went looking for Adamo. To tell him of her dream. Make some sense of it.

OPERATION DAMOCLES

The letter from Simon Wiesenthal. It arrived, as if by magik, one week after Otto's fateful encounter with The Mossad.

The Nazi Hunter stated that, although Otto Skorzeny had been a senior member of the S.S., there were no records of him having committed war crimes, and he was no longer the subject of any active investigations. He glared the sheet of paper for a long time. 20 years of being hunted. No more. Honour was finally satisfied!

Kurt visited *Die Wolfschanze* that afternoon, to brief him. "'Operation Damocles' is to discourage all German scientists working for Nasser, at Factory 333, by all means necessary."

Kurt stated the mission in two parts: "You will contact your friend President Nasser, offer to take over security at Factory 333. In order to create maximum workforce insecurity, you will assassinate the Head of Intra, Heinz Krug, in West Germany."

He knew Krug from his years serving as a C.I.A. asset in Egypt. Stocky fellow for a rocket scientist. Morose without schnapps; witty with it. "Why Krug, if I may ask? He is a paper-pusher, a bureaucrat. Pilz is the real brains behind Factory 333."

"We understand that Pilz, like all Peenemunde rocket-men, has an open offer to join Von Braun's NASA."

"I see," he said. He hid the thought: *So, I am to terrorise Pilz into Uncle Sam's Race for Space.*

Kurt cleared his throat. "We have, under the name 'the Gideonites', already issued death threats to Krug, and all concerned, by letter, and by phone, so he will be pleased to hear from you."

"You have been busy little bees."

"We are on standby," Kurt said, and handed over a business card. "This is the number to contact us on. Codeword: King Dionysius II."

First things first, he phoned the V.P. of the World Commerce Corporation, Ricardo Sicre, to explain developments, in detail. "*Mátalo,*" the Spaniard ordered.

The next call was to Allen Dulles, who did not mention any Nasa plans for Pilz, stating: "Krug has simply got to go."

His final call was to Reinhard Gehlen. The President of the *Bundesnachrichtendienst* was adamant: "Otto—halt that programme, before the Yids follow through on their threats to nuke Egypt, or worse, Germany."

To be the sword in Operation Damocles. The sword, hanging over the head of Krug. Suspended by a single strand of horsehair, which would soon snap. He phoned the number on the business card. Someone picked up, but there was no greeting. "King Dionysius II," he said.

"Enact Damocles on the 11th," came the reply.

So, Otto flew into Munich on the 11th September, using the Steinbauer West German passport.

Kurt, and two escorts, met him at Arrivals and drove him to the office of Intra on Schillerstrasse.

Otto went straight in, and introduced himself to Krug with a hearty handshake. "I have been ordered by Gehlen to ensure you are not assassinated by agents of a foreign power."

Krug accepted this explanation without question: "Thank you for coming, Skorzeny. I cannot tell you what a relief it is to have you as my personal bodyguard."

"*Kein problem,*" he said. "As the threat on your life is imminent, you cannot continue to work from the office, or go home. I have three men in a car outside who will escort us to a safe house. My boys will collect your wife later."

He directed Krug to drive his white Mercedes Benz south, out of the city, to the safe house in the hills round Starnberg. "A lovely old forest lodge," he said. "Belongs to Schweinsteiger, one of my Brandenburg boys."

What he did not say: It's the perfect site for an unmarked grave.

The escort car, a black Mercedes, followed discreetly.

"History is being made in Egypt," Krug said. "We are making great progress at Factory 333. We test-launched the *El-Kahir*, the so-called 'Conqueror' rocket, ground-to-ground, in July."

"I heard it veered 100 miles off-course—before crashing into the Sinai dunes."

"Hans Kleinwachter has been hired to work on the guidance system. He perfected the V2. Think of it—900 warheads, filled with cobalt-60, enough to wipe 'the Zionist Entity' off the map. The Final Solution will be complete."

"*Die Endlösung der Judenfrage.*" He pitied the poor fellow. Krug might be S.S., but he knew nothing of the Time War. If Krug could but see how small History is compared to Eternity, he would know the Final Solution was to be executed by the Sons of Belial—after the Erev Tav retook Zion, and rebuilt the Temple of Solomon.

Krug drove up into the pine-forested Bavarian hills. Forstenrieder Park.

Otto wound the window down, to breathe in the resin. "Pine cleanses the German soul," he said, "I have been too long in Madrid my friend, too long."

"This is truly the beating heart of the Reich."

For him, the heart lay not in Bavaria, but Wien. Still, two sentimental, old men stared out of the car windows and shared the dream of a Reich, built to last a thousand years. Atlantis reborn.

It was almost a shame to have to kill Krug a few miles up the road. "Take a right onto Romerstraße," he said. "The safe house is down a track, two miles from this junction, on the right."

Krug pulled into the shadowy pine-lined lane that led up to the lodge. The black Mercedes tailed them, drawing in close.

Halfway down the lane, he slid the Walther out of its holster. "Stop here."

"What are you doing?"

The Walther raised, head-high. "Stop the car!"

Krug braked, to a stop. "Have you lost your mind?"

"This is no safe house."

"Skorzeny—you are a traitor?" Krug shuddered.

Otto would flinch at the use of the word traitor. You—are—a—traitor. You. It angered him, greatly. "This has been sanctioned at the highest levels!"

"Then they are traitors to the Cause," Krug said. "The Soaps have bought you all."

A tightening in Otto's trigger finger. "Would you care for a last cigarette?"

Krug shook his head.

Otto shot. Three times. In the chest. The look was total surprise, not pain, quick.

The *Gnadenschusse* in the head, to finish.

Smoke curled up to the roof, as grey brain slopped down. Reeking cordite; copper-tang of blood a taste; until Kurt and the other agents opened the driver's door, and pulled the body out. Blood, dark red, smeared all over the leather of the seat. From the liver.

"We will take it from here." A blaze of righteous anger in Kurt's eyes: the wish to kill him also, bury two bodies in this hole, two Nazis for the price of one...

With a shrug, Otto sheathed his Walther, opened the passenger door. The cleansing scent of pine filled his nostrils.

He extracted a cigarette from a pack of Lucky Strikes, lit up, and smoked, observing The Mossad boys use a lump-hammer to smash in the mouth, then pour drops of hydrochloric acid to dissolve the teeth and sear off all fingerprints.

When the body was tossed into the grave, it was powdered white with a bag of ammonium nitrate. They shovelled in the dark, wet earth of the forest. It was naturally acidic, and the fertiliser would turn to nitric acid, speeding up the process of decomposition, eating the very bones.

They scattered quick lime on the topsoil to throw bloodhounds off the scent. Very efficient. Very professional. Nothing would be left in five years, except a human stain underground. To all intents and purposes Heinz Krug had disappeared from the face of the Earth.

The Mossad wished the disappearance—and the denial of a body to grieve over—to serve as a warning. The Jews, hearts hardened by the war, the torture of the camps, had now become the reflection of the Aryans. It therefore fell to him to show some mercy.

In the war, he'd had to write many, many letters to the relatives of his boys missing in action. It was a harrowing wait for the son, the brother, who never came home, so the next morning, he took pity on Krug's wife, and made an anonymous phone call, to inform her that her husband was dead. The very least he could do.

The Krug disappearing act did not convince Pilz to quit. Letter-bombs sent to him at Factory 333 at Heliopolis, one of which blinded his secretary-and-lover, Hannelore; another of which, killed five Egyptians—did not discourage Pilz.

Even a direct assassination attempt, on Dr. Kleinwachter by The Mossad, a botched job, did not shake Pilz's genocidal resolve.

Threats made to the children of another colleague, Dr. Goercke, about what would happen if he did not return home immediately, finally had the desired effect, the Exodus of Nazis from Egypt, but Pilz did not rush into the waiting arms of NASA, opting instead to go to the People's Republic of China, and found their intercontinental ballistic missile programme.

A Knight of the Feme; a Brother of the *Schwarz Sonne*; a Son of Belial, working for the fucking Red Monkey, Mao. *Some men would do anything for money! Had no honour.*

Wherefore Art Thou...?

Otto, International Man of Mystery. The dream-like encounter with the German played on Adamo's mind as he left the house, walked up Chepstow, onto Dawson Place. But then, he had to phone the letting agents, Dutch & Dutch. No answer, no answering service. A blow-out of a sigh. Who doesn't have fucking voicemail?

He passed a teen rapper on the corner, earphones on, beatboxing; envying the guy that carefreedomness.

On the doorstep of the Double-Mums', he rang the bell and stood there, staring at the big pink door, wondering: What are you going to say? He didn't want to sound mad, and yet everything had gone absolutely mental since he had been told he was going to be a dad.

It took a few minutes before the zombie of Helena answered the door, in black silk pyjamas. "I was beginning to take root out here!"

"I took a Xanax." She attempted a thin smile as apology. "Come in."

He hated it when she drugged herself up to cope with Nadine, but he hugged her, and went in. "Are you all right?"

"We were up all night, working."

There was a picture of a beautiful, naked woman propped up

against the wall. He couldn't help but notice. A snake had coiled all around her body. "Rats are back in the attic again?"

She nodded. "The show. I told her this Black Moon thing was no good for the soul. Dark energy."

The Black Moon reference meant nothing to him. Astrology meant nothing to him. Lilith meant nothing to him. There was a dull echo of his first-and-lost love, Lilit, but that was it. "Off her meds?"

"Tornado-mania. I had to help smooth things over with the set-up. She was driving everyone crazy. We got it done but..."

"—I wondered why you weren't here last night."

"You were here last night?"

"Yeah. We had our own emergency to deal with..."

"—What happened?"

"You wouldn't believe me if I told you."

"Over a cup of tea." She led him into the kitchen, flicked the kettle on, and set about ransacking a cupboard to find tea.

The kettle boiled. He outlined the details of the eviction-at-knife-point, in brief.

She scooped some loose tea into a teapot and poured the steaming water in, to stew. "That's simply ludicrous."

"If it hadn't happened, I wouldn't believe it. It's farce."

"How did he get in?"

"Who knows?"

"And you're squatting in that mansion, ha?"

"Eva is still there."

"You guys can stay here, with us."

"Yeah-yeah. I'll go get her. But, ah man, Blackcross Crescent is amazing. You want to see it. I wish we could stay there forever."

"We don't want you getting into trouble. Not in her state. That's not clever."

"Point taken. But what do we do about our flat? I mean—do you know any lawyers who could help?"

"Nadine will know."

"Speak of the Devil." Nadine entered the room as if she was treading the boards, on-stage. "I know everything, and everybody."

"Hi Nadine," he said.

Nadine's hair had changed colour from shocking pink to sky-blue.
Helena admonished her: "Were you listening at doorways?"

"I was. Eavesdropping as social-intelligence-gathering."

"Those who listen at doorways..."

"—Never hear anything nice about themselves. I know. I know. But
I do, dear, hear nice things about me. Everybody says nice things about
the Great Nadine Nadiri."

"Why didn't you just come in, and listen like a normal person?"

"I am not, and will never be, a normal person."

"Dear God. Give me patience?"

Nadine's arm reached up, her hand outstretched most theatrically. "I
am She-of-the-Black-Moon!"

Helena sighed. "Actually, you may want to just stay round there,
Adamo, given that this is currently a madhouse."

"Nonsense," Nadine said. "Come Adamo, come into my studio. I
want to show you the Black Moon. It's amazing. Isn't my show amazing, Darlink?"

"It is vee disturbing," Helena said, "nothing less than a genius explo-
ration of Fourth Wave Feminism."

Nadine nearly swooned with that praise. "What a show it will be.
Six-, seventh-, eighth-, ninth-, tenth-wave Feminism all rolling-in, one
monster-bitch tsunami, ah-yeah."

"It's very dark in there, Adamo," Helena said. "Tread carefully."

"I'm a big boy, Mum." It was dark as sin in the studio. He couldn't
see a thing.

"Let there be light," Nadine said, and there was light. Beaming from
a triad of holographic sculptures, light bent into frequencies, colours,
shapes. The stuff of nightmares.

'Dark Goddess': in the mode of Francis Bacon, there sat a shrunken-
down Nina Simone, with the body of a cross, tipped with a crescent,
playing a tiny piano to a lynch-mob of Ku Klux Klan ghosts.

He walked around the second sculpture, entitled 'Snow Black and
the 7 Abortions'. 3-D Dali-esque. A sculpted Marilyn-Monroe-headed
female, slipping out of a cracked glass casket, like a melted timepiece,
helped, by what could only be—an aborted litter of seven grey, bug-eyed
embryos.

'Mother Night-owl' was the third sculpture, Cubist, à la Picasso—a great owl-woman was breaking into a thousand shards, to escape from the glowing golden net that surrounded her. The shards had names written in light on them: Isis, Ishtar, Astarte, Ereskigal. Inanna, Lilith, Kali, Hecate.

"Wow, Nadine," he said. "Deep. Dark. Thought-provoking."

"The centre-piece is already set up at the heart of the gallery. It is a huge 4-D shrine to a Madonna-faced Lilith, Goddess of the Black Moon, dancing in a hula-ellipse of menstrual blood, the Earth, the moon, the black moon, all caught in the gyre of her hips, from apogee to perigree, from perigree to apogee."

"Sorry. The Black Moon is what?"

"The Black Moon is the moon which cannot be seen, except with eyes wide-shut. It is an entirely non-material object, a fictional planet."

A fictional planet!? "Oh?" is all he could muster.

"You want to see it, to not believe it, don't you, Darlink?"

"I do, of course, yes-yes."

"It is a post-structural, nihilistic masterpiece. An annihilating masterpiece, I tell you. The best work I have ever done representing the subconscious, or will ever do. There is a collection of pictures to go with it that I've called 'the Porn Maenads', featuring Dionysian orgies in which fallen women rip apart the men they are fucking, and eat their dicks. Raw sausage meat."

"I look forward to seeing it," he said, playing along with the batty-ness. "I didn't realise you were putting on two shows simultaneously like this. That's a lot to do."

"Two shows? Whatever do you mean, Darlink?"

"The Oops-art show you were preparing last time we were around?"

"Oops-what?"

"Out-of-place objects, yeah?"

Nadine looked at him, vacant as Lithium.

"You wanted to annoy the Christo-fascists by challenging Creationist propaganda. Dawkins—had—bought—some—pieces...?"

Nadine's face twisted into a scowl. "Are you trying to undermine me, Adamo? Are you one of patriarchy's little under-miners? Because if you are a fucking under-miner, you can go, you can go. Just—fucking —go!"

"You showed me and Eva the Oops-art."

"You've made a terrible mistake." Nadine covered one ear with one hand, and with the other, stabbed a finger at the door, repeatedly. "Go. Go. Go!"

"I'm not undermining you, okay?"

Nadine screamed: "Fuck you!"

He shook his head. Got out. From experience, he knew: Better leave the drama queen to her tantrum.

Helena met him in the hallway. "Dear God. What happened in there? Did you criticise her work?"

"I'm not an idiot. I just mentioned the Oops-art show."

"The Oops-what?"

"The stuff when we came around for lunch."

"The Black Moon work."

"No."

She shrugged. "There isn't any other work."

"Whatever. I am so out—of—here! I've got to sort out my own shit."

THE WALL OF THE
RIGHTEOUS

Kurt invited Otto to Jerusalem, City of the Morning and
Evening Star, to meet his superior, Joe Ranaan, Head of
Airforce Intelligence, and the Head of The Mossad, Isser
Harel.

"You cannot possibly go into that ghetto," Ilse said. "They will arrest
you for a show trial."

"Gehlen says I must go," he replied. "Operation Damocles is the start
of a new era of cooperation between West Germany and Israel."

Ilse smiled. "'Who dares wins', eh Herr Stirling?"

He laughed with her, in the face of death. *The fucking S.A.S.
motto!* Stirling: his rival to the title of 'Most Dangerous Man in the
World'. At times like these, Ilse was a humour-sniper, bang-on the mark,
mocking him. Also, he laughed, because death itself was laughable.

As a gift, Belial had shown him his death. Cancer of the spine, two
tumours. This fifth column would finally end his embodied existence.
In bed, surrounded by his boys, being drip-fed morphine. His final
words: "What—is—it?"

Stupid, because he knew. It was an alter-life, an afterlife, *plus-plus.*

Who would have thought that he would die in bed? Hitler's
Kommando, who survived some of the fiercest artillery bombardments

this world had ever seen. Fuel-air bombs, high explosive shells, turning huge swathes of the Russian Front into great fountains of frenzy.

Death fizzing through the air.

A sliver of shrapnel hit him in the head, scoring round under the eye. It burned. The metal, searing hot, cooking the cheekbone, frying his finger like bratwurst as he frantically tried to rip it out of his face. He felt he would die of this wound. Or be blind at best, wearing a piratical eyepatch over the empty socket like von Stauffenberg.

But he was stubborn. Most wilful. Rather than leave his boys, seek medical attention, he slugged down half a bottle of vodka and carried on, like an officer must.

The officer's primary duty: to set an example to his men. To be brave was mostly bravado, courage being a stubbornness that arose from within, a refusal to be beaten down, the erasure of death.

Thus, he took an early morning Lufthansa flight from Madrid to Lydda airport and was met in Arrivals by Kurt, who was in great spirits. They drove down into Jerusalem. The venue of the big meeting was a complete surprise. *Yad Vashem*. The Holocaust Memorial. Or as the Jews call the Holocaust—the *Shoah*.

Kurt led him down what was called the Avenue of Righteous Among Nations. He was aware that he was being closely observed. It was a very odd feeling being summoned here, feeling so in, and out, of place. Very much like when he was on trial at Dachau, Nuremberg, Darmstadt. Where as a 'Prisoner of Peace' he faced a number of different charges, all of them trumped-up.

The Americans tried, for three years, to hang him for putting the fear of God into Eisenhower, in their 'Battle of the Bulge'. The interrogations would go on for hours, in circles, like a puppy chasing its tail. "Why did you order your men to wear American uniforms, knowing that if they were caught, they would be shot as spies?"

He explained the details of *Aktion Greif,* meaning 'Operation Griffin' and repeated the answers until he was blue in the face: "My *Kommandos,* in the 150th, went behind enemy lines, wearing their uniforms under the enemy's uniforms. They were under orders to remove their American uniforms before engaging in any combat with the enemy, in accordance with the rules of war. The fact that you Americans shot my boys after they were captured, is the real war crime, if we are discussing war crimes. Tell me, do the victors ever get prosecuted for war crimes?"

To clear his name, took the sworn testimony of Wing Commander Yeo Thomas, a British Military Intelligence officer—who stated that in commando or resistance operations 'turning coat' was fair, and within the rules of war, and that the Allies had employed the exact same tactics on innumerable occasions.

"Did you order the massacre of 100 American P.O.W.s at Malmedy?" Date unspecified. Details were not forthcoming. A complete fabrication. "*Nein.*"

"Did you fly Hitler out of Berlin in a Storch in May 1945?"

Preposterous. World War Weird. "Hitler committed suicide, honourably, to release his soldiers from their oath to the *Führer.*"

He used these three years, behind bars and barbed wire, to write *Skorzeny's Special Missions: The Memoirs of Hitler's Most Daring Commando.* It was no *Mein Kampf,* because he was no Rudolf Hess, but it would sell, bought by wannabe-warriors, military historians, Neo-Nazis, members of the Ku Klux Klan, Mormons, the C.I.A.

His readership would be thrilled by his daring escape. His defiance. He never admitted in writing that he had S.I.S., O.S.S. and S.S. help in the execution of the break-out, which in the world of secrets and spies was an admission of sorts.

Freiheit. He used the Vatican ratline to get to Madrid, and had been on the run ever since. He had run all the way here. 33 degrees longitude. 33 degrees latitude. All roads led here, this place of remembrance. There was nowhere left to run.

Kurt walked him up to where the two Jewish spymasters stood in front of a wall of names. "May I introduce—Mr Harel."

Isser Harel acknowledged him with a nod.

Joe Ranaan stepped up, and shook his hand. "It is an honour to meet you, Skorzeny. I'm Joe."

Joe's amiability took him completely off-guard. He would always like Joe, and Joe him—Joe was the one Jew amongst the horde of old Nazis, German spies, and American spies, who would come to pay his respects at the funeral of 'Hitler's *Kommando*' in *Wien*. That little guy had chutzpah.

Isser Harel cleared his throat. "On behalf of the state of Israel, we thank you, Otto Skorzeny, for your service in decommissioning Factory 333. We have brought you here to the Garden of the Righteous to say this, for whosoever saves a single life, saves an entire universe, and you have helped to save many lives in Israel. We regret that we cannot officially acknowledge this or pin the Medal of the Righteous on your chest, even though you merit this award."

Ilse would have burst into hysterics: *A medal, from the fucking Yids, ha!*

His mind returned to when Hitler personally presented *Obersturmbannführer* Otto Skorzeny with the Knights Cross of the Iron Cross, with Oak Leaf Clusters, for rescuing Mussolini from the vengeance of his own people.

Truth is indeed stranger than fiction.

If only it had ended there like that, in a moment of reconciliation, but it did not, for there was an old Askenazi woman, standing near the Wall of the Righteous, and she was glaring over, hate in her eyes. "Nazi scum!" she shrieked, and ran over.

Isser Harel and Kurt grabbed her arms, and hauled her back by her prayer shawl, but she kicked out. "I know you. You are S.S. I know what you've done!"

Isser Harel stared at him. Hard eyes. Accusing.

The woman spat froth onto the dusty ground. "You burned the church at Yefremovka with 300 women and children in it."

"I was never there." He did serve with the *Leibstandarde S.S.* Adolf Hitler, and was all too familiar with the *Aktion*, even if it was not included in his memoirs. Peiper's men were always hyped up on Pervitin pills, and they certainly earned the nickname 'the Blowtorch Battalion' that day.

"Nazi pig! You should be shot!"

Joe Ranaan took him by the arm, walked him away. "Let's go get a coffee."

It affected him afterwards. This fall from grace. To have gone from pride to guilt to shame in so short a time. It bonded him to Joe Ranaan, who was on his side, and they would work well together, afterwards, but it niggled him: *Did they stage that little intervention at Yad Vashem?*

After the brief interruption of death, he could see it so clearly. Of course they had! As they had faked Wiesenthal's letter. *So very clever.*

Exemplary spy-craft.

It is forbidden to sleep alone in a house, and anyone who sleeps alone in a house will be seized by the evil spirit, Lilith.

THE TALMUD

Initiation leads to the mount whence vision can be had, a vision of eternal Now, wherein past, present, and future exist as one.

ALICE BAILEY, *Initiation, Human and Solar*

THE LANDLADY

H*angry, and some.* But Eva's feeder, Adamo, was nowhere to be found. Post-coital, and pregnant-primal hunger—*I could eat anything, my own hand!*—drove her down into the kitchen.

Hunter. Gatherer. Squatter. Thief. There was a crystal, a blue crystal, on the marble-topped kitchen island.

That had not been there yesterday. *What is it? Had Adamo found it? Left it there, for her...?* She felt the need to pick it up, and so, did.

In her fingers, a thrumming, a throbbing. A shift in the flux of the temporal field. Electrical expansion. Magnetic repulsion. Some of the soft hair on her arms stood up on end.

A loud banging upstairs. Rapping-tapping sounds. Odd-sounding. Muffled. Profound. Rhythmically clustered. Alien code, tapped out by a dead man.

This activated the orienting response in her brain. She listened for a moment, as if to decipher.

No, no, it was senseless noise.

The rappings got louder, much faster. *What the heck is going on?* They abruptly ceased.

She dismissed it. Dodgy plumbing. Chuckled.

A loud creak quickened her heart.

Bang! A door slamming violently, shut on another floor.

Was she alone in this strange house? This very strange house. She should not be here. This was not her house. She was not safe here. She listened intently for more noises. Suddenly able to hear with a clarity, an acuity that was preternatural. Owl-like. Convinced that she was hearing soft footsteps on the stairs, descending.

Peripheral vision. Short, sharp breaths. She saw, or imagined, a shadow flit around the threshold of the kitchen door. As if someone was there. Hovering. Waiting to come in. Making ready to attack her.

"Adamo?" she said. "If you are pranking me, you are a dead man." But, if it wasn't him...? The back door was open.

They'd left it open. So, anyone could have come in... Off the street...

She edged her way closer to the doorway, her hands forming fists, her self-defence training kicking in. Nurses were schooled in self-defence, because hurt begot hurt: there were a lot of attacks on nurses in hospitals. "Adamo? This isn't funny. If you're there, show yourself."

The full force of Eva Kadmon got to the threshold, and drew a deep breath, psyching herself up for confrontation. Whoever it is, is going to be sorry. She crossed the threshold.

The dining room was empty. She breathed easier.

Bang! A door slamming upstairs.

That made her jump, her organs inside. She backed into the kitchen. Made a be-line to the back door. Best leave now, she told herself, live to tell the tale.

The difference however between intention and realisation; time lagged at pivotal moments like this. Her hand was on the door handle when a stark-naked woman stalked into the kitchen, and said: "What are you doing in my house?"

"Ah." Beauty, real natural beauty, attacked the heart, was terrifying to behold.

"Answer me. What are you doing in my house?"

"Em." This must be the owner. Their landlady. And, she had been in here all the time. With them.

"How did you get in here?"

Run! She pressed down on the door handle.

"You shouldn't be in here."

In a state of mortification, a smile cut into her face, she realised the back door was locked. *I can't get out!*

"Now you're here, you can't leave."

I can't? That was confusing. The perfect woman was confusing; true beauty being utterly bamboozling. The stammering symmetry of that face: she seemed the epitome of womanhood, more precisely, the envisionment of womankind. A zenith, a triumph, unmatchable.

"That would be very silly of you. To even try..."

Silly? What? Try what? Eva didn't understand. Couldn't. Was struck dumb. The whole situation was crazy-mad-bonkers! Why did she listen to Adamo? They should never have come here.

The perfect woman smiled, a wicked smile, let it widen into an evil laugh. "It's okay. Don't worry. I'm not the owner. I was just fucking with you."

It took a moment to sink in. A moment, in which her nose wrinkled at the base note of burnt hair in the air. A reek not too dissimilar to sulphur. Deep in her throat, the volcanic scent diverged into a charred rubbery taste, salty, potent as sex.

"I'm a trespasser, a squatter, just like you."

Her panic subsided in a gush of empathy. "You are?"

"Yeah. I stay here, from time to time."

"You do?" She was only capable of two-word responses.

"Have you bumped into the old spy Otto yet?"

"No." Eva shook her head.

"If you do, he will ask you if you have seen the crystal."

"Otto?"

"Tell him nothing, yeah?"

"Okay."

"Otto is a fascist pig."

"Otto is a fascist pig."

"What's your name?" The perfect woman extended her right hand in friendship.

"Eva." She took the hand, and then recoiled, because it was disturbingly hot.

"Eva. Ah. What's in a name, eh? My name is...Lilit."

"Nice to meet you."

"Lovely to meet you, Eva. Do you want some jam? I love jam. I can't get enough jam."

"I like jam, yes."

"Jam-jam-jam-jam, yummy-jam." Lilit raided the fridge, taking out pots and pots of jams, and sliding them onto the surface of the island. "What's your favourite jam?"

"Strawberry."

"Strawberry?" Lilit laughed. "That's a bit conservative on the preservative, isn't it? There's a whole world of jams out there."

"Mmm."

"I love fig and pomegranate jam. Old-skool. Let's do a jam tasting session, test your limits, find out the true jam-love of your life."

She couldn't help but laugh, and then stared in an excruciated fascination as Lilit fetched two plates from a cupboard, and two teaspoons from the cutlery drawer.

Lilit twisted open some jars, and dolloped out different jams onto the plates, in spirals, not circles. "You ready for this taste-bud-extravaganza?"

She nodded, and was handed a plate and a teaspoon. She thought it odd, the strangest thing, to eat jam by itself, without bread, cake, scones —but she ate. Enjoyed the fruitiness. Floral notes. The sugar-hit made her smile. Or was that Lilit—that goading smile of hers? She could not tell.

"The green one is gooseberry," Lilit said, excitedly like a girl. "What do you think?"

She had a taste. "Mmm. Yummy."

DARKNESS AT NOON

What did any of it mean—if History could not be escaped, and he was going to die in Paris, in the glow of May? A vile thought, so unfair, and yet there was no getting away from the deaths-headed forces of History, the Nazis.

Hitler's stormtroopers were coming, but outside the window, the cherry trees that lined the streets continued to blossom. Pink petals swirling in the wind. So beautiful, so fragile. The sight made him giddy, nauseous. Will this be the last time I see spring in Paris? The Sakura. It was unthinkable, and yet he could not help thinking like this.

The name on his carte identité read: Arturo Koestler.

Hongrois was French for Hungarian.

It was stamped with a big, blue 'E' for Enemy Alien. Dated: 1940. Like thousands of Jews and refugees from Axis countries, he was rounded up at the start of 'the Phoney War' by the *Sûreté Nationale*, and imprisoned in a concentration camp at La Vernet. Unlike most people, the authorities eventually let him leave with a cachet de concentration.

Liberté it most certainly was not. Held in a state of virtual house arrest. The cherry tree framed in the windows of his apartment, shedding its exquisite petals, slowly, but surely. License could be revoked at any time.

Plain-clothes *Sûreté* officers kept surveillance on this Enemy Alien at Rue Dombasle, 7th Floor, in the XVth Arrondissement. They made a note of everything he did, Satan was in the specifics. They raided his apartment at dawn on the 2nd, kicking the door in, and scaring the dear-God out of him and his Lilith of that time, the sculptress Daphne Hardy.

In case Monsieur Koestler had written anything revolutionary, Les Flics confiscated his works, singling out the last gratis copy of his debut novel, about the Spartacus Revolt, *The Gladiators*. They seized a stack of anti-Nazi pamphlets in French. They stole Maesterlinck's *Life of the Termites*, the second volume of *Crime and Punishment*, Rauschning's *Hitler m'a dit*, and a rather racy illustrated volume called *Histoire de l'Erotisme en Europe*.

The filthy perverts also took into evidence the original German version of '*The Vicious Circle*', but miraculously, they did not take away Daphne's English translation of it because she protested: "That's my work, not his."

This rescued manuscript would later become published as *Sonnen-finsternis* in German. *Le Zero et L'infiniti* in France. And *Darkness at Noon*, in England.

"Why am I being investigated?" he demanded. "When can I have my possessions back?"

They did not tell the Enemy Alien anything. So, he risked a visit to the Prefecture, room No. 34 and the *Department de l'Eloigement de Étrangers* to argue his case, vigorously. "*Je suis un journaliste.*" He produced his press card. He lied about the scope of his influence, his presence at Ministry of Information briefings.

Les Flics humoured him. His throat was dry as Jerusalem, but they kept offering him Gauloises. In a fog of smoke, acrid as cedars, they tried to bribe him with a contre-enquête—a way out, if he informed on German émigrés he knew, prominent Left Wingers. Lion Feuchtwanger. Herman Hesse.Heinrich Mann. Walter Hasenclever. Ernst Weiss. Carl Einstein, no relation to Albert. His old boss, Willi Muenzenberg. Cold sweat stuck his shirt to his spine, but he of course refused, point-blank. Again. And again. Until, they bored of his pig-headedness.

Spending whatever political capital he had left, he approached Leon Blum, leader of *La Front Populaire*, and the former President of France. But the great man would not meet him in person. Too busy meeting colleagues. There was a war on. However, soon after, the Chief of the Aliens Department in the *Sûreté*, one Monsieur Combe, summoned Arturo Koestler to his office.

"What crime am I being persecuted for?" he asked. "Charge me if there is a charge, and discharge me if there is none."

Monsieur Combe picked dirt from his nails. Burped garlic, a whole bulb of gas. Did not excuse himself.

"There is obviously no case for my detention. To go on persecuting me is contrary to the law, arbitrary and infamous in any civilised country."

Monsieur Combe nodded. Sympathetically. "Be assured, I will look into your case most thoroughly, Monsieur Koestler."

There was no change to his Enemy Alien status—because Arturo Koestler had been, for over a decade, a member of the Communist party. Active in Germany, France, Spain during the Civil War, and England. The fact that he had finally, totally renounced faith in Stalin after the Non-Aggression Pact with Germany in 1939 made no difference.

To the *Sûreté*, he must have seemed an apparatchik. An agent in the service of a foreign power committed to worldwide revolution, by all means necessary. They likely had a thick file on him, courtesy of the Gestapo.

It was only a matter of time before they came for him again. He should have been terrified. All the remaining Juif he talked to were terrified, making plans to flee the City of Love. Instead, he viewed his impossible situation with an ironic detachment, and having lived under sentence of death before, in Spain, made a joke of it to Daphne: "Journalists love a deadline, and imminent death as a deadline, certainly focuses the mind."

She laughed, helplessly, so he added: "I will finish this novel if it kills me—and it very well might."

She stopped laughing and started crying, so he stopped joking, and wrote. About Russians. Like a man possessed. In German. While Daphne translated. Into English. They rushed to finish, and sent the manuscript to Rupert Hart-Davis, his editor at Jonathan Cape in London, before the total collapse of the country, which occurred on the 18th May, with the stark headline: *NOUS AVONS ÉVACUÉ SEDAN.*

The Fall of Sedan meant that the Maginot Line, France's version of the Great Wall of China, had failed to stop the barbarous Germans, whose generals decided to avoid such a large obstacle and smash through the 'impenetrable' forest of Ardennes. The massed ranks of pine trees failed to hold back the panzers of German Army Group A.

The Luftwaffe succeeded in terrorising Field Marshall Lafontaine's 55th French Infantry Division into a rout. His troops simply ran away. Stukas shrieking down. Only 56 men died in the fountains of earth churned up by the massed aerial bombardment, but the French ranks broke and ran, and ran, and ran. Home. *À Maman.*

German Army Group A proceeded almost unopposed. There were some pockets of resistance, but the weight of the Wehrmacht crossed the River Meusse en masse and with their superior air cover, they inflicted massive losses on the R.A.F. and *Armée de l'Air* bombers targeting the bridges. And so, when Sedan fell, all of France fell, and Arturo Koestler with it.

Two days later, the *Sûreté* rounded him up. Seized him and bunch of others drowning their sorrows in corn brandy at the Café Dupont, in the Place de la Convention. They dragged him into the back of a van. Dry heaves, a stomach in mutiny. It was not drunkenness. He feared most of all that it was resignation. *This—is—it.*

It was only bureaucracy that saved him from being reinterned as an Enemy Alien, and taken to a concentration camp. When *Les Flics* picked him up, he did not have his *carte identité* on his person—with the fatal stamp 'E'—and so without that evidence, they could not be sure he was really Arturo Koestler, and had to let him go.

Back home, he told Daphne to pack her bag, and stuffed his with books. And then, they left, abandoning everything else. "Where are we going?" Daphne said.

"To my friends." His good friends at Pen helped them get the necessary travel papers to Limoges. There, the happy couple joined *le Grand Départ*, which was happening earlier than expected this year. The great migration to the *Sud*. 10 million of the most petit-bourgeoisie, fussy, stay-at-home people in the world, took to the road to become tramps *à la guerre*.

The roads were crammed, all communications jammed, with their little Citroëns and Peugeots, five, 10, 15 years old, and inside these tin cans were rammed a jumble of old men, young women, saucepans, babies, sewing machines, cuckoo-clocks, grandmamas, accordions, dogs and cats.

On their rooves, the refugees carried their mattresses, wrapped-up in toile ciree against the misery of frequent spring downpours. That broke Daphne's heart. In Limoges, she was sitting with him on the terrace of the Café de l'Orient, facing the Place de la Mairie watching the never-ending procession of misery, when she bemoaned in true British fashion: "Think how fussy Frenchwomen are about their mattresses and pillows and *plumeaux*. They'll never get over it. What a revolting war."

The dogged Belgians surrendered.

A lot of those hitching rides south were deserters, or *isolés* —men who somehow became separated from their units in the heat of flight. The French planned to regroup down south, and fight back. The British had other plans. General Lord Gort's 'Operation Dynamo' called for the evacuation of the British Expeditionary Force, and the last of Charles de Gaulle's Free French, from Dunkirk. 338,000 men would flee to England to fight another day.

High on Pervetin, the amphetamine that put the blitz in the Blitzkrieg, German Army Group A made a mockery of the Weygand Line, crossed the Somme, the Aisne, the Bresle, the Seine. Reims gone.

Rouen. Pontoise. Panzer commanders were stunned by how fast they could travel on completely empty roads. The only thing to slow their advance into Paris was refuelling. The French government fled its own capital on 13th June. Paris became an open city, which the Germans occupied the next day.

Final surrender on the 22nd.

8 BLACKCROSS CRESCENT

DIVERSION: KELIPOT TREE SURGEONS. Adamo was halted on Blackcross Crescent by this sign. The pavements on both sides of the street had been cordoned off with day-glo orange plastic barricades. The road cleared of the cars that normally lined the kerbs.

A chainsaw roared into life up in the canopy.

The sun caught the saw-blade as the tree-surgeon held it up, fiery.

He would stand there, in a state of exile, yes, exile, from his parents, his home, his own self, watching the chainsaw eating into the bark, spraying of white pulp out each side.

"Timber!" Lopping off a thick branch, which fell, cracking on the road below.

A tree-surgeon on the ground dragged up the branch over to a shredder.

It was turned on and, with sweetness of sap exploding everywhere, the tree was reduced to a spatter into the rear of a green dump-truck.

Black Moon? He'd have to take a different route back to Eva. Along Trevor Place. *Entirely fictional planet?* Turn onto Brompton Road. *Nadine is Mad Jack McBonkers!*

He wondered if his mum was okay, if Nadine had calmed down.

How did Mum get herself into living with that level of insanity...? How on Earth did he survive that madhouse as a boy?

Turning right onto Blackcross Street, he was stopped in his tracks by a man dressed in desert fatigues...

"Adamo, my boy," the man said. His voice, deep. His German-accented English, harsh. He looked like Otto, but somehow younger, fiercer.

"Otto...?" A great heaving in his intestines told him: It is not possible to meet someone who has grown younger since your last meeting.

"You are returning to the house?" The deep scars on Otto's cheek twitched when his lips moved, and afterwards too.

"To get Eva," he answered.

Otto held out a chain threaded with an amulet. Pale metal. "You will need this."

"What is it?"

"Element 115." Otto stepped forward, trying awkwardly to loop the chain around his neck. "Wear it round your neck for protection, my boy."

He ducked. "I'm not your boy."

"Take it!" Otto tried again with the chain.

He flinched away.

"She wants the baby. She will seize it when your wife gives birth." Gathering the chain and the amulet in his palm, Otto offered it up.

The baby? How can he know that...? Nobody knows that, yet.

"That house is haunted by the Mother of All Demons."

Mother of All Demons?

Otto sighed. "I know this is difficult to believe, but there is no time to explain."

"Is it a full moon today or something?"

"You must listen to me, my boy."

"You're as bonkers as Nadine."

"You have been possessed by her." Otto thrust his hand out, a flash of silver. "I must exorcise you."

"Exercise yourself." He turned on his heel, and pelted away, fast as his size-12s would carry him.

Otto pursued him, bellowing out: "Out Lilith. I adjure you, Lilith.

In the Name of the Lord, blessed be He, and in the names of the Three Angels who guard the threshold."

He slowed around the corner onto Backcross Crescent, but sped up again on the straight.

Otto was quick, right behind: "Remember Lilith the vow you made —that whenever you find the Three Angels you will cause no harm, neither you nor any of your kind."

It was a long time since he'd sprinted for any length of distance. His lungs were burning by the turn into No. 8, his thighs dead-heavy, lactic acid loading.

Otto caught up. Grabbed him by the shoulder. Lifted him off the ground, single-handedly. "I adjure you, Mother of All Demons, to cause no harm to this man, nor his wife while she carries a child, nor when she gives birth, nor to the children born to her, neither during the day or by night, neither through their food or their drink, neither in their heads or in their hearts."

He struggled, trying to break the iron-grip of that hand. Impossible strength. Inhuman.

Otto looped the chain over his head, around the neck. "By the strength of the Holy One, and the power of the Three Angels who guard the threshold, I so adjure you, Lilith, and all unclean spirits, to obey this command."

A reflex. His arm flashed out, impossibly quickly, cobra-like, striking Otto in the neck, right in the Adam's Apple.

Otto let go, gagging in pain.

Adamo was running as soon as his feet hit the path. Through the gate. Past the Zen garden. Up to the kitchen door.

Leaning on the wall, one-handed, listening for sounds of pursuit. None. Trying to catch his breath. Sucking in oxygen in diaphragmatic heaves.

The amulet dangled under his chin on the chain. He seized a hold of it. Three angels, all attached at the wing tips. There were letters engraved into the angels' bodies, Ancient Hebrew. "Out Lilith. Adam is Eve's!" Otto said.

He did not simply hear these words; he felt them, broad spectrum; through time and into space; across every sense, hearing, seeing, smelling, tasting and touching, and the sixth sense that makes sense of all the senses. He could not know what this connection was, how mere static electricity had become ecstatic power, or how it was triggered by the coda of the exorcism.

Otto was standing off-path, in swirls of Zen. In his grip, fire. Searingly bright white.

Adamo could not take his eyes off the light. *What is that? A wand? A wizard's wand?* He backed towards the door. His hand fluttered to the handle.

Gripped. Clunk. It opened.

He darted inside, pulling the door shut and locking it. He instantly felt safer. Secure. Protected. No place like home. *There's no place like home! Even though that was crazy thinking. Because...? Because. You met Otto inside the house, idiot!*

My Name is Legion

The name Arturo Koestler would get him shot. The end of the Phoney War meant he could no longer be his true self. When authenticity is impossible, what then? How might an author, who lives by his reputation, escape his name, be born anew?

Cinema would give him his answer: *Le Grand Jeu* (1937). A few years before the war, in Paris, he'd seen this famous film, in which the hero, played by Jean Gabin, spends all his money on a Parisian beauty, goes broke, joins the Legion as a last resort. He would remember the exact words of the sergeant who processed the hero: "Whatever your past has been, from this moment it is dead. In the Legion, we are all *des morts vivant*."

To die to yourself, and come back to life as a real fictional character: this would be Arturo Koestler's immediate solution.

Literally an hour after the surrender of France was announced on the radio, life would imitate Poetic Realism, and he was walking through the gate of the *Caserne de la Visitation* in Limoges.

Less than an hour later, he came out as Legionnaire Adamo Elyon, former taxi-driver, born in Berne, Switzerland, to Franco-Italian parents. The price Legionnaire Elyon would pay for this miraculous transformation: the next five years of his life. From June 17th 1940 until June 17th 1945, he would belong to the Legion.

Desertion carried the death penalty, but he absolutely, utterly, completely, intended to desert. Or be demobilised, in effect disarmed, by the Germans. Whichever option presented itself first.

Legionnaire Elyon's Swiss accent was suspect, but the surname Elyon was the name of the Chief of Police in Limoges so, it would pass muster. A huge, black walrus moustache might help. He started to grow it.

Le Grand Jeu meant 'The Great Game' even if it sounded like the 'Grand Jew' in English, and the sergeant who signed Adamo up on the day of capitulation, was perceptive enough to read between the lines of the joining forms. "Do you want to beat it before the Boche get to Limoges tonight, Legionnaire?"

Legionnaire Elyon nodded, emphatically.

The sergeant got the doctor to perform a medical examination tout de suite. "All legionnaires are supposed to report to Angers," the sergeant advised. "But, the Boche are already in Angers. Débrouille-toi."

Literally: Go your own way.

So, Legionnaire Elyon went his own way. He and Daphne packed their bags, again. Less is more. He threw any papers related to Arturo away, manuscripts, notebooks. And—every—last—book. They headed to the railway station. It was closed. There was nothing to be done but thumb a ride.

They hitched, until they got to the Perigueux, where he left Daphne at the bus station, and went in search of the Caserne Busseaux for rations. The plan was to argue he was an isolé, and should be taken *en subsitance*, housed, and fed until further instructions. To this end, he showed the orderly sergeant his new Legion papers.

"Do you think I do not know what you are doing, uh, you Israelite?" the sergeant said. "*Encoulé!*"

He did not let his anger show. "*Le Capitaine, s'il vous plait.*"

Le Captaine was a kindly man, and agreed to play along. "A uniform might make Legionnaire Elyon's story more convincing to the Boche."

He was handed the uniform of a legionnaire. The blue tunic of the 15th Algerian Rifles. Too tight round the chest. The red tar-brush hat, replete with a sickle moon and the number 15. Too small. Still, he hoped Daphne would be aroused by the sight of a man in uniform, sporting a half-decent moustache.

"You look like Charlie Chaplin dressed like a Turk," she said.

Sex was therefore not forthcoming.

So sharp. Sometimes he could forget that Daphne was only 22. She had devised their whole escape plan. It relied on the likelihood that after the Fall, the Legion would be dispatched to Africa—to police the French colonies. Legionnaire Elyon would bring Daphne over to Africa with him, because she had a sister who was married to a Frenchie, who lived in the Interzone, Tangiers.

Secretly, he wished Daphne to leave, leave now for a port, any port in this storm, jump on a boat back to Old Blighty. 22 was far too young to die. 22 was too young to be tortured or raped to death.

The escape plan changed drastically that night when he returned to barracks. "The Boche are coming," Le Captaine informed him. "Here." He was handed a pay-book, the pay-book of Legionnaire Jean Rouzier, and told to desert. "Tell any Boche you might meet you are French, not some Swiss called Elyon who signed on the day of the Armistice."

Daphne packed only the most necessary things. All else was litter strewn on the road of flight. Let the dead bury the dead. And they hit the road, heading for Bordeaux, the temporary seat of Viche France.

According to rumour, there were many rumours and counter-rumours flowing around, there were still British ships in the port there, taking refugees who wanted to join their army.

There were many checkpoints on the road to Bordeaux. Army. And gendarmerie. All main roads were sealed off. They were forced to try the back roads; dusty lanes across country. 30 miles. Snails move faster. By the time they reached the city, the last British ship had sailed, gone a mere 36 hours hence.

It was a bitter pill to swallow, but there would be bitterer pills to swallow—for this was the time of despair, of fatigue, of the malaise of *Je m'en fous*, sometimes translated as 'I don't care', sometimes as 'the Devil take you'.

Many of his old friends—players in The Great Game of the Haves versus the Have-nots—would take their bitter pills, rather than fall into the hands of the Gestapo. These brave men and women took the last journey, into darkness, and he could not help but feel tempted himself.

Il fallait en finir. This was what the French kept saying about the Phoney War: 'It had to end'. If he didn't have to look after Daphne, he would end it too.

One must be careful what one wishes for in this life. Because one will get it, with interest, compounded. At the American Consulate. There, on very neutral ground, he met Daphne's knight-in-shining-armour, the 1933 Pulitzer Prize winner, Edgar Ansel Mowrer, from the Chicago Daily News, who was most definitely on Hitler's hit-list and must escape.

Mowrer had just bought a stately car left behind by the British Consul. He offered to take the pair of them out of the city under cover of darkness. He was heading for Biarritz, and from there, Spain.

Arturo Koestler could not return to Franco's Spain. All his bridges were burned there. He tried to convince Daphne to go to Spain. But she refused to leave him. Floods of tears from her.

Salt, kissed from her cheeks, burned his lips. He retired to a lavatory, had a sort of nervous breakdown, because he already knew that he must leave her. Mowrer was a good man. Mowrer would look after her. Mowrer would get her out.

Koestler was a spy.

Koestler would get her killed.

Down the road, a gendarme at the second checkpoint challenged his papers.

"Go Mowrer!" he said, and got out of the car. "Do not look back!"

Daphne began wailing.

This is the right thing! He put his hands up.

The gendarmes escorted him to their van. Do not look back! Not if you are a real man.

Mowrer drove away; mercifully speeding away into swirls of dust.

Being heroic was truly, awfully lonely. Upon his release from the Biarritz Police station——he got drunk for four days. Solidly, on Pernod. Drowning his sorrows, which were Legion. Waiting for a boat that never came. Remembering the misery of Cell No. 40.

Solitary confinement in Seville prison.

The long hours by the window. Existing under sentence of death for four months. This was the harrowing experience that via the alchemy of the Koestler unconscious, he spun into gold—the worldwide bestseller, *Darkness at Noon*.

The Nazis and Commies burned any copies of it they could lay their black-gloved hands on, which had to be a sign that it was a good book. A good book, based on pure evil. The irony, again. Irony was his lifeblood. Irony, the only protection against the horror of being captured by Franco's Rebel army as Malaga fell.

Taken under the Union Jack, at the villa of Sir Peter Chalmers-Mitchell. Arturo Koestler was known to them—thanks to an incident at a hotel full of German airmen, which prematurely ended his last *tour de España*.

The Rebels were also acutely aware of his tourist guidebook, Spanish Testament—naked Communist propaganda, encouraged by his mentor, the Head of West European Propaganda for the Comintern, Willy Muenzenberg. The Rebels were fully aware he was a Communist spy operating under the cover of Correspondent for the British News Chronicle.

This was why he tried to commit suicide in the police station, with a stolen hypodermic syringe and some pills. He would have shot Arturo Koestler—if he were the Rebels. And, they were shooting everybody, after summary court-martials. Lining prisoners up in apathetic rows.

Anarchist P.O.U.M. G.P.U. Communists. Socialists. International Brigades. All of them, *los rojos*, marched, kicked, beaten to the firing squad after midnight. A last cigarette. Bang, a bullet through the chest. Bang, the coup de grâce blown right through the face.

All executed, except for Arturo Koestler. Special case. Saved by a greater power, for a higher purpose. The concept of free speech in Liberal Democracy. His purpose: to be a symbol of the Free World under the threat of Tyranny—despite being a Communist in disguise.

Thanks to the unceasing nagging of his wife Dorothy, the British media kicked up such a fuss everyone knew the name of Arthur Koestler. Like King Arthur, he became absurdly famous in his absence, because of his absence.

Arthur Koestler was an innocent man. Sat around long tables, the governments of Britain, France, and Hungary protest—insisted that Arthur Koestler's status as Prisoner-Under-Sentence-of-Death must be reversed. Reporting the news was not a crime! The diplomatic furore made Franco opt to exchange him for a high-ranking prisoner held by the Republican government forces, the beautiful wife of a Rebel fighter ace.

The fighter ace personally flew this spy to the exchange to make sure he got his wife back. It was something of a romantic, happy ending for the patrician couple, although this officer and a *caballero* was shot down and killed a few months later. Professional soldiers had such strong death wishes. *C'est la vie, c'est la guerre.*

Lucky-lucky Arthur got to go back to London. To his saviour, Eve to his Adam, Dorothy. And to celebrity, glory. Ecce Homo! He was indeed the man of the moment. Off the back of this fame or infamy, he sold *The Gladiators* to Jonathan Cape, for the princely sum of £125, and secured their interest in the follow-up, '*The Vicious Circle*'.

A man of the moment must act in the moment. And so, he did, he rose to the challenge of Modernity. He left London for the Sud, to live out a writer's fantasy, or was it destiny...? He wanted to write '*The Vicious Circle*' in a villa with amazing light, inspired by a new muse, young Daphne. He would write it and be damned. After it was finished, he would fight in the coming war. To experience war first-hand, up-close, and personal.

That fantasy had brought him to Biarritz. Soldier-boy-drunk in Biarritz. Trying to board any ship at the Commission du Port. The sentries, yelling, warding off desperate *isolés*, bayonets fixed.

There were no ships. And there was more dreadful news— ships that sailed have been torpedoed by U-Boats, all aboard drowned. Convinced that Daphne and Mowrer had taken one of these sunken vessels, he tried to drink himself to death with a killer mix of Pernod and corn brandy.

German panzers rolled into Biarritz.

All French troops were confined to quarters, but full of Dutch courage, he flopped over the back wall to take a look. His first reconnaissance of the enemy turned his stomach, acid-burn. The Panzer III commanders were teenaged boys. The officer in charge of the grey column looked goppy in his black goggles, had a lop-sided smile.

It was therefore impossible to hate these German youths, though the urge to kill them was strong. *To kill Nazis, and die in a hail of bullets.* It was because he saw himself the way Nazis would see him. *Ragged, dirty, a beaten dog, a coward who could only run away, a son-of-a-whore. A Frenchman.*

All French troops were ordered out of occupied territories, tout de suite. *Dépêchez!* And so it was, that his ragtag company of *isolés*, the 22nd, marched out of the town, taking the back streets.

On the march East, into unoccupied France, the officers ordered their men to ditch their weapons in a big pile and leave them there, under the blazing sun. This was to honour the terms of the Armistice, and make sure the Germans did not engage the company en route to the demarcation line at St. Palais.

Men deserted fast as Spanish flies. 60 out of 200 vanish in the first two days, zuzzing off into the hedgerows and culverts.

On the third day, Legionnaire Elyon's feet came apart in his ill-fitting boots. He had to stop for treatment at a *pharmacie*. The company did not wait. After he got patched-up, he flagged down a Peugeot.

The old man and woman allowed him in, but he had to pay for their kindness in curses. "Curse that Israelite Blum, the source of all France's troubles," the old woman griped.

He nodded along.

"Hitler had to invade, to save us from the corrupt, Jewish, Marxist scum," the old man grizzled.

"The scum of the earth, Jewish Marxists, oui!" He would curse his race until he was blue, white, and red, in the face. There was no other way to catch up with his company at their objective, Mauleon.

'*Problème:* The 22nd left Mauleon.' The Mayor told him: "The 22nd marched on to Navarreux."

10 extra miles. He tried to find them, no skin on his heels. The ghost company was nowhere to be found, so he was forced to join a cantonment of *isolés* at Susmiou. He found shelter in a barn, and a sense of safety amongst these strangers, for the next days.

Roughly a third of these *isolés* had been captured and released by the Germans, and had good things to say about their treatment.

"The Germans are so very efficient."

"Their tanks are better."

"Their guns are better."

"Their troops are better trained."

The masochism of defeat. The rout was all the fault of the French generals, the incompetent officers, the Jews, refugees, Socialists and Communists. The ordinary soldier from the countryside did not blame Hitler or the Nazis at all. Flabbergasting. It was as if Goebbels has brainwashed all of Europe!

Legionnaire Elyon held his peace—to preserve the little piece of peace he had found. These idiots would find out soon enough, after demobilisation, what horrors the Nazis had planned for them, and their families.

Legionnaire Elyon hid behind his moustache, twisted it at the ends. Drank—*like a fishy in Vichy*—to escape the vicious stupidity of his comrades. The trick was to blend-in, survive the next month in-character, long enough to let his ruined heels heal, and his moustache bush out into a splendour that demanded daily topiary.

Legionnaire Elyon was a good Christian, prayed every night. "Lord, if you get me out of France to Africa, I'll be a much better man. To my fellow man. And, women. In general."

August: like an arrow in the blue, orders from on high were sent for him, and six others, to move out to Marseilles, and on to Algeria. He couldn't quite believe he might escape. *To hope that much. Es ist verboten!*

The soldiers who were with him were thinking the same things, and their doubts were prophetic. The four Spaniards, two of whom were wounded fighting for France, were looking forward to their 1000-franc bonuses upon discharge, but instead, were interned in a concentration camp. The Turk and the Romanian were forced to join a labour battalion after their demobilisation. Working for 75 centimes a day, until the Liberation.

GESTATIO
ACCELERATUS

Full frontal nudity. *Where to look?* Eva did not know where to allow her gaze to alight, what body part. *And what to say, what to say. What constitutes polite nudey conversation?* All she could manage was: "Eh? Mmm."

"Do you fancy some steaming, Eva? Let's steam in the steam room upstairs, followed by a sauna, jacuzzi, and then, a massage."

"That would be amazing."

Lilit twirled the necklace with a silver pendant hanging between her breasts. Light flashed off the crescent mounted on a cross.

The sigil drew her eye. "That's such a beautiful piece."

"Custom-made. Would you like to try it on?"

She shook her head. "No, no."

"I insist." Lilit reached back, unclasped the necklace.

"Seriously?"

"Seriously." Lilit moved behind her, slid the hand with the necklace around her neck, connected it to the other, pulled the ends together, clasp.

Her hands were drawn to it. Tingly. There was real charge of electricity to it, static, felt through the fabric of her dress. "Feels good."

"Yeah."

"Yes."

"Keep it."

"I couldn't."

"Yes, you can. And yes, you must. And yes, you will."

"Aw, Thanks, that's really nice of you."

"Hey, I am a true giver. You'll see that. Now, let's go upstairs and get all steamy and sweaty, and oily." Lilit took her by the hand, and led her upstairs, into the gym and spa area.

She liked to be led, in truth. There was a strange tingling sensation in her scalp.

Lilit helped her pull her dress over her head, and before she could object, unclipped her bra, and pulled her panties down.

"There. As naked as Eve in Eden—before the Fall."

She laughed some of the rising sexual tension away.

"I love getting wet, don't you?"

She swallowed, nodded, and giggled. The female as sexual predator. It was different. No less overt, but less threatening than when a man tried it on. She found the difference...stimulating, it repulsed her, and yet attracted her, at the same time.

Everything had been turned on before—steam room, sauna, jacuzzi, because Lilit knew everything that was going to happen here. They would steam first, becoming lost in the clouds, the mists of time. "Sit on the ledge. Lie down."

She lay down on the tiles. Her body absorbed all the heat of the ledge, into the muscles, the sinews, the organs, the very bones. She sighed, deeply.

Lilit let her soak up the heat, the steam for five minutes before she said: "Sauna-time."

They journeyed into the desert heat of the sauna to bake like mud bricks, spread out on wooden benches for seven sweltering minutes. The heat made her heart beat harder, and she felt the thump-thump in many places.

Lilit announced: "Jacuzzi time."

She shared a shower with Lilit before the jacuzzi. The foaming water was jaggedly cold. Invigorating, opening all the pores of the skin so it could breathe. It was like bathing in Champagne, being born again in glorious bubbles.

"I'll give you a massage." Lilit pointed to the bench.

"Wow. Really? You're spoiling me rotten here." She lay down on the bench, face-first.

"I'm an expert masseuse." Lilit fetched a bottle of frankincense from a rack of oils. She warmed a slather up between her palms, nice and hot, before smearing it onto her shoulders, and rubbing it in.

"Ah, magic fingers," she said.

Lilit's fingers did indeed work magik: plasma crystals penetrated the membrane of the skin, and branched out into arrays through flesh, interfacing with the nervous system.

Interconnection felt like a warm glow inside her because of the massive energy transfer. 'This is what they called *iccashakti* or *shekinah* in dimmed, distant pasts.'

The network of luminosity spread, seeking out the womb within the woman, enveloping it in a web, throwing open the occulted *muladhara* and *svadhisthana* chakras, flooding in plasmoids on an intracellular level, to fuse with the D.N.A.

The one-month-old foetus fed on this universal power source, growing another 'month' older, in mere minutes.

"I think I've died and gone to heaven!" Eva heard herself say. "Adamo will be well-jell."

ESTADO NOVO

Marseilles, a sight for sore eyes.

Marseilles: the spiritual home of the Marseillaise. Revolutionary anthem the world over. Those lyrics would never leave Arturo Koestler; sung by a French prisoner in Seville, on his way to being shot. *Aux armes, citizens. Formez vos bataillons!*

How he'd wanted to join in from his cell, Cell No 40: *Marchez, marches! Qu'un sang impur, Abreuve nos sillons.* But, he did not sing. Nor did any other prisoner who heard the song. No one, not even the most committed anarchist, wanted to join the condemned at the post, blindfolded in the darkness.

Besides, the meaning of *Qu'un sang impur, abreuve nos sillons*: namely 'So that the impure blood, waters our fields' had always struck him as a tad fascist. *Impure blood? Inferior race? Nation? Volk?* He would never denigrate the anthem at a Party meeting, but he had private doubts, pan-nationalist, crypto-Jewish doubts. *Marchez.* Marseilles.

It was nine o'clock in the morning when he walked out of Gare St. Charles, knapsack chafing his lower back. The crowds in the streets of the great harbour town made him feel dizzy and excited. The buzz of the hive, the terror of being discovered, helped him shake off the false sense of peace he had found in the Pyrenees. He was alert again, on high alert.

100 yards up from the station, outside the Hotel Normandie, he heard: "Halt. Arturo Koestler."

His own name literally scared the life out of him, and he flinched. But he had to walk on, as if he'd heard nothing. Head down. *Leave me alone.*

His accuser pursued him, grabbing him by the elbow. "What is this Koestler—fancy dress?"

"You are mistaken sir. My name is Legionnaire Elyon, Adamo Elyon."

"Hah!" The face of an old friend. Smirking at him. Walter Benjamin, a writer from Germany, a fellow Marxist, from a Frankist family, to boot.

"Christ, Walter! You scared me to death."

"I knew it was you under that ludicrous moustache."

"I won't have you mock this bush—it has saved my life."

Walter laughed. "Care for a drink? I'm staying here, in the hotel."

"What else do writers *do* when they get together?"

Walter led the way to a room on the third floor. A single room. He pointed to the bed. "Sit, my friend."

He flopped on the mattress. "So soft. I haven't slept in a bed in...I don't even remember."

Walter pulled a bottle of Courvoisier cognac out of the bedside drawer. "Nothing but the best."

He sat up. "Walter—you are a good egg, as the English say."

Walter poured two hefty glasses, and handed over one.

Tilting the glass. "*Heil* Hitler."

"*Zeig.*" He took a slake. The after-burn luxuriated its way down his throat, swilling round in the stomach. "Ah. Nectar of the gods."

Walter recounted the tale of his escape from Paris, by train, to Marseilles. Two long months ago. He had secured a visa for the U.S., but it was so hard to get a damned exit permit. He planned to go walk over the mountains, following *El Camino*, the Way of the Scallop Shells, to Santiago di Compostela, and on down to Lisbon. From there, he would go on the pilgrimage thousands of other Jewish refugees had taken already, to New York.

"Best of luck with Franco." He drained his glass.

"*Gracias.*" Walter refilled the glasses.

He would ask about their comrades, the fellows the *Sûreté* had wanted him to rat out. "What news of Feuchtwanger?"

"Feuchtwanger—lucky devil got away. To America. On a boat."

"What about Weiss?"

"Weiss was not so fortunate. He was old, did not run, committed suicide by taking Veronal."

"Hasenclever?"

"He cut his wrists in a concentration camp."

"Willy?"

"Two men walked Willy out from a concentration camp near Savoy, into the woods. Later, mysteriously, his body was found hanging from a tree."

"Gestapo?"

"G.P.U.? French? By his own hand...? The end is the same, whatever the means."

God! He needed more brandy.

So did Walter.

There was none left.

Walter's parting gifts were some black grapes and 30 tablets of a morphia compound. "Take with alcohol, yes?"

He would not know whether to thank Walter for this quiet way out or punch him in the face. "*Gracias.*"

"*De nada.*"

Back in character, Legionnaire Elyon was incredibly drunk by the time he reported to the Legion's H.Q. in France, Fort St. John.

It was midday, time for *dejeuner*, and after handing over his papers in the office, he was shown to a large refectory, painted all around with gory battle pictures of the Legion's victories in Algeria, Morocco, Indochina and Senegal.

Legionnaire Elyon sat down at a long table, both sides lined by soldiers in check skirts. One of them bellowed: "There's nay bloody salt in the soup again! Bastards. I havenae tasted any decent soup since we've been in this bloody country."

"Why, you lot are *Scots,*" he declared.

"Highlanders, Laddie. Highlanders."

"Och aye the noo. Yer bum's oot the windae, lassie!" he said. To be this uproariously drunk, at midday was mightily impressive to the Scots, so the conversation flowed, and he made two new, good friends: Lieutenants Byron-Hadley and Macpherson.

"We were bagged at St. Valery by Jerry," Byron-Hadley explained. "Poorly guarded. 60 of us escaped. Only to be interned by the French here in Fort St. Jean."

"We won't be here long." Macpherson winked. "We're not spending the war as P.O.W.s. We are for getting out of here, back to Blighty, and no mistake."

"I want to come with you." He was blotto enough to confess: "My name is Arthur Koestler. I am an author, a journalist for British newspapers."

"Arthur Koestler." Byron-Hadley laughed. "I know you. Of you. You're famous, Old Pal."

"It is decided," Macpherson said, "The famous Arthur Koestler is coming with. There's a newspaper story or four in that. We want to be famous too."

The lieutenants had recruited two other adventurers, the dour Staff Sergeant Stewart, and Captain Pierce, the rather aptly named regimental medical officer. The various preparations for desertion and departure took a fortnight in all. "A fortnight of days and nights in a fort, eh?" Macpherson quipped.

Puns—Great British humour. Funny-punny. What was not-at-all-funny-punny were the acts of repression and *destruction* that were perpetrated in that fortnight to unmake *Le Republique*. People were barred from buying spirits at bistros in the name of anti-alcoholism. "Fascist bastards!" cried the Legionnaires. The French trade unions were dissolved—in the name of the workers' interests. "Fascist shits!" declared the Communists.

The first Jewish shop windows are smashed in Marseilles in the name of the National Revolution. "Nazi scumbags!" decried the Jews. And, the Luftwaffe blitzing London with incendiary bombs—well, that really-really, really annoyed the Tommies. "Fuck Hitler," said Staff Sergeant Stewart. "Wait 'til I get to Berlin. I'll kill that wee runt wi me bare hands."

The daring escape plan was for five men, wearing civvies, to get on two different fishing boats across to Oran, in the North West of Algeria. The leather-skinned captains of these small boats were Riffi fishermen, hashish smugglers, until this summer, when refugees suddenly became a much more valuable commodity. "We are *the* prize catch." Byron-Hadley made the sign of cross in the air at the Riffi. "Behold, I will make you fishers of men."

They crossed on a calm, sunny day, but Arturo Koestler let the side down, desperately seasick. *Must have lost two stone in weight.*

From Oran, they made for the Moroccan border by the back roads, in two groups—to lessen the risk of capture by the gendarmerie, or Legion patrols. They rendezvoused in the town of Oudja and hitched a lift on the back of a lorry, through the rugged peaks of the Middle Atlas range, bypassing the garrison towns of Fez and Meknes to their ultimate objective: the free port of Casablanca.

It was a good plan. A damned good plan, and it worked—because the Vichy regime had yet to establish itself effectively in the colonies. Everyone made it through, in one piece. They celebrated their 'score' with wine. Awful Moroccan red wine from the Rif. Which was clearly mixed with dust, the way it clogged the throat. The wine was served up in a dingy bar in one of the side streets down by the docks.

They were met in the bar by a member of the Secret Intelligence Bureau, Foreign Affairs. The British Imperial *apparat,* which had been re-classified as the 'Special Operations Executive' by summer 1940. The spy's name was 'Henry'.

Henry arranged for them to smoke some *kif* in *sebsi* pipes to relax, and then for all of them, drunk-and-drugged, to stowaway on a fishing trawler that was leaving for Lisbon, Portugal, that evening.

"Oh please, not another rowboat," he moaned, going green just thinking about the voyage. "I have nothing left to purge."

"It's a 270-tonner," Henry said. "There will be 50 other escapees on it. Cost us a pretty packet so, *bon voyage* chaps."

Over the next four anxious days—many hours spent rolling on deck as a lookout, scouring the waves for submarine periscopes—the Atlantic tossed them past the U-boats, into safe harbour at Lisbon. They hurried down the gangway. When he set foot on dry land, the neutral soil of

Portugal, be let out such a huge sigh of relief the loss of oxygen was dizzying. "Free."

Byron Hadley crossed himself. "Thank you, Sweet Jesus."

Free. But the famous Arthur Koestler had assumed too much. Too soon. His *Odyssey* was very far from over. Just as Homer was cruel to his hero, positioning many obstacles in the way of Odysseus: The Cyclops, Sirens, The Roc, Circe, The Lotus-eaters; so it was to be for him. When he visited the British Consulate—although the Consul General, Sir Henry King, congratulated him on a daring escape, and thanked him for the help he gave the chaps with organising the fishing boats to Oran, he would discover he was not going to London, England. Not without a visa.

To get a visa he needed identity papers. And he had none. "I know you are Arthur Koestler," Sir Henry said, "but we have to be able to prove that Old Boy, and as you can't, you're rather caught between a rock and a hard place."

"Scylla and Charybdis."

"I will go into bat for you," Sir Henry assured.

It hurt, deep in the core of comradeship, when the chaps flew out the next day, leaving him completely alone in a strange city. A man without a past. A man with no present. A man without a future. The author in him conceived of a novel about this place. He renamed it 'Neutralia', though in truth it was anything but neutral. The Portuguese, like the Spanish, had become very pro-Fascist in their '30s, under Corporatist leader, António de Oliveira Salazar. They spat the word: '*Judeu*'.

It was said that over 1,700,000 desperate save-our-souls passed through labyrinthine Lisbon on the way out to America, and life, and freedom. Life, the preservation of life, became an industry to the Portuguese administration, and entrepreneurs. He noted this in his pocket diary. The country, which had been dirt-poor before, suddenly in one year, became the must-see tourist destination for all of Europe, and riches, gold, diamonds, American dollars, flowed into the coffers.

The trick to this ruthless get-rich-quick-scheme was to delay exit—the *holiday* must be a prolonged stay—to enable the transfer of all the riches of these asylum-seekers to the Portuguese. And there must be the constant threat of arrest, deportation and death to ensure it worked. An expanded, vigorous secret police, the *Policia de Vigilância e Defesa do Estado,* was the key to making the machine of terror as productive as *humanely* possible. That, and letting the *Abwehr* and *Gestapo* in the back door.

The *nouveau riche* Portuguese enjoyed *milking* the Jews, more than the politicos, the gypsies, the homosexuals, the blacks, the Slavs. They justified it by insisting that the banks, which were all owned by the Jews, had been milking everybody for centuries, bleeding them dry in fact. Like leeches. This rationalisation allowed them to sleep soundly at night: they were so righteous that the sheep counted them.

Estado Novo! 'New State' as they called this state of affairs. He found the Portuguese as despicable as the Falange regime in Spain. They were *collaborateurs.* It pained him to learn, and speak, their derivative language. But he did. Because he needed these words to defend himself should the P.V.D.E. come for him.

Watching. Waiting for the P.V.D.E. Keeping a low profile in his little hotel room. In the café, down on the quayside. In his favourite bar. All he did was *wait* in these places. He sometimes imagined Walter Benjamin, walking with a shepherd's crook, on a goat path in the mountains of the Basque country, striding towards salvation. The statue of Lady Liberty blazing in his eyes.

Sir Henry asked the Home Office to consider issuing a visa.

The H.O. refused. *Stark. No control whatsoever. His fate in the hands of madmen.* He abided like this for two whole months, abided by the rules.

Sir Henry approached a personal contact, higher-up the chain of bureaucracy, arguing: "Arthur's soon-to-be-published novel, *Darkness at Noon,* proves the fellow is one of us, anti-Communist and anti-Nazi."

Result: visa refused.

Sir Henry admitted: "They will not budge." The British Secret Intelligence Service, the very people who saved his life by helping to get him out of French possessions, were not letting him set foot on English soil, because of his Communist past.

The only good Red is a dead Red, Old Chap. Walter's pills: the temptation to mix the pills into his Amontadillo was strong, to put all hope out of its misery. But, he resisted, committing to experience the crippling sherry hangover at dawn the next day. *Where there was life there was hope.* God, he was the man who had found hope in cell No. 40. *Valor, hombre.*

Wearing an iron crown of self-inflicted pain; that was when he heard that Walter Benjamin, having finally managed to get across the Pyrenees, had been arrested on the Spanish side by the *Guardia Civil*, and threatened with deportation the next day. Poor Walter gulped down the 15 morphia pills in his cell rather than be delivered into the hands of the *Gestapo.*

Enough! It had to end. He could not wait another minute on their mercy. It was unbearable. He took the pills, washed the first two down with warm dregs of the sherry, tried to swallow. They were large and hard in his oesophagus. He gagged, retched. Swallowed a handful more, gulped them down, eager to get it over.

But, the god of head-shrinking-stomach-frying-hangovers, Dionysus, demanded an immediate libation, pitching his disciple onto the floor. To vomit up the most vile-tasting yellow bile and bitter white-powder mix *ever.* The wracks wrung every spit of the poison out. He hovered over the sickness, gibbering. Vision swimming in it.

Pride. Lumpen. Stupid pride had nearly killed him. Backhanding the drool off his mouth, he pushed himself to his feet. *You need to beg. Get down on bended knee and beg for mercy.* He cleaned himself up. Went to the British Consulate. Waited two hours to see the Consul General.

When Sir Henry King rose from behind his oak desk, offering his hand, he did not shake hands. Instead, he got down on bended knee. "Help me escape, and I'll do anything the you need me to. I'll spy for the British. I'll parachute into Berlin. Kill Hitler. Anything."

"God loves a trier, my boy."

With Sir Henry's connivance, and help from another Walter, Walter Lucas, a friend and correspondent for *The Times*, the famous Arthur Koestler managed to sneak past security, and board a Dutch K.L.M. flight, bound for Bristol, England. Those last 20 minutes of waiting before take-off were the longest, and then soaring up, up, above the clouds, heavenwards, staring at the sun and wonder. "Thank you, God!" he said, crying.

Tears of joy and sorrow and anger and hate and forgiveness, deep gratitude, every damned emotion, seizing him, all at once vivifying. The Portuguese businessman beside him frowned, *tsk-tsk.*

THE TEMPTATION OF ADAMO

B reath fogging the windowpane, Adamo stared out the kitchen window.

Crazy Otto was *not* trying to get into the house. *Why would he chase you all the way here, only to stand sentry in the garden?* Still as a statue. Otto The Younger.

It couldn't be fear of the non-existent security system...? There must be a reason. Another reason. Haunted House. The Mother of All Demons.

He shrank away from the window, out of line-of-sight. Sweat clagged the small of his back like a sheaf of chill, wet leaves. *W—T—F, Otto? Why stand out there?*

This was nutso! Had everyone gone nuts? Bonkers. Some sort of mass psychosis? *Or is it me?*

Me? As if in answer to his questioning, there was a hot prickling sensation at the base of his neck. An itch that needed scratching right away. Maddening.His hands clawed at the nape, scrabbling at the skin that surrounding the collar bones, fingernails catching on the links of a chain of the amulet.

He had to get this off. Pulling the chain taut, out past his chin, so that he could see the three angels, he yanked it away from his neck.

The chain did not break, not a single link separated.

A second, harder tug. All that did was jar into a cervical vertebra, drag his head forwards; mini-whiplash; ozone in his nostrils.

He slid his thumbs under the chain and lifted it up, trying to get it over his head, but it wouldn't fit over his chin. It was stuck. *How could it not fit?*

He gripped the angels' bodies, applied all up-force possible, grunting, as he tried to fit his grimace into the loop. The chain bit into the skin on his chin. It must have shrunk. Or his head must have grown... *Mr Potato Head.*

He let the chain drop back to rest on his chest; would have laughed at the absurdity of his situation, but for the realisation that he did not know what the amulet was, had no way of knowing what hung round his neck.

Otto had said it was for his protection, but it could *be* anything. A weapon. It could *do* anything. The horror of not knowing. *Eva. Maybe Eva could help him get it off?* Four hands are better than two. *Yeah. Eva.* He thought of her still asleep upstairs in that big bed. He would go and waken her up. He would tell her what had happened, all the craziness with Nadine, and they would find a way to deal with this drama-drama, together. To that end, he abandoned the kitchen, and ascended the stairs in twos, up, up, up, up to the third floor.

Gusting with effort. Finding the master bedroom, empty. The bed made-up, hotel-pristine. As if it had never been slept in. No clothes. None of her stuff lying around. Not even the scent of their sex in the air. He advanced into the en suite. It had been perfectly sanitised too. Regarding his reflection in the big wall-long mirror, he frowned in puzzlement. It was as if they never spent the night here. But this was the room. Definitely. "Eva?" he called out.

The silence in the mansion was measured in thousands of square-feet-cubed. *Otto. Maybe Otto got to her, before he came after me?*

This volume of silence served to amplify his fears. *The landlord. What if she got caught, was banged-up in a police station right now?*

Silence, dystopic, and vast as the effect of an extinction event. Post-cometary-impact. *What if he got caught in here?*

What could he say? Forgive me my trespasses, Detective, I got lost looking for my wife, who is missing, a missing person... He shook his head, or rather his head shook itself. Eva probably just left, went around to the Double-Mums' for breakfast.

He checked all the bedrooms on the third floor. No sign of her. He headed downstairs. Stopped dead-still, on the second-floor landing. "Eva?"

Listening out. Trying to regulate his breathing. Trying to determine if anyone else is in the house. Find a direction to go in. Heavier. Deeper. Breaths. From the diaphragm.

Not a peep.

So, he made his way down the hallway—to the first open bedroom doorway on the left. Stood there. Staring into the room. Stood there.

Tense, motionless, waiting for something to move. Stood.

Staring in.

Stood there on the threshold.

Because, there—she—was. In *that* bed. Asleep.

Long hair cast out like a net over the pillow, over her naked back and shoulders. There, she lay. In this room. *Why? Why would she have moved rooms?*

Stood there, like a statue. Like Otto. Frozen in time. A forever of waiting.

In his mind's eye, he saw himself from the interior of the room, stood back there in the doorway, staring in. This loop played out slow-mo', like a dream.

Thinking of the eternity as a looping dream. A dream, in the half-life of waking. Every second distending into an aeon. A terrible clarity. The loneliest knowledge. Gleam of a skull. The death's head grin. Death, chuckling like a boy, through clenched teeth. He tried not to not think of it but, that was all he could think of.

The need to be with her was a sudden, violent reaction to this thrown-outness. To go to bed with her. To sleep with her. He undressed, a frenzy of limbs in the doorway. A pile of clothes, and longing was stark naked, raw.

Slipping in between the sheets. Spooning into her back, wrapping his arms around her warm body.

A face full of hair. The summer-meadow smell of shampoo. A

strange scent. Not her usual brand. The newness of it was alluring. Arousing him into a hardness, against the squish of her buttocks. Brushing aside her hair, to kiss her neck. She stirred, moaned.

All he wanted was to hold onto her, like this. Forever.

SHOAH

error prays hardest. Terror prayed that they would not send Enemy Alien, Arturo Koestler, straight back. Terror was praying like a priest when he surrendered himself at Bristol Airport. Terror was praying like a bishop, when he handed the Immigration Officer a written statement from the British Consul General, Sir Henry King, explaining his case.

Terror was praying hard as *Il Papa* when he was immediately arrested, taken to Bristol Police station. Therein, Terror abated, because Prisoner Arturo Koestler had survived many a worse cell than this English cell. The bed was as hard-as-nails; no pillow, no blanket; still, Prisoner Arthur Koestler would sleep like a baby. He had concentrated dreams about *La Vernet*, but wakened up smiling: *Just dreams.*

The Duty Sergeant could not believe how happy the prisoner was when informed: "You will be taken, under armed escort to Cannon Row Police Station, London, where you will be formally charged with Illegal Entry into Great Britain, and possibly, Espionage."

He was arraigned in court on day two, a mere formality, and remanded in custody.

Pentonville was hardly the Ritz of prisons, but it beat Seville hands-down. If he had to write a Baedeker guide—'Prisons of Europa'—he would award Pentonville 3-stars.

The facilities were Victorian, Guvna. The plumbing, highly suspect. One had to share a cell with another inmate, which is excruciating on the toilet. The screws are bleedin grumpy. And, worst of all, a chap couldn't read before bed—the ruddy lights go out on your wing every nightfall to enforce the blackout. In case any of the suspected Nazi spies being held here, were indeed Nazi spies. Light must not bleed into the night, to draw the eye of bombardiers aboard Heinkel He 111s.

Blackout or no blackout: two incendiary bombs, courtesy of Field Marshal Goering's *Luftwaffe*, crashed through the roof one busy night of the Blitz, only to get snagged up in the safety netting between floors. *Near miss.* Trapped in dark cells, that rattled the population somewhat; a near-riot, until the bombs were defused.

There was no safe place in a world at war. Even under the threat of being Blitzed, he would not swap Pentonville for all the modern accommodations of Seville. *A cell to himself, hah. The relatively comfortable beds, hah. The working water-closets in each cell, hah. The spacious exercise pavement, exclusive to those few long-stay cases under sentence of death. Hah!*

And, although it was lovely being able to purchase wine with one's meals by bribing the warders, he did not miss the sound of doors opening in the hours after midnight, and prisoners calling for *madre, madre, socorro, socorro* as they were dragged out to be shot, or hung, or stabbed, or garrotted.

The Brits only executed one man in the six weeks he spent at His Majesty's pleasure in Pentonville. This German spy, convicted after a fair trial, was hanged by the neck until dead.

The night after they hanged the spy, he had a nightmare about Pentonville. There were no other prisoners. Koestler was serving a sentence in every cell. Koestler was every prisoner.

In one cell, he was being held for being a Zionist agitator, an agent of *Irgun*, right-wing forever.

Next door, he was banged-up by the Israelis for advocating a two-state solution to Zion, and worse, writing the anti-Semitic, *The Thirteenth Tribe*, about how modern European Jewry were not Semites at all, but the Khazars, late economic converts to Judaism, intent on avoiding ludicrous laws against *usury*, the crime of Christians lending money to fellow Christians.

Further down the wing, he was incarcerated by the Germans for being part of a Communist cell that assaulted multiple Brownshirts of the *Sturmabteilung*, in a beer hall.

Across the suicide netting, he was in-clink for anti-Stalinist agitation on behalf of the Congress for Cultural Freedom, a C.I.A.-backed front to counter a Cominform campaign for world peace through nuclear disarmament.

A level down, off-left, he was imprisoned for being a pornographer, under the false name Dr. A. Costler.

Down on the ground floor, kept in isolation, he was accused of rape. The rape of Gill Craigie, the wife of his friend Michael Foot, the Leader of the British Labour Party.

Up on the top floor, he was being held for effectively campaigning to end the death penalty in Great Britain and the Commonwealth. Evidence: *Reflections on Hanging* (1956).

Right next door to that, he was in a cell for writing *A Guide to Self-Deliverance* for the pro-euthanasia organisation EXIT and wanting to end his own suffering—advanced Parkinson's and terminal cancer—by committing suicide in pact with his much-younger, third wife, Cynthia Koestler (nee Jeffries).

In the oldest, darkest cell, he was held on the charge of Crimes Against Humanity, for summoning Lilith from the Firestone to do his bidding, demanding an after-life of his own choosing, in of all places, Zion.

Prisoner Arturo Koestler was technically not allowed visitors, but Daphne wangled her way in to visit with some page-proofs in his second week in-clink, and the famous journalist was granted special dispensation by the Governor to edit his novel in his cell.

His National Registration Card was an early Christmas present from His Majesty, conferring the right to exist in Great Britain and the colonies as 'Arthur' Koestler, the rather kingly, Anglicised version of his name.

King Arthur was released on the 21st. Freedom came in the form of

Daphne to collect him in a car, at the main gate. She was full of good news: "Jonathan Cape are very excited about the initial response to *Darkness at Noon*."

"*Darkness at Noon*." This was when he first said the English title of the book out loud. It was Daphne's choice, suggested by Job 5 v 14: *They meet with darkness in the daytime and grope in the noonday as in the night*. He kissed Daphne, pulling her in tight, to feel that he was free to do what he wanted to do. And, it did feel that way. Truly. In his body. "I want to drink champagne and take you to heaven and back a few times. Are you with me?"

She raised an eyebrow. "Like Lilith was with Adam."

Cigarettes. Champers. Cocktails. Daphne's 22-year-old luscious body. He fell into her, lost in flesh until the next day, when he announced, cigarette twitching on his lip: "I'm going to sign-up for the British Army."

"You're mad," Daphne said. "Are you trying to get yourself killed?"

"I want to fight. Freedom is worth fighting for." So, he *did* apply. And, became Private Koestler in 251st Company, Pioneer Corps. The last 'Alien Company' formed. Stationed way out West. The patronisation infuriated him; his talents were totally wasted.

In time, Private Koestler did some home-front propaganda work for Whitehall. The Political Warfare Executive. Waging a war of words, same old story, since the days of the K.P.D. and his stint at AGITPROP.

It wasn't exactly satisfying. He wanted to be like Ernest Hemingway or George Orwell, a *real* fighter, not just a paper tiger, but he consoled himself with the knowledge that writers write, and the pen would be mightier than the sword—in the end.

Darkness at Noon was a weapon of war, a *totally* political novel, written in the authentic language of the Party, by an ex-member, about the horror of secular religions and totalitarian governments. Ironically, Communist attempts to bury the novel resulted in it becoming a huge commercial success.

In England, the only country in Europe in which Marx believed a truly bloodless revolution might occur, *Darkness at Noon* sold a modest 1,000 copies in the first year (1940) and then it ran out of print. The *plop!* of a pebble in a village duck pond.

In 1945, the French translation *Le Zero et l'Infiniti* broke all post-war publishing records and sold 400,000 copies in the first year—precisely because the Communist Resistance Movement, the *Maquis*, took so violently against it.

When death threats against the publisher, the translator, and the author (*Le Traiture de le Prolétaire*) did not stop the publication or retail of the book, the Party ordered up entire stocks from bookshops, and burned them, in secret at first, then in public.

Backed by Stalin, the *Maquis*—numbering under 600 in 1943, but having recruited hundreds of thousands by the end of 1945—were trying desperately to consolidate a stranglehold on power in France, after their bitter struggle against the Nazis.

With an armed paramilitary wing behind them, the Communist Party became the strongest political party in France, and in 1946 called for a referendum on the future form of the constitution.

Arthur Koestler took great pride in the controversy. *Le Zero et l'Infiniti* was cited by many 20th Century intellectuals as the *most* important factor which led to the defeat of the Communists. It was written into History how he, and his novel, came to symbolise freedom of speech.

He believed he survived the Fall of France for this purpose. Surviving, when many of his friends and comrades were captured, sent to Auschwitz-Birkenau, Mauthausen-Gusen, Bergen-Belson, Dachau.

Worldwide acclaim, household-name-fame, and rags-to-riches sales of 500,000 copies at 10% of the retail price, ameliorated his survivor guilt. For a while. *There, but for the grace of...*

Let there be also among the people the Lilitu,
Let her snatch the baby from the lap of her who bore it.

THE EPIC OF ATRAHASIS

The entity was among the Sons of Belial, who used the divine
forces for the gratifying of selfish appetites.

EDGAR CAYCE, *Reading 3633*

COMPLICATIONS

Eva woke up on a couch, knackered. Totally shattered. Woozing in, and out, and in, of consciousness. Her head felt like a roasted marshmallow. *The last thing she remembered clearly...?* Lilit giving her that magic-fingers-massage. It felt so good.

She could taste that metallic tang of dope, like tinfoil in her mouth. So dry, parched. It felt like she was on the worst comedown ever, from a high, but: *When did we get high?*

"Ah, look who's back in the land of the living," Lilit said, coming over, and kissing her on the lips.

She was taken aback by the kiss, this show of intimacy, but tried to smile.

"Pregnancy sure does take it out of a mum," Lilit said, "but we have a baby-scan party to host."

"Baby-scan party?" Her hands went to her tummy, which seemed bloated. She had absolutely no idea that her baby was the size of a lime, that she was now 'three months' pregnant, in no time. "Sorry. Did I miss something?"

"Darlink! I invited my friends around for a jam-tasting bash, to celebrate us finding out the sex of our baby. It's raging—in our kitchen."

"Fuckballs." She shook her head, as if this might help orientate her in time and space. *What comes after fuckballs?*

Helicopter head-spins. "Oh—My—God."

"Aw, you're tired. Should we let you sleep? My Yummy-mummy needs lots of sleep."

Yummy-mummy? She looked very uncomfortable. Struggled to sit up. The desire for order. To be in control. To situate herself in time-space as herself. Eva Kadmon. "What day is it? The I.C.U. I'll be fired."

"You're worrying me now, Darlink," Lilit said. "You're off on the sick. High blood pressure. We don't want pre-eclampsia. Remember?"

"No."

"It's as well I have memory enough for the two of us then, isn't it? Why don't you come downstairs, meet the others? They're an interesting bunch. Weird, even for weirdo West London."

"Eh, no." She could barely string a sentence together.

"Oh, come on. Everyone is a member of this group called 'Possess'. You can join in."

"*Possess?*" she said.

"It's a bit like Occupy," Lilit explained. "Except we take over vacant property in London, owned by rich Arabs or Russian scum, possess it, as a form of political protest."

Occupy. Name recognition. She knew what *Occupy* did, direct action for global justice. "Activism." She slurred the *-ism*.

"More than that—we are Anarchists," Lilit said, mockingly punching the air with a clenched fist. "We do anal. A-nal. A-nal!"

'Uh. Are you really...drunk?"

"No. Haven't touched a drop. High on jam, maybe?"

You're not drunk? She wanted to ask: *Then why are you shouting: A-nal! at me.* But of course, didn't, because it seemed terrifically complicated.

"A.N.A.L. stands, or rather *squats*, for the Autonomous Nation of Anarchist Libertarians."

Anal. Libertarians. It was like Lilit was reading her mind. Which was even more disturbing. Magic carpet paranoia. Desert dunes flashing by below. Speeding over a sea as dry as death. Velocity combined with vertigo and she wanted to be sick. To purge her system of whatever it was she was on.

"You look frankly bedraggled, my dear," Lilit said. "Don't fret. I have engaged the services of an expert."

"Mmm-hmm" was the best she could manage.

"Dr. Walter Freeman II is possibly the world's greatest brain surgeon, ever. So, we are in good hands. I cannot wait until the scan tomorrow. To know the sex of our baby. Then we can name him."

Him...? She felt the blankness on her face like a dry mud-mask. All muscles relaxed, but the skin drawn tight.

An anxious swooning, a fainting away, as if her body no longer belonged to her, as if she had been possessed by forces unseen. Worse. Spirited away.

THE GREAT DRAGON

Insanity, 'The Great Dragon', could be slain. Liberation from life's pain, could happen. If, there was consent.

Enoch Dannecker *must* consent.

For, without the husband's consent, Dr. Walter Freeman II could not, would not, perform the lobotomy on his insane wife, and then, Mary-Mary-QuiteContrary would have to be confined to a mental institution.

Joining the other 600,000 patients, wasting away, in mental hospitals across the United States of America in 1965. A total waste of humanity. The sheer productivity lost to society, and industry. Millions of dollars-worth per annum.

It was the civic duty of Dr. Walter Freeman II—the self-appointed 'Saviour of America'—to persuade Enoch of the necessity of his brain-child, the trans-orbital lobotomy, to save Mary from the scrapheap of defectives, but it was proving hard work in this case, because these folk were Mormons.

"I dunno, Doc," Enoch said, holding his head in both hands. "It's a lot."

Doc? He would correct the man. "Doctor Freeman, if you please."

"The Bishop says she's demon-possessed, that what she needs is an exorcism. Are you sure this will work for her, Doc?"

Lobotomy vs. Exorcism. There were certain similarities. Except, lobotomy was a scientifically proven method of treatment. He had explained the procedure to Mr. Enoch Dannecker *ad nauseum.* The poor fellow understood 'pre-frontal lobotomy' because of his own surgery, but on the new 'trans-orbital lobotomy', he seemed somehow, blocked.

Resistance to Progress was to be expected amongst the Church of Jesus Christ and the Latter-day Saints. To combat stalwart dogma, he had a manila folder that was full of black and white photographs of schizophrenics wandering the wards of nihilistic institutions, lost in the realm of demons.

A keen photographer, he took these photos of the *treatments* used by caretakers in these places. As a record of modern medieval tortures perpetrated by these caretakers. They were not doctors or alienists or psychiatrists, or any of the other grandiose names they gave themselves, to justify doing nothing to heal, or cure, the mentally ill, and lots to harm them.

Enoch was horrified by the photos. Several pictures of 'bowssening': buffeting the patient, blows to one side of the face, then the other, in rapid succession.

A series of images showing metrazol injections, and the extreme seizures produced that sometimes fractured bones, even spinal vertebrae.

Next up: the ice-baths series, recorded memories of naked, white, female patients being held down by black, male attendants; half-drowned, in freezing water. This proved too much for Enoch—this man who had stared death down on the battlefield—paled.

"Compared to a lifetime in one of these all-too-real hells," he argued, "lobotomy, and the good-life thereafter, is a cake-walk, a summer breeze."

"I just want my wife back, Doc. For this illness, this bad spirit, to be lifted, you know?"

"Lobotomy is effective in treating 93% of patients exhibiting early signs of psychosis."

"I know it works. I *know*." Enoch sighed, an exhale that deflated him totally. "She can't be calling the Bishop *evil* anymore. It's caused a lot of problems at Temple."

"She won't. Go, fetch her in, and we'll have a talk, so I can assess her."

"Okay." Enoch got up slowly, went to the door, turned. "I worry about her soul. How might this affect her soul?"

He played with his goatee, twisting the beard hair. This was a good question. *Was this surgery of the soul?*

Good answers to good questions were always difficult to articulate. "The most basic role of a doctor in human society is to relieve suffering. If a soul is tortured, and the torturer is the self-same soul, do we allow this suffering to go on indefinitely? If the person is stuck in misery, if nothing is learnt from it? That would seem to be Hell, and this isn't supposed to be Hell, is it? Hell is supposed to be in the Hereafter."

Enoch left, and returned with Mrs. Mary Dannecker.

Mary was a tremendously self-conscious, preternaturally beautiful brunette. Her face had a fierceness to it, the features were angular, striking. It hurt his heart to look at her. *This is how a man falls in love.* A woman's face became an obsession, and all of a sudden, he would be imagining himself in a future with her, the faces of their children flashing in her eyes.

This was what must happen, this compulsion of the species. It took him over, far more potent than any one individual's will. He knew full well that he *would* sleep with this patient, biblically *know* her, code of ethics be damned, double-adultery or not. "Hello, Mary. Take a seat. You can wait outside, Enoch. This won't take forever. Maybe 15 minutes."

Enoch nodded. "It'll all be okay, Sweetheart."

"Okay."

Grimly, Enoch left, closing the door behind him.

All the fear of being left alone with a doctor—one's life placed in the hands of another—flashed in those green eyes of hers, and that thrilled him. "Could you tell me today's date please, Mary?"

"2nd April, 1965."

"Correct. And, where are we? Which state?"

"Utah."

"Good. So—your husband tells me that you're having some troubles coping?"

Mary bit her lower lip.

The erotic charge from that little bite shivered down his neck. "Is that fair comment?"

"Yes, Doctor."

He did not normally indulge patients by asking this next question. *Because this was not psychotherapy.* "What seems to be the problem—from your perspective?"

"Life is...somewhere else."

"Yes?" *Dissociation.*

"I feel like a complete stranger to myself sometimes."

That was quite the statement. *Rational? Certainly self-aware. Paranoid? Schizoid? Normal?* "Mmm. Don't we all?"

"I keep thinking—I am not in control of my life. The stranger is."

Said with complete conviction. He nodded. Sometimes this kind of split happened with schizoids or manic depressives. He knew this from his own experience. When the mania seized a hold, it was as if he possessed too much energy for one person. The power seemed to come from elsewhere. *Devils? Angels?*

"I am losing my mind. The stranger is stealing it from me, bit by bit."

He had cracked-up twice. Into a series of Dr. Walter Freemans, I, II, III, IV, V. The first schizz was a standard mid-life crisis. The second nervous breakdown; a shattering into many irreconcilable parts, followed his dear son Keen's drowning.

Nembutal—a nightly dose to knock him into a dreamless unconsciousness—was the answer. Though oftentimes, it did not work, and he saw Keen pitching over the head of the falls.

Some mornings he was tempted to perform the procedure on himself, exsecting that memory once, and for all. "Who is this stranger, Mary? Have you given her a name yet?"

"Enoch is a hero, a good man. I just want to be a good wife."

"What is her name?"

"Lilith." Her face twisted into a mask of pain, and rage, outrage, as if she had been administered a low voltage electric shock. "The Bishop calls her 'the Mother of all Demons'."

Demons. That old story, raising its ugly head again. Hydra-like. Strike off the head, another two grew in its place. Mankind had always been plagued by the idea of demons. They always seem to take up residence in the head, the brain, gripping the imagination.

The earliest soul-surgery known to Prehistoric man was called 'trepanning', or 'trephining'. Specimens of skulls carbon-dated to prehistoric times showed evidence of this technique. It was believed that medicine men of old, shamans and brahmans, intuitively bored into the cranium, exposing the *dura mater*, trying to release evil spirits that were driving people mad.

Dr. Egas Moniz refined this technique into the leucotomy, and won the Nobel Prize. And a very clever fellow, Dr. Walter Freeman II, developed both the pre-frontal lobotomy, and his trademark procedure, the trans-orbital lobotomy from this primitive trepanning.

"Do you believe in demons, Doctor Freeman?"

"I do not *believe* in anything. I only know, or do not know, *yet.*"

"You will."

He doubted that. *The Greek word daemon meant 'one who knows'.* He knew that—the way he knew that schizophrenia was the diagnosis in this case.

It was a no-brainer.

COITUS MALEFICARUM

Awakened by Adamo's embrace, she slid down, under the duvet. Her long hair being the last thing to disappear, into the world below.

Like the tail of some beast.

The surface was disturbed humps, waves of motion, but beneath, she was kissing her way down his chest, little pucks, sending tremors through him.

Teeth nipping at his belly: or at least, that is how he perceived it, given that all he could see was the impression of her.

Deprived of sight, the super-sense of sight, denied of the source of the sensations, made her caressing of his inner thighs somehow much more intense.

Eva wasn't a biter, hadn't done that before. He closed his eyes. In the widening gap between reality and imagination, the thought occurred: *This could be anybody.*

That dissociation was permission to imagine it was another woman licking a trail along the skin that sheathed his hip. A new lover.

A filthy fantasy partner, who would do anything to pleasure him. This lover licked down his abdomen, past his throbbing cock, to his balls.

She sucked a testicle into her mouth, and rolled her tongue around it, maddenly hot and wet. Releasing it, with a swak.

Pointy-tonguing its twin, gorgeous, glorious flicks. 'Oh—My —God.'

A hand encircled the shaft of his cock, right under the head. Firmly.

Another hand, fingers fondling his balls. Lifting them up, to lick the sweet spot under there, the root. The softness of her tongue.

It drove him crazy, reduced him to a twitching, mess in seconds. Legs tightening. The muscles so tense. His hands gripped her head under the duvet, held it there.

She stopped, pulled away.

"Don't stop," he said.

But she disobeyed. *The bitch.*

Just breathed hard on his balls. Teasing him.

He tightened his grip on her head. Don't—stop?

She shook her head free of his grip. Reared up; tenting the duvet. Swished her hair on his thighs, back, forth. Such a thrill.

Both her hands gripped the shaft of his cock, one above the other, and she began—slow strokes, up and down. The rhythm drove him into shudders. She sped up. A frenzy shook him beyond his own limits.

She let go, both hands. Full—stop.

God!

The pause only lasted for 10 seconds, if that.

Still, it was long enough for him to feel abandoned.

Forsaken.

Left out on the shoulder of a mountain to die.

And then, suddenly, she took him in her mouth.

All of him. Down, down to the root.

The infernal softness of her throat.

Gagging on him. Choking off her air for him.

Too much.

Too intense to hold.

He wanted to see her face. "Look at me."

She kept bobbing her head up and down, forcing him down deep into the flesh of her throat: constriction, release.

"I'm close." He yanked the duvet back to see her face, but hair covered her face. He brushed it away.

She was down there, lapping at the throbbing head of his cock.

Long, flat tongue, teasing.

He was going to cum! Except.

That.

Is.

Not.

Eva.

Right on the edge of orgasm.

Lilit!

His Lilit...?

But how? She would swallow him. The world dissolving into neon explosions. She swallowed all of him.

PSYCHOSURGEON

I t doesn't take one to be a brain surgeon to perform brain surgery.

Dr. Walter Freeman II was *not* a brain surgeon.

Not a qualified brain surgeon anyway. Although, *sans licence*, he had performed more brain surgery than most certified brain surgeons ever would. 3105 procedures, before Mary Dannecker's trans-orbital lobotomy.

Despite the protests of surgical colleagues, and the objection of his own partner in private practice, Dr. Alan Watts, he had learnt how to operate on the brain by trial and error. He did not need a hospital. Experimentation, a combination of Moniz's and Fiamberti's techniques. He did not need an operating theatre. *Practice makes perfect.* He did not need a surgical team. He began by using an Uline Ice Company standard ice-pick, borrowed from his wife Marjorie's kitchen.

He did not need expensive anaesthetics. He used ElectroConvulsive Treatment, good old E.C.T., to knock 'em out cold. The nice thing about the region around the eye was that it was relatively sterile, so post-op infection was rare; the strict regime his illustrious grandfather imposed on American medicine—anti-sepsis and draping, was not required.

Dr. Walter Freeman II was not shy. Showmanship: he made instructional films—*Trans-orbital Lobotomy* (1950), took great pride in exhibiting the technique in public or on camera, using Look-Mom!-both-hands, ambidextrous synchrony.

He had done so, so many lobotomies he could literally perform this operation with his eyes closed. In fact, he had tried this in his office, secretly of course, with an unconscious, negro, 'agitated depressed' patient. And, it worked. Eyes wide shut. That negro did not die, she was never institutionalised, so something of a life was salvaged. Admittedly, the procedure would leave her indolent, petulant, puerile, and irresponsibly incontinent, but she wasn't seeing U.F.O.s, or hearing aliens telling her to come-fly-with-me, come-fly, come-fly-away, anymore.

Mary Dannecker's trans-orbital lobotomy. It would happen, like this: the day after her assessment, her husband Enoch delivered her up onto Dr. Walter Freeman II, like Abraham offering up his son Isaac, as a sacrifice pleasing to God.

All surgeons have something of a God-complex going on. He was not ordinary. He was extraordinary, an exceptional person, with higher powers. Life-giving powers. A third-generation doctor. Following in his fore-bears footsteps. Standing on the shoulders of giants. In the Land of the Free, the Home of the Brave.

His grandfather and childhood idol, Dr. William Williams Keen, was a brilliant brain surgeon, a true pioneer of the medical world, a trailblazer, always-always-always striking out West, West, to subdue the unknown, to make it known.

He wanted to make his mark in the world like that. That inspiration made him sit down and write for a year, the early bird, 4.00–7.00 A.M. ever workday. The end result: a book co-authored with Watts, entitled *Psychosurgery: Intelligence, Emotion, and Social Behaviour Following Prefrontal Lobotomy for Mental Disorders.*

The book cover was finger-painted by a lobotomy patient, Mary Lawrence. Marjorie proposed the colophon—which appeared on the title page and dust jacket—a holed skull with black butterflies flying out of it. The French for having the blues is *'J'ai des papillons noir tous les jours.'* The startling claim on the cover: *This work reveals how the person-*

ality can be cut to measure, sounding a note of hope for those who are afflicted with insanity.

Grandson sent Grandfather a copy and Dr. W. W. Keen wrote back, telling him what a great book it was to read, how proud he was of his descendant, and lastly, annoyingly, warned against hubris. *Hah, hubris be damned. That was the curse of the heroes of the Old World.*

It was a source of great, personal, *American*, pride to him that Grandfather bore witness to him making the pages of *Time* magazine, before the old fellow unfortunately lost his mind, outlived his usefulness, and died. Grandfather knew him in the end as his world-famous grandson. *The New York Times* called lobotomy: *Surgery of the Soul, History-making*. Dr. Walter Freeman II had become literally a living advertisement for the organisation Dr. W.W. Keen helped to build: the American Medical Association.

"May I take your coat?" he asked.

Mary was agitated, taking her coat off awkwardly, perspiration turning her white blouse see-through in blotches.

He sat her on the heavy gurney, patted her on the arm. "Everything is going to be fine, Mary. Lie down, now."

He used leather straps to secure the patient's legs, and arms, to the gurney because the E.C.T. causes violent muscles spasms; contractures, which can snap femurs—even on the relaxant, curare. He had been sued more than once for this, in the early days. *Expensive business litigation, if one is adjudged negligent.*

He strapped her head in place. She had a look of such consternation on her face. "It's perfectly safe," he said.

Singlehandedly, he administered the dose of the muscle relaxant. Succinylcholine. It did the job, in seconds. He really was these days what his dearly departed mother used to call him as a boy—'the cat that walks alone'—and did not even employ a nurse, to help handle patients.

He was more than capable of administering the electric shock to the temples. It usually took a few jolts. Women, three or four. Men, five or six.

One shock. She tried to jitterbug out of the straps, thrown about by the current like it was unheard Swing-ding-a-ling music, jaw-clenching tight, eyes in full Chinaman squint, then fell still.

Two shocks. The body convulsed manically, but the straps held her in place.

Three times—there was no escape, to make sure she had been rendered unconscious.

The patient coughed, hacked, the diaphragm kick-starting, breathing again.

He pinched her cheek, to test the muscle tone. Complete relaxation. She looked younger, released of all anxiety. *Younger, and more beautiful. Pale skin. Dark hair. She could be Snow White. He could be her Prince Charming.*

Thou shalt not covet thy neighbour's wife. He picked up his leucotome. It was an instrument he himself designed, which Henry Ator, a Washington machinist had cast in gold and imprinted with his name. Modelled on the original, standard icepick; incredibly sharp point, and cutting leading edges.

He peeled back the right eyelid, held the epicanthic fold up, and slid the tool round the white eyeball, so that the point addressed the orbit, parallel to the ridge of the nose.

Two taps of a gold-plated hammer, a crack that would make even the most experienced surgeon wince, and he had fractured the skull at one of its thinnest points, the transorbital bone.

From there, he steered the blade into the buttery grey matter. *No deeper than 5cm.* Then he pulled the handle of the instrument as far laterally as the rim of the orbit permitted— in order to sever the fibres at the base of the frontal lobe, the connections to the thalamus.

He returned the instrument halfway to its previous position and drove it in a further 2cm to 7cm from the margin of the upper eyelid.

The ticklish part came next, for arteries were within reach. Keeping the instrument in the frontal plane, he moved it 15 degrees to 20 degrees medially and about 30 degrees laterally. Hardly any resistance, as he returned it to the mid-position. He had to keep pressure on the eye upon withdrawal, to prevent haemorrhage.

Right lobe—done! He walked around the patient to create the best angle for the operation on the left side. He peeled back the left eyelid, aligned the leucotome. *Tap, tap* with the hammer.

Crack! Push it in 5cm. And—that—was—when—it—happened.
Reflexes made him lurch back in shock.

An eye, the pupil a slit, slid down into view, struggling to focus on the golden blade sticking out of the socket.

"Mary. Can you hear me? Blink once for yes."

Not a flicker.

In the old days of the pre-frontal lobotomy, he sometimes—Watts thought, inappropriately—asked patients mid-operation, to recite the Lord's Prayer as a brain function test. He would insist: "It is a good measure—everyone having learnt their Our Father by rote."

Watts accused him of being 'dark', 'a tad sepulchral'. *Dark?* "What's going through your mind right now?" he once asked a patient being given a 'Minimal', as opposed to a 'Radical'. The reply was: "A knife." *Now.*

That.

Was.

Dark.

"Mary—blink, if you can you hear me," he asked.

Blink. Slit eyes.

Snake eyes. One reptile-eye, trying to close around the leucotome. He drew it out. Three blood-tears ran from the eye, and she started to growl, a guttural non-human noise: "Her gates are the gates of death..."

Goosebumps prickled over his arms. The hackles rose on his neck.

"...and from the entrance of the house she sets out towards Sheol."

In shock, his whole body began to jitter.

"None of those who enter there will ever return..."

Red lightning surging through his central nervous system, adrenalin dump.

"...and all who possess her will descend into the Pit."

Make it stop. Make it stop. He seized the head-strap with the E.C.T. electrodes in it. Zapped her back into unconsciousness. Several minutes passed. Looking at her body. *Stay still, for Chrissakes.*

Signs of unconsciousness. *But...*

Those eyes.

Those words.

A curse. She cursed you.

He picked up the leucotome to complete the procedure. Peeled back the eyelid. There was only an egg of red-threaded white rolling about in the socket. The relief he felt was beyond words. He thrust the blade in, operating with utmost haste.

BABY SCAN

All flouncy in a pregnancy dress, she let Lilit guide her into a hospital room. *Yes, it was a hospital, although the journey, how had they got here...?*

"What hospital is this?"

"Why is it nurses make such bad patients?" Lilit replied.

The hospital room was replete with an ultrasound scanning device and bench; surround-lilac-curtain, and a crappy, little desk, computer and chair, in the far corner. All the props one might expect.

There was also a doctor in attendance. Old. Bald. Bespectacled. Goatee-bearded. Wearing blue latex gloves. "Would you take your top off Eva, and mount the bench, please?"

She would comply. Sluggishly.

Lilit drew up a chair, bunny-hopped it in as close into the bench as possible. "Go ahead, Doctor Freeman."

A squirt of gel onto the bump."Sorry, it's cold." Dr. Freeman applied the scanner.

She watched as the black-and-white world inside her lit up, sounded out. It was possible to make out a tiny human form in the confines of her womb.

"There's your lil' baby," Dr. Freeman said. Directly. To Lilit.

"Awww, cute. My lil' baby," Lilit said.

My baby! Eva thought, and immediately felt bad about thinking that way about her life-partner. Being possessive.

Lilit smiled. "So, my love, light of my life, fire of my loins, my sin, my soul—we want to know the sex, right?"

"We do," she heard herself answer, as if from a distance.

"We want to know the sex."

"Your wish is my command." Dr. Freeman nodded. "We'll take a look around all the major organs before we get to the sex organs."

"Suspense," Lilit said.

"The head, the brain, the eyes. All normal."

She lay, and watched the scanner lighting up the alien world in her belly. Morphic resonance. The borders of this world changed with the angle of view. They swam, in a sickening surreality. There were strange shapes, faces that appear, around the form of the baby.

A skull.

A dragon.

A hideous, visage, open-mouthed, silently screaming.

It was like she was inhabited by a legion of demons, possessed. Insight made her gorge rise, hot in her throat and her skin shrink, and grow cold. "What is going on?"

"It's okay," Lilit said.

It's not okay! It is not okay. The scan was telling her something profound about the nature of reality. Everything around her was sound. Distorted frequencies. Her fears were literally taking shape. "What's wrong?" she asked. "Is there something wrong?"

Dr. Freeman shook his head, but did not look away from the screen. "I'm just checking the heart. To be sure."

Scanning and re-scanning. Minutes pass. All that occupied the screen were different views of the little heart pumping, pumping, pumping. "Everything looks good with the heart. I'll just check the sex now..."

They waited to see.

"It's a boy," Dr. Freeman said. "For sure."

"He is huge." Lilit said. "Hung like a horse. Print us off a shot, and we can stick it on the fridge."

That was laughable, but she didn't laugh. Couldn't laugh. It was beyond her.

"For the proud parents." Dr. Freeman printed off three images from the scan.

"Thanks, Doc." Lilit took the scroll. It unfolded into two full body shots. "They'll look good in our kitchen."

You should be happy. You should be over the moon. Wiping the gel off her belly, she pulled her pregnancy dress down, and got to her feet. She should have been overjoyed...

Hand-in-hand, Lilit led her out of this room, waving the pictures. "He looks like a Samael to me."

"Gabriel."

"Samael. Samael. Samael."

"Let me see the pictures."

Lilit handed the scroll to her, this projection of a life yet to come. "We should get a 4-D scan. See Baby's face clearly."

She nodded. *A 4-D scan makes babies look golden. Pure gold. Molten gold.* "Sure."

"But next on Mum's to-do list is: antenatal classes." Lilit's voice, so joyful. "We are talking organised labour here."

THE EXORCIST'S
POSSESSIONS

T hou shalt not commit adultery. Thou shalt never stop thinking about having her. The growling her, strapped to the gurney. That snake-eyed devil-woman. For many months after that fateful procedure thou shalt be distracted by thoughts of lifting her skirt, ripping down those panties, and... Her awakening, the words spoken, haunted his very dreams. *Her gates are the gates of death.*

Dr. Walter Freeman II was a man of science, not a religious man. He therefore did not know the gates of death were to be found in Proverbs, as translated from the Hebrew into Greek, and thence into English and thence into American-English. He came upon *the gates of death* when his mind emptied itself of science.

He found distraction in his work, his vocation. His *calling*. He indulged in another of his 'manhunts': following up on an unusual case at St. Elisabeth's in 1939. A schizophrenic patient who had what he dubbed 'Atlas Syndrome'. His given name, or at least the name he gave for the medical record—Frank Overhoser.

Frank was institutionalised because he believed that he was fated to hold up massive objects such as the Statue of Liberty, and the Empire State Building. Standing at their bases, arms extended. Exerting himself to the utmost.

Holding up the sky.

Just before the procedure, Frank decided that this was his job. To hold up the very sky, like the Great Sinner, Atlas. He lay in bed, arms outstretched, fingers clinched. Under observation, he began to sweat profusely, his tongue poking out between his teeth, eyes loaded with the sheer weight of madness. When pressed on his arm, Frank exclaimed: "Don't you think I am holding up enough already?"

He had often wondered what became of Frank after the procedure. He endeavoured to track him down, as a distraction from Mary, but he couldn't find a trace of him anywhere, nor could the private investigator whom he hired. It was as if poor Frank has disappeared off the face of the Earth.

Leaving no one to hold up the sky.

He had a vivid dream in which Frank had been crushed by the weight of the world. Into a man-pancake. Standing atop it: Mary, Mary, naked and contrary.

He determined to drug himself dreamless. *To not see her.* He had always prided himself that he'd never needed more than three tablets per night. He was not an addict. He was *not*. But to be sure, he would up the dose to five Nebutal.

Five should fell the proverbial elephant in the room. Still, she found a way into the bedroom of his dreams, lay down beside him in a state of undress, and tormented him by just lying there, open-legged.

China Doll Syndrome occurred in patients sometimes, as a side-effect of lobotomy. Usually in lethargic, near-catatonic, long-stay institutionalised patients. But sometimes, it could occur in those who presented as more active.

This was what happened to Mary Dannecker. She was rendered lifeless as Galatea. A beautiful statue. An inert doll. This was how Dr. Walter Freeman II recreated her. This was how he returned her to her husband Enoch that fateful day.

Enoch shrank away from the lifeless body, fell to his knees and wailed, wailed like an infant crying for a the mother he killed at birth.

Dr. Walter Freeman II would console Enoch, trying to reassure him, but it brought tears to his eyes. The tears he could not cry at the deaths of dearest Keen, and poor Randy, Randy whose funeral he could not bring himself to attend. To survive his boys. For him, those were the keenest of all cuts, in a life that would seem like the death of 3,000 cuts by the end, cuts to the very quick.

He broke down with Enoch Dannecker, this Elder of the Jaredites, that lost tribe of Israel that sailed to the New World 1,500 years before Christopher Columbus was recorded to have discovered those continents. This breaking down, breaking through, loss of face, abandonment of male pride, bonded these two as brothers of a sort, at least to Enoch, who from thenceforth shared his pain.

The secrets of the dark heart. He would learn that Gunney Ryman took this name, Enoch, who was also known as Jared, because of a spell in the American Lake Veterans Association Hospital. The V.A.-doctors there diagnosed him as suffering from retrograde amnesia as an effect of shell-shock. He simply collapsed, like so many Marines after they took Okinawa, and was shipped home for treatment. Kill, or be killed.

Thou shalt not kill. Live, and let die. *Thou shalt not kill.* A commandment broken, numbers beyond knowing killed. He learnt that the Japs even killed themselves down in their caves, blowing themselves to pieces by grenades rather than surrender, even the women, children. *These yellow devils. They were not the same race. They could not be the same species. They had no humanity.*

Gunney Ryman suffered no wounds to the body, but his mind, and any moral sense, was hideously maimed in the madness of war.

The War on Madness—Gunney Ryman spoke about what peace meant to him. The four months of wandering the wards and corridors of American Lake being tormented by returning, horrific memories of hand-to-hand fighting in the long grass, *"Banzai! Banzai!"* the V.A.-doctors, concerned about the onset of psychosis, and the potential for homicidal mania, in these returned Marines, gave him a prefrontal lobotomy.

No prisoners.

The lobotomised Gunney Ryman—two months after his good conscience was deep-cut—had a very American dream. In his American Dream, he was reading a book, a lost book of scripture, not included in the Bible, and in this book a truth was revealed to him and he became whole again.

It was called *The Book of Enoch*. He believed in this apopheniac vision and had his doctor find him a copy of that book. He read it, and understood. *The Book of Mormon* came next and, by accepting Jesus Christ into his heart, he became one of the People of that Book, a Latter Day Saint, a prophet of God Himself.

Dr. Walter Freeman II, evangelist of the lobotomy, who converted the American Veterans Association to perform 2,000 procedures, to return war casualties to the world, with a two-thirds success rate, was as much the saviour of Enoch Dannecker as blessed Jesus himself.

Still weeping, Enoch picked Mary up like a rag-doll, and left the Lobotomobile. "I will nurse her back to health," he said. "God will deliver her, you'll see, Doc."

The miraculous recovery of Mary Dannecker took the next two months. Enoch was a man of his word. A man of God. Named after one of the few men of God ever to ascend to heaven in a fiery chariot. Enoch's God does deliver. That was the semblance of it.

The trouble was that Mary did not see it that way. Sure, she gave thanks to God, but there was no great love in her altered mind for her nurse. She only had this soaring love for her doctor.

A perfumed letter, addressed to *Dearest Dr. Freeman*, winged its way to his office as if Cupid had delivered it personally. In it, there was a poem dedicated to him:

Gentle, clever your surgeon's hands
God marks for you many golden bands,
They cut so sure they serve so well
They save our souls from Eternal Hell
An artist's hands, a musician's too
Give us the beauty of color and tune so true
But yours are far the most beautiful to me
They saved my mind and set my spirit free.

He dabbled in poetry occasionally and it touched him, the simple gratitude contained in this one verse. The tremendously good news of her recovery. It stirred up the desire for her anew. He wanted to go West and see her, checkup on her, but...

Thou shalt not.

Until, she sent a package to his office. Within was a beautiful silver fob watch, hunter case, with a silver chain. There was an engraving on the inside of the lid: *In Time...*

That did it. He could not resist the temptation any longer. He went West. Devising another plan to follow-up on lobotomy patients out there, a great many of them negro females. He would take the R.V. for a spin, and execute said plan.

Thou shalt not lie. Marjorie had cooked dinner that evening: *poulet a la crematorium.* She drank red wine when she cooked, the alcohol dulling her, so she hardly batted an eyelid when he announced: "I'm off tomorrow, Dear."

It was not out of the ordinary. He wandered off, crisscrossing America all the time following-up on patients and recording their life stories for posterity. He went off on solo fly-fishing trips, for trout. *Why would this trip be any different? He had slept with patients before. Even Blacks.*

But, this was *so* different. He was lying. A lie of the heart. And he knew the consequences of this black lie of the heart for his marriage would be catastrophic, but he lied anyway.

2081 miles from Washington D.C. to St. George. But, so what. He loved driving long distances, road trips across this Big Country. The open road was therapeutic. Whatever he was doing. Wherever he was going. Whether it was *un tour de lobotomie*, heading to conferences to lecture about lobotomy was a frontline weapon to beat back the enemy. Or taking the boys on vacation to Yosemite or Yellowstone Parks to instil in them a sense of adventure and self-reliance.

Driving allowed a man to switch off, leave all his cares and woes, life and wife, behind. That feeling that one could go anywhere one wanted in America, just make a left or a right, truly freed a man.

Before the damned Interstate Highway system was built, obviously.

St. George. He reached the city limits around midday. He drove to Mary's neighbourhood, Red Bute Canyon. Got out of The Lobotomobile at a payphone, and called her up, banking that it would be her who answered—because it was midday, and Enoch should be at work, unless he was ill, or staying home to look after her...

"Hello?"

"Hi, is that Mary? It's Dr. Walter Freeman II here."

"Oh—my—God."

Her response was everything he hoped it would be. "I'm in town on business. Could we meet up? I thought we could maybe go for a constitutional walk up into Zion National Park?"

She agreed. Completely.

Lobotomy patients often showed a lack of trustworthiness, and loyalty. As well as other 'virtuous' traits such as helpfulness, friendliness, courtesy, kindness, obedience, cheerfulness, thriftiness, bravery, cleanliness, and reverence. Truth was—they didn't give a damn what other people thought of them anymore.

Doctor and patient rendezvoused up in the visitors' car park of Zion at 2.00 PM. There was over an hour to kill for him.

Listening to country music, tortured love songs full of cheating and broken hearts. He sang along to '16 Tonnes' by Tennessee Ernie Ford: "You load 16 tonnes and what do you get, another day older and deeper in debt. Saint Peter don't you call me, coz I can't go... I owe my soul..."

Enoch. Gunney Ryan. Dr. Walter Freeman II felt bad about going behind his back. Enoch didn't deserve this betrayal. Nor in fairness, did Marjorie. It wasn't his wife's fault he was bored to tears by her. But, all was fair in love and war. Kill, or be killed. Fuck, and be fucked.

Mary drove up, got out of her Caddy. Even more impalingly attractive than he remembered. The sight of her looking at him and smiling was like a slap across the cheek. "You look the very picture of health," he said.

"I am feeling a lot better," she said. "Thanks."

"The black butterflies have flown away then?"

It was clear she did not completely understand the second question but nodded. "I am much, much happier."

"The pursuit of happiness is one of your three inalienable rights as an American. Life, liberty..."

In a giddy rush, she hugged him. "It is good to see you, Dr. Freeman. I have been wanting to thank you in person for giving me back my life."

He squeezed her tight to him, Tabu perfume masking the musky scent of her, the heat of her body pressing against his. He patted her on the back, fatherly, pulled away as desire hardened him. "Shall we walk and talk? I love Nature-walking."

"Yes, yes. Let's."

The erotic charge amplified as they walked the walk, talked the talk, on the winding path up into the foothills. He deliberately stopped at a promontory.

Gazing out over the lushness of the slopes, the sheer greenery under that big blue sky, it relaxed him a little. The astringent scent of the pine trees on the whispering breeze was truly invigorating, opened his heart 100 miles wide. *Or was that her...?*

"The Great Outdoors," she sighed.

That *punta de vista* was where he first kissed her.

She was surprised by his boldness, but kissed back, hard.

He fondled her breasts, let a hand slide to her buttocks.

She moaned into his mouth, her spit sweet as soda.

He manhandled her off the trail, kissing, fumbling a way into the pines. This was exactly what he fantasised doing.

In many cases that Dr. Walter Freeman II followed up, lobotomy increased the sexual desire and response of female patients. Less second thoughts, less anxiety, less inhibition. He greatly enjoyed testing out the sexual responses of ex-patients and he intended to test the very limits of how slutty Mary Dannecker had become.

Under the shadows of the canopy, she undid his flies and hunkered down. She licked and lapped at his prick, looking up into his eyes as her tongue flicked over the tip. "I want to eat you up," she said, her pupils narrowing into slits. "Eat you alive."

"Do it."

He watched as her lips rolled over his prick, her tongue wrapping round, until it hits the exquisite softness at the back of her throat, and she was fucking him with her face, her beautiful face, until she choked, gasped for breath, but then took it all down again to make herself gag on it.

"Oh my God," he said, looking up, into the canopy and the blue ecstasy beyond the branches. *Do not come. Do not come yet.*

"Treat me, Dr Freeman." She got to her feet, wiped a translucent cord of spit from her lips with the back of her hand.

He watched, a man-possessed, as she slid her panties down, and discarded them like trash.

She leant up against a tree trunk, pulled her skirt up to show the orbs of that exquisite rump. Her eyes were beseeching: *Take me.*

He seized her from behind, and using her hipbones like handles, thrust into her slick-smooth insides.

"I want your seed in me."

The demand for his semen drove him insane, hips bucking into her ass, ripples of flesh rolling up either side of her spine.

"You must say my name when you come."

He seized hold of her hair and yanked it back, so he could see half her face. "Says who?"

"You must say it. Say you will say it."

"I will say your name." He thrust into her harder. Making her his. Only his. The concatenation of flesh on flesh.

"Lilith. Say it."

"Lilith?" His rhythm slowed. *Lilith.* "Say it. Say it now, and sow your seed in me. Lilith."

Lilith? The lobotomy, dear God, it had not worked.

"Say it. Lilith."

"Lilith," he said, and it happened—like—that.

WHO WOULD BE A FATHER?

nd the dead shall eat the living: she had his engorged cock clamped between bared teeth. The worst sight he'd ever beheld. Eye-watering, searing pain, sharper than anything he'd ever felt, but the fear, the naked terror that she would bite down, unman him. Truly unbearable.

Just.

Don't!

Those eyes, wild with power. Raging-amber, those eyes, pupils huge like owl's eyes, glaring up at him from between his legs. And, there was small scar on her right temple, a little black mole he had never noticed before. When she was alive. A black hole mole, sucking in the nearby skin, making her left ear twitch. A black hole in her face.

Tell me, A-K... the black-hole-mole said, *Would you give your own life to save your wife and your unborn child? Would you die for your family?*

The desperate thought: *If I grab her by the hair, pull, maybe she'd let go?*

As if reading his mind, she bit down, harder. He heard himself howling, shrieking, then sobbing. But she did not for a second let him go.

Answer me!

"Yes," he sobbed. "I would."

So be it.

In a single, fluid movement she released his manhood, and mounted him, her legs straddling his torso, a powerful clamping around his diaphragm. Both her hands pinned his wrists to the bed.

He instinctively tried to break her grip, struggled as hard as he could, twisting his hips, bucking, kicking out with his legs but, he could not get out from under her. Deadening weight. Weakness, the weakness of resignation. The profound acknowledgement of his first love. Living, again. She was here. *But how? That's not possible. You're dead. Dead, Lilit.*

"I will have my baby." Tendons protruded in her neck, an impossible lattice of wires and cords beneath the skin. Her jaw tensed. Her face reddened to a fury. "You will be the father of my baby."

Her mouth opened wide. A retch, a dry heave. Dry, but for one translucent strand of drool stringing down from her red lips, latching onto his chin.

Oh Christ. He tried to wrench an arm free to wipe it away.

She held him down like gravity. Gulping. Swallowing. Another heave wracking her ribs. She leaned in.

She's going to puke over your face. Head weaving side-to-side, to try to avoid that vileness, at all costs.

She arched upwards, mouth wide open, until, she horked up a red, slimy blob onto his chest.

For a moment, all he could do is stare, not even breathe; as revolted at his impotence as with the gobbet, there, on him. He shuddered. Thrusted up his shoulders, shook it off.

It rolled off into his armpit.

He could feel it there, sticky-wet-icky. Bristling by his ribs. Pressing against his bicep and side. Throbbing, it had a pulse, a heartbeat. *It is alive.*

The sudden realisation: *It's growing in there.* Swelling.Like a manifestation of his own panic.

He jerked, kicked, thrashed, trying to roll off his back.

To counter his escape attempt, she rammed her left elbow into his neck, clamping him in place, and used her right hand to yank the thing out of his pit.

She showed it to him. It had unfolded into a red-capped mushroom, pulsating. "This is the Dragon."

She jammed it into his mouth.

He wanted to bite her hand, sink his teeth in, but shock stopped him biting down.

She rammed the mushroom down his throat. And further: he felt a bulging out of the oesophagus, and he choked. Swallowing, swallowing. It seemed to wriggle its own way down into his stomach. Sucking in air, a *whoop* of blessed relief.

She released his arms, one hand snatching up the angel amulet, snapping the chain, casting it away.

The relief. Not having to bear the gravity of her was so profound a palliation, it was almost like he had become disembodied. *So light.*

She stood there, glaring at him, naked contempt.

I don't care. I'm free. Of all sensation. And he was, out-of-body, almost fully transcendent, until he coughed, felt his chest convulse, spraying an aerosol of droplets out of his lips, a mist which exploded into a jet of flames and shot over the bed, to stick like a torch, on the wall.

A fit of coughing followed, and everything caught; the bedroom raging into an inferno, flames flowering, blooming red and orange, all over him, all over her, but they did not burn.

Impossibly.

Nakedly.

Aflame.

Novos Ordo
Seclorum

T*hou shalt not kill.* Public records state that by the end of Dr. Walter Freeman II's career, in 1965, this 'Saviour of America' was responsible for 100 *operatio per mortem* and 490 post-lobotomy deaths.

If the Freeman family had not been one of the 13 Illuminati families, neo-Atlanteans, dedicated to 'The Science', oathsworn to implementing *Novos ordo seclorum,* it would have been noted.

If Dr. Walter Freeman II had not been an active Freemason of the 33rd Degree, Scottish Rite, Northern Jurisdiction, attaining the 28th degree of Prince Adept, someone would have said something.

If Dr. Walter Freeman II had not been secretly working for the C.I.A. whilst conducting all those lobotomies on W.W.2 Veterans, the beans might have been spilled.

If Dr. Walter Freeman II had not been a founding member of the American Psychiatric Association, serving on the boards of innumerable other professional bodies, including the American Medical Association, another doctor would have reported him for malpractice or misconduct. But no one came forward.

If he had not been so protected, so untouchable, the Fourth Estate would have exposed him. It was decades before some hacks, briefed by public relations experts in the employ of the pharmaceutical industry, then in its infancy, went to print with the *expose* that Dr. Walter Freeman II was worse than Dr. Mengele, the Nazi 'Angel of Death', that lobotomy was 'stealing someone's soul'.

The Mengele comparisons were most unfair! He was not experimenting on live patients in some death camp, or off in the jungles of Brazil after the war, with the sanction of the C.I.A. He was trying to save people from themselves. The procedure was never a cure, but it allowed two-thirds of afflicted patients to live outside of the walls of an asylum. *That was surely worth doing...?*

Dr. Mengele, and German doctors like him, would simply have killed these defective people. Dr. Walter Freeman would learn about the Nazi's state-sponsored euthanasia programme for the mentally ill from his tour of Europe in 1941. Their approach to suffering was sickening. To fall ill was to lose one's right to live.

Thou shalt not kill. His very last victim, Helena Mortenson, died of a brain haemorrhage, three days after the procedure, her third lobotomy. It was reported by the press that 'Dr. Death' negligently left her in the care of a junior doctor at Herrick Memorial, and went on vacation. The hospital suspended his surgical privileges after that, and no other institution would have him either.

Dr. Death! It was not reported that Helena Mortensen had been one of his first trans-orbital patients back in 1946. The first lobotomy allowed her to be a productive member of society for a decade. She requested a second lobotomy after a relapse in 1956, and returned to work, until a third breakdown in 1967.

The Press—'De-Press' as he called them—declined to mention that, but for being reborn, being redeemed by his hands, Helena Mortensen would have been institutionalised for decades. *What could one do?* He was a one-man-band, charging less than 100 bucks per procedure.

'De-Press', by that time, was firmly in the pockets of the multi-million-dollar Madness Industry. Jew psychoanalysts. Jew psychiatrists. Huge, new pharmaceutical companies, looted from the Germans. The cost of what they marketed as a 'chemical lobotomy' in pill form = $2 per day.

Chlorpromazine. Discovered and developed at the *Val-de-Grace* military hospital by a Frenchman, Dr. Henri Laborit who described it as 'inducing a state of artificial hibernation'. *Laboratoires Rhone-Poulenc* launched it in France 1952, tradename: Largactil.

Launched in 1953 in West Germany by Bayer, a part of the liquidated Nazi conglomerate I.G. Farben. Tradename: Thorazine. Named after the Mighty Thor, Norse god of Thunder, because like his hammer, *Mjollnir*, it would knock patients out.

The F.D.A. approved Thorazine for use in the U.S.A. in March 1954. This was the beginning of the end of the trans-orbital lobotomy. This was the beginning of the end of the world famous, controversial, brilliant Dr. Walter Freeman II too. It did not matter how much he raged, raged against the dying of the light. He knew deep in his heart that this was his decline, and fall.

He wrote prophetically of this in his memoirs, in his mid-30s, when he divided his life into three distinct phases: Preparation, Accomplishment, and Decline. He did not know how much he had staked career, reputation, happiness, self-esteem on this one procedure, and how far he would fall. Into the Abyss of infamy. Nor how many people he would drag in with him.

Thou shalt not kill. He never meant to. Did not consciously mean to kill his wife Marjorie. She did not want to leave her circle of old friends in Washington, but he shipped her out West with him, to a new house in the hills of Los Altos, because his career was stagnating in the East.

He worked all the hours that God sent as usual, and the isolation would not be good for her. She had no job, no children to look after, so slow emotional annihilation became heavy home-drinking. She used sherry to numb herself from the accumulation of grief and life's disappointments. *Sherry, as chemical lobotomy, chéri.*

"I should have divorced you,'" Marjorie railed at him. "You should be ashamed Walt, at your time of life."

"I am not having an affair," he insisted.

"I know full well about this Lilith you are seeing—because the bitch-in-heat keeps phoning you."

He told her: "Mary Dannecker is mentally ill. Have some compassion, Woman."

What sort of man tells his wife about his fantasy sex life? Especially, sex dreams. And Lilith came to him, on him, below him, in torrid sex dreams. The Nembutal blocked most dreams, but the nocturnal visits she made to him were so vivid, lucid, in his mind when he was awake, to discover he had ejaculated in his sleep. *Milk, spilt.* The succubus told him what she was doing while she was doing it: "I'm milking you."

One night at the dinner table, caustic as Drano on that deadly second sherry, Marjorie called him: "Liar. The Father of All Lies".

There was a ray of hope. Majorie fell and broke her arm, not long after they move to California. While the cast was on and afterwards, in physiotherapy, for all those seven weeks, the recovery period, she abstained from drink and returned to the charming, intelligent wife he admired. But hope was as short-lived as lab mice. She required institutionalisation several times due to alcoholism, stomach pumps. Once, she ended up on a psychiatric ward, which was embarrassing. Soon, she was spending 20 hours a day in a ratty bathrobe, watching T.V., drunk, more and more confused, and forgetful. One morning, in late 1967, five sherries unsteady, she stumbled in her bedroom, and broke her hip.

He would use the time when she was 'indisposed' to write a new book, *The Psychiatrist.* It was lucky for Marjorie that he was writing this non-bestseller in his study, not at hospital, when she inevitably fell, otherwise she would have been lying there in pain, for hours and hours. She might have died all alone, of shock.

It was mighty fortunate for Marjorie that her errant husband had Paget's Disease, a rare illness, which looked like anal warts, but was closely associated with colorectal cancer. The treatment: surgery to resect his colon, a colostomy bag for three months, and resting at home for six months. His misfortune was thus her fortune.

Upon publication, *The Psychiatrist* was dismissed by the critics as 'light bedtime reading, but neither a good history nor good biography'.

Suicide. A subject close to his heart at the end. A close study of it—and he ascertained that psychiatrists are eight times more likely to commit suicide than Ordinary Joe white males. Eight of Freud's close associates committed suicide: that was what first drew his attention to this epidemic of self-destruction, or so he told himself.

The A.P.A. poo-pooed his findings. He insisted—because it was *all too true*, and Psychiatry, as a new Jewish religion, would not acknowledge this truth about its high priests and their tendency to self-destruct.

He had long been convinced that insight was a terrible weapon, so few know how to use it constructively. "When people realise what stinkers they are," he would argue, "it takes only a little depression to tip the scales in favour of suicide."

His final attempt to garner the attention of the world was the submission of a paper to the *American Journal of Psychiatry* entitled: *Fungal infections may be the root cause of schizophrenia and other mental illnesses.* His peers cited this is as proof that he had gone insane.

After a few weeks in hospital, Marjorie was taken to a nursing home. He admitted to a friend in December: "Marjorie has nerve damage, might never be able to live at home again."

That was not the whole story. The anger. The depression. The confusion, and the forgetfulness. He omitted that he'd misdiagnosed his own wife, the mother of their six children, the person he knew most intimately in all the world, possibly because her descent into alcoholism disgusted him so much.

Senile dementia. These were all classic symptoms of senile dementia. Bedridden, in the nursing home, she developed a circulatory blockage in her left leg.

His children tried to get him to agree to an amputation, but he knew this is only prolonging the agony, for her, for him, for them, and threatened a legal battle over her limb in court.

Eventually though, he assented to their pleas. Marjorie was taken to hospital to have the amputation, and returned to the nursing home to convalesce. As often happened with the demented after a hip fracture, she lost a lot of weight, diminished to the point where she contracted pneumonia, and succumbed on April 22nd, 1970.

Thou shalt not kill. It was a terrifying statistic: 85% of all disease has mental or emotional causes. Dr. Walter Freeman II had written his memoirs, sketched out his thoughts, told others of his struggle towards gnosis, but his emotions, well, he had never been an open book in that sense, had always been in a state of dis-ease.

The fixed, and must-fix-it, state of American hyper-egotism, lost in the illusion of constant self-improvement in linear time, but always walking around himself and others, in circles, blowing goat-horns, hoping the walls of Jericho would fall, to reveal all, as it was.

Thou shalt not...

First Marjorie, then Mary Dannecker.

He did not mean to hurt her either. He *cared*, he wanted more than anything to save her from herself.

Enoch got in touch. "I declared Mary a missing person. She just lit out. I came home after work about a month ago and she was gone."

"I'm sorry to hear that. Maybe she needed some space? You know women. Don't worry I'm sure she'll be in touch soon."

"She thinks of you as her saviour, Doc. I have a feeling if she is gonna reach out to anyone it will be you. Let me know, please."

"Will do. Of course."

Lilith did indeed reach out to the Doc, at his office in Palo Alto. She made an appointment. Waited in the waiting room. "She is dressed like a street-walker," his receptionist warned.

Dr. Walter Freeman II was disgusted, and aroused, to see that she was indeed dressed like a prostitute. She reeked of sex, as if she had been doused in semen.

"I'm pregnant," Mary announced. "Pregnant with your child."

"That's crazy-talk."

"We had sex, and I'm pregnant. Those are the facts of life."

"Mary..."

"—Lilith. I am Lilith. Say my name."

He cleared his throat. "We had sex four years ago, Mary. The human gestation period is nine months..." He let the impossibility of the biology sink in.

"We have sex all the time."

"*We* do not. Maybe in your mind..."

"—In yours, you mean. I'm talking about in *your* mind, where you fuck me into submission every day, every night."

The animus in her voice. He stiffened at the word, *fuck*. He wanted to slap her face, and grab her by the hair, and...but instead, he said: "Do you need some money for your trouble? Is that what you want?"

"No. I'm having our child, whether you like it or not."

"But what about poor Enoch?"

"I cannot go back there. I haven't been with Enoch since you first took me."

Diagnosis: a major psychotic break from reality. Normally, he would use E.C.T. to jolt her out of fantasy-world A.S.A.P., but she might actually be pregnant and that ruled out shocks.

Involuntary commitment, the only option. He phoned Herrick Memorial and arranged for 'the men in white coats' to come and take her away.

A sneer on her face. "This changes nothing,"

"You're ill. You need to get better."

Her parting words: "You are mine. I am yours. We are one. Not even death has the power to separate us."

He phoned Enoch to inform him where she would be held. For her own good.

After her institutionalisation, she came to him at night, just as frequently as before. But, these visits were more forceful, demonic. She overpowered him, stripped him. She brought whips, flails, bats. She brought restraints, chains, a straitjacket even. She gagged him. She beat him. She fisted him. Unclenched her hand deep inside him, and clawed his insides, ripping through his guts, seeking out his heart. When she had a hold of it, and he was overthrown, she whispered to him what he would do in story of a future Adam and Eve, and it was more dreadful than anything he had done so far.

Thou shalt not kill. Oneself, especially. But he became even more fixated on the idea of suicide seven months later, when he was notified that Mary Dannecker had passed, giving birth to a dead baby. A breach-birth. The umbilical cord had strangled the infant. The doctors could not stop the haemorrhaging.

Was cancer a strange form of suicide? Were tumours festering clusters of the soul's sorrows devouring the body? In the end, when cancer took him, like it took his poor father before him, and his illustrious grandfather before him, lying in bed, weak, and high on morphine, he wished for a better death. For he knew when he should have died, rightly.

Dearest Keen. Forever young. He had forgotten to fill up the canteen with water before beginning the ascent to the top of the Vernal Falls in the Sierra Nevadas. That was what killed his son.

He led the expedition of his three boys up there. It was a very hot day, a scorcher. Keen was thirsty, stopped on the Merced river's edge, near the crest of the falls, knelt, and plopped his canteen in. The canteen. It must have slipped from his little hand. He must have lunged for it, lost his balance, called out.

He turned to see the boy being swept along by the flow. He froze. His heart. *If you had not frozen... If you had had the presence of mind to act, to run, vault the railing, leap into the water...*

Like Dale Loos. The 22-year-old ex-sailor, who heroically did just that, in spite of the jeopardy.

15 feet from the brink of the falls, Dale Loos seized Keen by the neck, trying to haul him back.

On the bank, another man rushed to the rails, held out a hand for Dale Loos to grab a hold of. "Take it! Take—my— hand."

Dale Loos desperately struggled to find purchase on the rocks, reached out with one hand, and then lost his footing, was swept away, carrying Keen with him.

The paralysis broke, he rushed forward to the rail. Keen's face as he went over the edge: mouth open, the boy seemed to be calling for his father to save him, but the words would be ripped away.

In their place—a cry of horror from the small crowd of tourists at the top of the falls.

"Keen, Keen, you're dead, you're killed," he cried.

Randi and Jef clung to his legs as that reality sunk in. He was sure of it. *No one could survive the 325-foot fall.*

So, it proved.

All Marjorie's prayers come to naught.

Denial was denied. The bodies of Keen and brave *brave* Dale Loos were found several days later.

He would return to this place many-many times on hikes, pilgrimages to the very brink, wishing God might grant him a do-over, as one father to another. He built a cairn of smooth pebbles each time to honour Keen's memory, and felt strongly that his son forgave him, the spirit of his dearly-departed son, but he could never forgive himself.

This was always his problem, all through life. *Ego.* The hurt. He never allowed himself to be compassionate, to love himself, warts and all. To be fully human. At one with the Divine. Good. Not even on his deathbed.

Then a serpent who could not be charmed,
made its nest in in the roots of the huluppu tree.
The Anzu-bird set his young in the branches of the tree,
and the dark maid Lilith built her home in the trunk.
The young woman who loved to laugh, wept.
How Inanna wept.
(Yet they would not leave her tree.)

THE EPIC OF GILGAMESH

Man has no individual 'I'. But there are, instead, hundreds and
thousands of separate small 'I's very often entirely unknown to
one another, never coming into contact, or, on the contrary,
hostile to each other, mutually exclusive and incompatible.

PYOTYR OUSPENSKY *In Search of The Miraculous*

THE GREAT MOTHER

S even-months-old, in no time. Baby would be approximately the size of a pineapple at 'seven months', which explained Mum's big belly.

Baby would weigh three-and-a-third pounds, and measured 16 inches from head to heel, but not for long, his growth would spurt in the third trimester.

Not long to go now, at all. Pregnancy was becoming an all-consuming experience. Mum's sense of being Sister Eva Kadmon, having been anyone else in fact, was lessening daily, hourly, minutely, secondly.

Her baby was speedily taking possession of her. She was becoming something bigger than herself. Vast. The Great Mother. A universal archetype, a role, a programme, which dwelt in every woman, in the womb of every woman, waiting to be primed by the baby occupying her.

Squirming in Mum's belly, Baby was a much more belligerent guest than Mum expected. Testing the limits of her womb. Kicking, harder and harder. Moving his head side-to-side. Pushing out with his arms, if not punching. Swimming, spinning in the amniotic fluid. He was keeping her awake at night, the little devil. Well, the couple of nights that she could recall, for they all seemed to have merged into one long, looping night, in which she could remember a recurring dream, about giving birth to him, only to discover he was actually a book, with a owl in flight embossed in gold, on the black leather of the cover.

Breasts: the fountains of youth. Mum had begun to leak colostrum, pre-milk, from her left breast. Only the left. Spoodging her blouse. Turning her nipple a scabrous green. She wondered: *What's going on with the right one, is it on strike?*

Mum was having contractions. Irregular spasms in vagina. 30 seconds long. *Weird. Painless, but freaky.* The first one nearly gave her a heart attack—*Is this the onset of labour?*

They were called Braxton Hicks contractions, after the man who first described them, and were perfectly normal at this stage, but still, the fear every time, was they were the real thing...

"So, you want a natural birth, right?" Lilit said.

"I want a water birth," Mum replied.

"Okay, since God decided to greatly increase your sorrow and pain in conception, it's time for us to start doing some breathing exercises."

"Yeah-yeah, I want to go to a Lamaze class. Will you come with me?"

"Lamaze? No."

"What? Why won't you come?"

"Lamaze was a patriarchal asshole. He based his Conditioned Response techniques on Velvoski's research, which was based on Pavlov's Dogs. You've heard of Pavlov's Dogs?"

"Yes. But..."

"—Do you want to be treated like a little bitch?"

"No."

"The School of Behaviourism is for purely mundane minds. We will indulge in some practices from the age-old school of Spiritual Midwifery."

"Okay."

"I'll teach you to consciously breathe, to draw on your inner reserves. We'll use meditation techniques to break the fear-tension-pain cycle, and to build your confidence I'll teach you to chant through the pain of the contractions."

"Sounds good."

"You need to move. Lying down is no good. Moving around, standing, squatting, on all fours, whatever works to get the baby in the birthing position, so you can bear down."

"I can move."

"And I'm going to help you to open up your *manipura* and *anahata* chakras. That's your navel and heart energy centres. The *kundalini* will flow freely through the lower four from here on, up the *Ida* and down the *Pinghala* serpents, so you will embody the Mother Goddess."

"Where did you learn all this stuff?"

"Yoga class."

"*Right.*"

"I have been preparing for this since the very beginning," Lilit said. "There is nothing I would not do for my baby."

DEVOTION

'Cynth', as he called her, poured a triple of Hine. Because 'Art' as she called him, would only drink Hine brandy these days. From a snifter. He had become such a sniffy snob in his dotage. She set his snifter on the silver tray, beside hers.

The little green bottle of Tuinal, she placed in between. Her fingers locked on its surface and before her eyes, her very eyes, her hands greyed, and cracked. Into that archaic word, 'smithereens'. Cells falling apart, and away. Shedding. Dust to dust. Like the body had already been delivered to the crematorium for a Sunday-roasting. Ashes to ashes, the fires of hell, come days early. In the mundanity of their kitchen.

It was not the first such premonition she'd experienced. Nightmares were usually confined to the night, that was the convention, but the closer to her death she came, the more they popped by in the daytime, looking at first as ordinary as the postman, walking up the garden path to the doorway, but then peeling off their human masks, to reveal their true, demonic visages, and what they wanted.

Which was...

Her life, her very life.

Life itself.

Feminists would say: "He made her do it. He forced her to. Koestler was a bastard of the First Order of Bastardry."

She pitied these women, self-empowering women, the women of the Future. For they had never known true love. Love as sacrifice. Love as *suttee*, the burning desire to sacrifice everything for the beloved, the way the ancients lived, and loved, one another. The Brahmans. 'Sati' was the verb. Throw oneself on the pyre. Devotion to death. Through death.

Through Time. And on—

...Into Eternity. A Feminist could only know the smallest part of the Eternal Feminine. Feminists, it seemed to her, were forever stuck-in-time, acting-out, as teenage daughters do. These liliths never became The Mother, let alone The Great Mother. These lolitas could never unlock that Motherlove in themselves. The unstoppable, undying love.

That transformation, that transcendence, even the aspiration, remained beyond their grasp.

She understood the why and how of the trap of that thinking. Fear of men. Anger at men. Hatred of men. This man's world of men, the patriarchy, the impaling phallocracy, it was so easy to let that get in the way of loving. Of being love. Of being Woman. The Feminine as opposed to the Masculine. She was glad that she had moved ahead, and out, of that cruel world, like a dolphin riding the breaks of a bow wave, effortlessly carried along, by its forces, and yet able to veer off at any time, steer a different course.

"Service, please," he called, from the sitting room.

"Coming." Like a good little waitress, she ferried the deadly silver tray from the kitchen, up the wood-panelled hallway, and into the sitting room. Serving him was one of the last things she would do, so she took care to do it well. Even though she was drunk. Drunk as a skunk. They both were. Three bottles of Burgundy having fortified them with French *courage*. "Now, what we need is some proper, old-fashioned Dutch Courage. Would you be a dear?"

Your wish is my command. And so, it was dearly done. Like a witch preparing a potion for a spell, she did it—*hey presto, time-shift!*—placing the tray down on the table between the his and hers Queen Anne armchairs.

"I do love my fine Hine," he said. "Socrates chose tea, hemlock tea, to exit. Give me Hine, any day of the week."

"Only the best poison for the world-famous Arthur Koestler." She grandly presented him with his snifter. Made sure that his grip was sure on the bulb. His hands were weak, full of the tremors of Parkinson's.

"Why thank you, Angel." He smiled, the most fantastic smile, at her. To her. For her. Right through her.

Angel. She smiled back, in all the glory of this sadness. *I love it when you call me that.* She firmly believed in angels. The angelic. Being his angel. Him, being hers.

People nowadays called belief in angels, stupid, but what did they know. *Modern* people. Empiricists. Imperialists. Materialists. Atheists. Scientists. Socialists. Communists. Fascists. Nazis. Technocrats, all.

Once, long since, when she was reduced to a Romantic cliché, contemplating taking her own life because Art did not love her, could not love her, would not love her, her own Motherlove had convinced the Despairing Lover archetype within that she was loved, always had been loved, always would be loved, and that everyone she'd ever met had been an angel, a messenger of the Lord, bringing her a message; whether she wanted to hear their message; whether she could understand what they were telling her; whether it cut her to the very quick with its truth. They were angels. Even if they looked or acted like demons.

Her Irish father had been an angel, when he had blown his face off with a shotgun, and she'd heard the shot, aged 10, and knew his damnation, and screamed, and screamed at her mother, sitting there, simply sitting there in their parlour. *How could she sit there like that? It was so passive. So bourgeois. So damned Jewish of her.*

She hated her parents for a long time.

Father, the most. For leaving her, abandoning her like that, when she loved him so much.

Didn't he know how much she loved him, and needed him? But then, she met Arthur, and little by little, forgave her father, stopped seeing him as a demon who had ruined her life, and started to see him as an angel, an angel with whom she had wrestled, as Jacob wrestled with the angel, and won for himself a new name, and a destiny as—'Israel'.

Love springs eternal, yes the most human hope of all, springs eternal in and of the struggle, if you let it. And so-believing, really being the believer, his Angel embodied, she picked up the bottle of Tuinal elixir, popped the stopper, and poured half, roughly half, perhaps more it into his snifter. Enough to kill a man, she felt sure. She would make-do with the leftovers for her exit.

He raised his snifter, sniffed at it. "Bitter."

She poured the barbiturates into her snifter and sat down on the edge of her chair.

"*Santé,*" he said, joking.

"*A la votre,*" she replied.

"I love you to death, Angel." He was always joking; never had a mind and a heart been born and bred so extraordinarily sharp. Sharp enough to cut through anything. Even steel. The 'Man of Steel', Stalin.

"I love you more than life itself, Art," she told him.

"You don't have to do this, you know," he said, one more time. "I don't want you to die, even if it is just for a moment." He felt he had to protest because he didn't think he was worth it.

"We two are one." This had been her every reply to all his doubts, his fears, his anger.

He argued, until he was literally blue in the face, wheezing. "But you can live such a comfortable life after I'm gone. I have provided for you. And you know we will see each other again. For now, it's enough that you are with me."

"We are man and wife," she said. "Adam and Eve."

And so, in a strange kind of shared fascination, they watched each other drink down the bitter, burning elixir together. In gulps.

It took only two swallows for her to finish, showing teeth, *aaaaaah.*

He had more difficulty swallowing. It pained him, the cancer had wormed its way through him. "More like Calvados than Hine, you think?" He coughed, spluttered, wheezed. "Christ."

"Finish it," she told him. *Thanatos. Angel of Death.*

"I've never had to be told to finish my drink before." He gulped it down. "Now then, let us go gentle into that good night, like poor Dylan himself."

She could see him thinking of their friend, Dylan, drinking himself to death, occupational hazard, after all that rage-rage against the dying of the light. Poor fellow had died alone in a strange city, on the other side of the world.

No way to go. She was so glad to not be dying alone. She hoped it had not been painful for Dylan to pass, but she was glad to be at home, dying together with her beloved, in the knowledge that they would meet again. In the afterlife. In the Promised Land. The Land of Milk and Honey. The Holy Land. Where wandering Jews were finally welcomed home.

She stood up, set her snifter back down on the table. She plucked Art's away too. Then she tucked the blanket in, tight around his legs, and kissed him on the forehead.

His old hand, skin like paper, reached for hers.

His lips were twitching.

His eyes, glistening.

He didn't have to say a word, she knew everything he was feeling, the veil was torn, there was nothing between them. It was as it should always have been, and it was enough. This moment. This one moment of knowing. *It won't be long now*, she thought. She held his hand, tightly. Knelt down before him.

1000 milligrams each would come on strong. That 50/50 mix of secobarbital sodium and amobarbital sodium. Sold on the street as 'tuies', 'F-66', 'Double-trouble', 'rainbows', 'nawls', 'jeebs' or 'the heebie-jeebies'. It would put you to sleep.

Mercifully, like they put dogs to sleep. Like David, their Lhasa apso, who she'd brought to the vet's yesterday, to be put to sleep.

Sleeping together. Their last sleep on Earth. They were both well aware that 20 X 50mg—with 50mg being the prescribed dose of Tuinal —would be fatal in minutes, for they had both written the handbook for suicide for EXIT.

He had dictated the text, as always. He was Dictator. She was the listener, had taken shorthand, typed it up afterwards. This was the way they wrote books. Their tried and trusted method. Art was the narrator. She was his writing instrument. Mightier than the sword. '*The* Cynth' as he called her, in this context. She wrote his books. She was their mother, and he was their father.

Not all of them, though.

Not 'The Darkness'.

Her predecessor, the lovely Daphne Hardy, wrote his finest, most famous novel, *Darkness at Noon*. It was her who got to translate the German version into English; her who posted the novel to London and saved it from the French fascists.

She had learned not to be jealous of his many lovers, indeed had made a policy of befriending them, but she could never forgive Daphne for birthing The Darkness. How she would have loved to mother his magnum opus, more than flesh-and-blood children, but she was only a stepmother to it, and a bitter stepmother at that.

1000 milligrams of Tuinal per person, on top of the alcohol excess, would kill them both soon. Dying would start with a heavy drowse, an inability to control the mouth, digits, limbs. A falling out of the body entirely, into a weightless darkness. Swoons in, and out, of consciousness with each short sharp breath.

"Nadheshda," Art moaned.

She looked up, as if that was her name, though she knew it not.

"I denounced you." He was looking right at her, his pupils hugely dilated, the deepest wells of the deepest darkness. "Forgive me."

His head, splitting into three faces in a row, four in a semi-circle. More. Multiplying, bubbling up and out until they were a terrifying swarm of eyes, all looking down at her. "Nadheshda?"

She pushed him away, or rather pushed herself away from him, sliding numbly down onto the floor, to face his slippers.

At the end, red slippers. So furiously alone, and red slippers.

Wind And Fire

The Fire Brigade was called in to tackle the blaze at 8 Blackcross Crescent, but it was already a raging inferno by the time the firemen leapt out of their red engines.

The firemen hooked up a hose to the mains, directed the jet of water into the wall of flames that had replaced the sundered frontage of the building. The water knocked the source of the conflagration, back into smoke, into darkness, but it re-ignited after the water was directed away.

A fireman in a breathing mask rushed in, tried to pull what he reckoned must be a burns victim out, and was engulfed. Thrashing around in agony, trying and trying, unable to extinguish the flames. Because these were no ordinary flames. This was Dragon-fire. Fire that would not go out. Not with all the water in the world.

The Dragon exploded out of the Door of the Angels, leaving a dragon-shaped hole in it, edges glowing orange. Rage, rage, raging away from screaming firemen. Streaking out down the middle of Blackcross Crescent, causing a Range Rover to swerve and skid to a halt. The driver and passengers screaming; man, woman, children; like they were on a roller-coaster.

The Dragon headed for 9 Dawson Place, the Double Mums'.

Knocking, scorching the pink on their door into a bubbling black. Helena and Nadine answered, but they did not recognise their own son.

Helena slammed the front door shut in its face. Blowing it open, seeking out what is needed, the embrace of the Mother, inhaling her—being invigorated by—her maternal love. Cremating her. And, then the Other Mother. The Great Nadine Nadiri.

Without them, and bereft of Eva, who am I anymore? What should I do? I don't know what to do with myself? The Dragon stood at a crossroads, literally, and virtually. Trying to decide on a direction to take. *Straight. Left. Right?* There were so, so many places to go.

That was when the police caught up with the Dragon. Two officers jumped out of their patrol car. "Stop!"

So the Dragon did, because strangely, it thought the Law still applied to it.

They tried using a fire-extinguisher to put it out.

In a retardant fog, The Dragon fell against their car, and the heat, the sheer heat, set the petrol tank off.

The explosion scattered bits of car, and bodies, across the road.

Flaring bigger and brighter for that instant, it glimpsed the global potential of its life. A glorious inferno. For this was what the Dragon was. The End. And so, it exploded again, a huge incendiary bomb, blitzing the West of London to ashes and embers the way the Nazis never did.

The Dragon hated the City, all the cities of men. It was the wildest beast, and desired to be to be free in the mountains, the forests, the wild places. It heard the sea in the flames. Hissing. It wanted to see if it could set fire to the water. *Does water burn?* Steam. *How much steam would rise into thunderclouds?*

The thunder, perfect mind.

It started to rain, black rain, and would continue to, for the rest of that first annihilating night, but the Dragon was so hot it melted footprints into the tar on the roads it travelled.

The authorities used this to track it down to the coast.

It was not long before there was a horde of followers trailing down the road to Brighton. The police. The fire brigade.

But, near morning, the Dragon got away onto the South Downs. It walked out into the heather. The wind rose. Beneath its feet, the heath caught fire, and flames and dust and smoke hampered its pursuers. Fire and wind. Wind and Fire. Roaring on the earth.

Over the next week, water-bombing planes were the only things that kept up with the Dragon as it scorched a path down the coast, across heathland, woods, crop fields, buildings, bridges, and farm animals. They deluged the fire with water. They could not put it out.

A Sky T.V. news helicopter joined the chase. Whirling up there, journalists yelled their stupid questions:

"Are you the Beast?"

"Are you a destroying angel?"

"Is this Armageddon?"

In trying to answer the Dragon spoke in tongues of fire, and their machines exploded and dropped to the ground, in pieces. Fire and Wind. Wind and fire.

The British Army was called out to stop the Dragon's relentless progress. Sheer military might met it in Dorset, on a plain that may as well have been called Armageddon. They ordered: "Stop! Or we will open fire."

The Dragon could not stop. It tried to tell them: *I am fire, with the wind at my back,* but instead it showered them with a giant fireball.

Soldiers, guns, tanks, jeeps, and jet fighters high in the sky, melted or exploded. Great Britain. Europe. The world. All obliterated in time and space. Everything, in an instant.

Not a single soul survived.

Except the Dragon, burning in the darkness.

Light and dark. Dark and light. The world turned upside-down, inside-out. Tendrils of fire licked up the crumpled roof of a car. The slishing of the sea into shingle. Waves of life and death.

The others were in the car with the Dragon here, Lilit and the Berbers, and it cremated them, before erupting out of the car, scattering bits of policemen all over the road, and went raging off into the long grasses, through the shrubs and wind-bent trees, until it was elemental in ancient oak forests. Free in the mountains. The mountains of West Cork. Amongst burning trees, the pillars of a new temple in the old world, dedicated to Fire.

With the incense of godhood in its nostrils, it looked back down on the black plains and around at the smoking slopes. Everything in sight was either fired or ablaze. Through the smoke, the Dragon beheld the sea. The ocean. The Atlantic.

It saw its face moving out over the waters, was suddenly afraid of the ocean. *What if the fire goes out?*

It cannot go out. It must not.

The Dragon's appetite for devastation was as strong as ever. All the land. The whole of Ireland. West and East. Arya of Atlantis. North and South. The compass encompassed. All of space-time.

Time-space. Across the oceans. It wanted to be everywhere, all at once, and therefore it did not know which way to go.

Where will it all end? Adamo's own voice.

When everything is gone—heaped on the pyre, The Dragon answered, and was suddenly, massively sad, wept tears, beads of fire, onto the spoiled earth, and stood in the ferocity of its own sorrow.

Extinction happened quickly: Adamo opened his eyes—he was back in their living room, the Kilburn flat, lying on the sofa in front of the T.V.

He held up his hands. Flesh. He looked down at his body. Shirt, jeans, work clothes. He was human, fire no more. He laughed. *Like a hysterical donkey. Jesus.*

Fu-huck, was that crazy.

An absolute nightmare.

Smack-bang in front of him, frozen on the T.V. screen, paused somehow, was good ole Agent Cooper, as if he'd been trapped in the goggle-box forever, trying to escape from behind those shivering, red curtains of the Black Lodge.

Twin Peaks: The Return.

Talk about life imitating art, Lynchian melodrama. Wait till I tell Eva.

DICTATORSHIP

Miss Cynthia Jeffries had always wanted to be a writer's secretary, and there it was. Opportunity knocking. The advert in the *Herald Tribune* read: *Author, Fontainbleau area, seeks part-time secretary. Write. Box 888.*

She applied. Writing a letter in her own hand, because the blasted typewriter at her Romanian friend's apartment was an ancient one, and being continental, all the keys were in the wrong place.

She was quite proud of her curriculum vitae, aged 19: a firm of solicitors, an art gallery, Warner Bros, and Dr Ishlondsky, a psychiatrist, who was writing a very dry book on Pavlovian theory.

Of course, that was not the sort of writing, or the sort of writer she had in mind. As a child, she had always been happiest when reading. Her favourite people were the imaginary heroes of books, rather than than those living around her. They were larger than life. More alive. More real than real.

At 12, she decided to write a Historical Romance, *a la* Georgette Heyer's *Regency Buck*, which everyone was reading at school. She shut herself away in the loo—the only private space at public school—and begin scribbling in a notebook, with a blunt pencil. The first paragraph described the hero, the clothes he was wearing, because that seemed important to know what sort of regency buck he was. She got as far as his 'sky-blue waistcoat', but there, the words stopped. The flow of words, which she expected to flow forth from the pencil tip, never came. She gave up.

At 15, the muse visited with her once more, and she found herself writing a play. Inspiration took the form of fine fellows, galloping about on fiery steeds, spouting expressions like 'egad', 'methinks', and 'forsooth'. People didn't speak like this. Not anymore. Not in the colonies. And so, her romantic fantasy could not persist. She tore it up. *The closest you can get to writing,* she determined, *would be to work with a real writer.*

Three weeks passed before a letter arrived, requesting her to come to interview at an address in the 17th arrondissement. It was signed: *Daphne Woodward.*

The most suitable clothes to wear to the interview would be clerical grey, so she put on her grey coat and skirt, a paler grey pull-over and a grey beret. Choosing the clothes made her late, and tardiness compounds itself, so that she was 30 minutes late, and thoroughly mortified, by the time she presented herself.

Mrs. Woodward, Daphne, was not impressed. Dark circles ringed her eyes, and she had a slightly melancholic expression. "Mr. Koestler is a stickler for punctuality."

To test her shorthand skills, Daphne read out a passage from *Darkness At Noon.* She got one word wrong. 'Effix' instead of 'ethics'."Mr. Koestler will be interviewing applicants at the Hôtel Montalembert at 5 o'clock, on Thursday."

After the interview was over, she went to see her Romanian friend to ask him about this author. "Ah, Arthur Koestler..." he said. "This is dangerous, to work for him."

"Why?"

"The Communists will assassinate him."

The pen is mightier than the sword. She was terribly impressed that a writer could be so Political, that one man might matter this much. Her mind raced. *What would he look like? With a kingly name like Arthur, he must be very tall. With a beard and a rugged-red face.* She imagined taking dictation from him, in his study, under the eaves of his house, lined with books and, beside the small window, a writing table, with a lamp glowing on it.

The days literally flew by in a quiet determination: *I am going to get this job, no matter what.* To avoid lateness, she wore the same grey ensemble, and set off ridiculously early. A bus took her from the Right to the Left Bank. As it crossed the Seine, she wondered about aspirations, how necessarily—to get anything done—they thrust one forwards, out of time, into the world of make-believe.

She got off the bus in the Boulevard de St. Germain and walked to the Hôtel Montalembert. It was 4.30, but she went to reception. *"Pardon. Je suis Cynthia Jeffries. J'ai une appointment avec Arthur Koestler."*

The receptionist pointed to a room which led off the entrance lounge. She went at sat down at the entrance. Inside, the room was nearly empty, but on the far side, sat a couple, facing her.

The woman was dark, and extraordinarily beautiful. She was looking intensely at the man, leaning towards him.

The man, however, was bored, his gaze trying to escape hers. He was handsome in a dark, fierce way, if a tad small.

She began to wonder about the couple. They had either been together too long or did not know each other very well at all. *The latter*, she decided. He was taking her out for the first time, and it was awkward. Listening in—the words 'train', 'Melun'— they were talking in English, which made it more interesting. The woman had a Southern American accent. The twang of it floated across the room when she phonetically murdered: 'Font-ain-bleu'.

Oh my Lord! She realised with horror that she had been staring at Mr Koestler, while he was interviewing another applicant.

He saw her staring aghast at him—this was the first time they locked eyes—and called out: *"Concierge. Est-ce que quelqu'un m'attend?"* His voice carried easily. His French—*parfait*.

She felt she had to get up and go across. "I'm awfully sorry," she said. "I'm early, and I thought you were in the other room. I'll go next door and wait."

"Quite," he said.

When the other woman left, with a glare in her direction, it was her turn. She sat down, face still boiling red with embarrassment, at the table, with the great Arthur Koestler.

He was frowning. "Daphne—whom you've met—is going to be away for the summer. So, I need someone competent to take her place. But only for two months."

"That's fine by me."

"You're sure?"

"Never been surer."

"Do you really think you'll be able to do the job? You don't seem to have much in the way of confidence."

She blushed even more, flushed even with shyness. "I can do it."

"Would you like a drink?"

"No, thank you."

He looked displeased. "An ice-breaker? I need one."

"I'm sure." She knew she'd done the wrong thing—this was not an interview with a businessman—but, it was too late to change her mind.

He ordered his drink.

"Mr. Koestler, ever since I was a little girl, reading books, it's been my dream to work with a writer."

That heartfelt plea, the word 'reader', the writer's ideal person, seemed to move him. His face softened. "We could try you out for the day, I suppose."

"Yes, yes."

"I'm driving back to Verte Rive tomorrow morning. Meet me at L'Opéra, and we'll take it from there. I'll give you some letters to type, and we'll see what you can do."

She went home to mother's place on Rue Copernic. They had dinner. "I have no doubts you'll get it," her mother said, the particular way Jewish mothers are supposed to. Why was it then, when she was convinced that she was the best secretary in the world, she could not will herself to sleep?

Hayfever. Playing up. All night long, sniffles, snuffles. Running into the dawn and beyond. She had to bring the Benzedrine inhaler with her, and a handbag full of handkerchiefs.

By the time she met Mr. Koestler, and his friends—Paul Winkler,

Head of Opéra Mundi and his wife—she looked like Helen of the Troy, still a-weeping over the loss of her beautiful Paris.

"You look like I feel," he said. His manner was so unnervingly direct. Brusque.

"Thanks."

"I need to buy lilos," he said. And so, he took her to the nearby Galleries Lafayette for some breakneck shopping.

After that they went to the car. The sun gleamed off the chrome. They got in. He drove very fast. Out of Paris. At 60 kilometres per hour, minimum, along busy streets. So madly fast, that she could not think of a single word to say; so hard was she hoping he would not crash into any of the cars, bicycles, or pedestrians that kept hurling themselves at him. *Don't crash, please.*

There was less swearing, less blaring horns in the countryside. The roads were lined with trees, sometimes forming a green tunnel, which rippled by in the rush of his desire to get somewhere.

"This car goes well," she said.

"It's got good brakes," he replied tersely, never taking his eyes off the road.

She wondered vaguely what he would be like in bed. *This urgent? Or slower, as he took control.* But such a thought seemed beyond any stretch of the imagination. He was married. *Perhaps he had children, even...?*

"We'll have lunch with Daphne, and her husband, Henri," he told her. "She'll brief you before we attempt to do any work."

She nodded. *Que sera...* As she'd already made an idiot out of herself in front of Daphne, she didn't have anything to lose.

"Verte Rive," he said, pointing at an ugly villa, set back a little from the narrow lane. Trees shaded the gravel drive that he skidded to an abrupt stop in.

A big Boxer dog bounded round the side of the house, barking.

"Sabby!" As soon as he got out of the car, Sabby jumped up to greet him.

He gave the dog a big hug, and a kiss on the forehead. "How is the silliest girl in the world? Yes. I missed you too."

Sabby came over to sniff her hand. "Hello Sabby," she said, and they made friends. Dogs were so much nicer than humans, more polite in their own ways, nosings aside.

He picked up the lilos from the back seat. "We'll go round back," he said.

When she turned the corner, she saw why he had bought this place. The garden sloped down from the villa to a landing stage on the Seine. The river rippled by: its tide powerful, wide, blissful. On the opposite bank, forest stretched as far as one could see, like a silvan scene from a painting.

Above the landing stage, in the garden, lay a canoe, keel side up. Made of wood, with long flowing lines and graceful curves, it seemed to glow in the hot sun. "I'll kill her,'" he said. "Happily slay her."

"Who?"

"Madame Grandin, you old scarecrow! What is my kayak doing roasting out in the sun? It will shrink." In a blistering fury, he hurried into the house to remonstrate further with his housekeeper.

She stood outside. Then she thought: *It might do to drag the canoe into the shade.* So, she did.

He came back out, and nodded at what she'd done. "Read my mind."

Pleased to have seized the initiative, she flushed deeply.

"Help me with the lilos," he said.

They blew up the inflatables. Before long, she was out of puff, breathless with blown-out red cheeks, but he seemed to have bellows for lungs.

Soon after inflation, Daphne and Henri arrived from Paris. Henri was quite charming, very easy-going, an industrial designer, and he attempted to put her at her ease as they drank aperitifs. Daphne was much more matter of fact, did not hesitate to speak her mind to her replacement. "You realise—you will have to run Stalin's gauntlet."

"Don't scare her off, Daphne! The Reds will never try anything here."

"You need to warn her, Arthur," said Henri.

"Consider yourself warned, Miss Jeffries. Don't worry. We'll take precautions."

Mr. Koestler is so startling, she thought. Every time he spoke she nearly jumped out of her skin.

Lunch was served by a grumpy old woman dressed in black. *Madame Grandin*, she supposed. Black pudding, followed by black stew, and a salad of greasy dark green lettuce leaves. *Tasty, but nothing special*, she thought, *What Mother would call 'Pleasant peasant food'*.

"*Madame Grandin—trésor national,*" he declared. Clearly, trying to make up for his earlier tirade.

"*Vrai,*" Madame Grandin grunted, and returned to the kitchen.

After lunch, they abandoned lilos, and went down to the stage. They clambered into a rowing boat. He rowed them out, across the river to the Forest of Fontainebleau on the other side. They walked through the old trees, until they found a bright clearing, where Daphne and Henri spread out some rugs to sit down.

"*Una siesta literaria,*" he said, lying down on his back, closing his eyes tightly. After a few minutes, he was soundly asleep, breathing quietly.

She did not feel at all sleepy. *One ought not to fall asleep in a job interview. One ought not to sleep with one's employer.*

Henri asked her questions about herself, her background, where she was living in Paris. It was like he was conducting a second, much more genial interview. "I think you will get along fine. Arthur is quite the character. You couldn't write him, no one would believe such a man existed."

Speak of the very devil. As quickly as he had fallen asleep, he awakened, and hustled everybody back to the rowboat.

Before the guests left for Paris, Daphne laid a hand on her forearm. "Be careful, Cynthia."

She could see fear shine brightly in those eyes, and intuited another secret in the secretary—*Daphne was not coming back, no sir.* The threat was too much, she had too much to lose.

The threat of losing one's life... There was already such a thrill to knowing Arthur Koestler, he positively radiated risk, and that edge—*so cutting the edge of Life's knife*—she knew she could not resist. Here, sharply, undeniably, immediately painful, the way you know it, was love.

The love of her life.

His study was on the first floor, his desk by the window, overlooking the Seine. They went up to work. He dictated one-sentence replies to six letters, which she anxiously typed.

He read them through, and signed them. "No errors. Not much of a test, but...you'll do. It'll be two days a week to start with."

"So, I have the job?"

"Post these letters when you get back to Paris. We don't use the local post office."

She took the letters, stuffed them into her handbag.

"I'll take you to the station." He drove her, at ludicrous velocity, to Fontaine-le-Port train station and left her off with the words: "You start Tuesday, at ten. Change at Melun for Gare de Lyons."

It was a tiny, deserted, French country station. She walked up to the platform and sat on a bench, waiting for the train. Through the rows of pollarded trees on either side of the line, she could see the bend of the river.

Tears filled her eyes. Her nose and eyes were prickling with pollen. She took a drag of the inhaler. The Benzedrine rush made her heart flutter fast as fruit bats in her chest. All the way home, that light-headed, giddy sensation would build, swelling, until her mother's prompt: "Tell me all about Arthur Koestler."

Going Into Labour

Giving birth had been the death of millions of women. Anything could go wrong. The littlest thing, and you could lose the child, or your whole life. To give birth was to be at your most vulnerable. Mum was terrified, rightly so, but the mix of antipsychotic drugs Dr. Freeman prescribed, clozaprine, risperidone, haloperidol, and Lilit's joking around, calmed her. "You're *yuge*, Mum," Lilit patted the bump. "*Yuge*. Ready to pop."

"I'm going to insert an I.V. line into your left forearm," Dr. Freeman said. "It will release a mild sedative and pure oxytocin—the joy hormone —into your system. This hit of prostaglandins will help with the induction process, provoking contractions of your womb."

"How soon will labour come on?" Lilit said.

"All too soon." Dr. Freeman inserted the I.V. and released the drugs.

The sedative relaxed Mum; all tension left her limbs, and then her torso, made her *aaaahhh*. So light. Floaty. Birthday. Due-Date. It was incredible to think that it was nearly over. This miraculous pregnancy seemed to have taken no time at all. *Where did all the days go, uh? Nine whole months...? Missing. Not like losing a necklace, though. No. Here today. Poof!* She had no idea that the sedative drugs included the powerful muscle relaxant succinylcholine.

"I'm going to try to manipulate the baby while your muscles are relaxed, turn it around in the womb." Dr. Freeman lay hands on the bump. He tried to turn the baby, and again, and again.

"That tickles," Mum laughed.

"I can't get it to budge." Dr. Freeman flashed Lilit a look. "It's definitely going to be a breach birth."

Lilit nodded. "A breach birth."

"We're going to have to do a C-section, okay Mum?"

"Okay." Mum was, as they say in Ireland—away with the fairies.

"We don't want the umbilical cord to strangle Baby, do we," Lilit said.

"I will use E.C.T. to kill the pain," Dr. Freeman said.

"It has the positive side-effect of inducing powerful uterine contractions."

Mum's faraway voice: "Easy T...?"

"Electro-Convulsive Therapy. This method of anaesthesia is usually reserved for female patients who have severe psychiatric disorders like schizophrenia, but I have experimented extensively with it in the past and found it extremely effective."

"Schizz...?" Mum hissed through her front teeth.

"Yes. Schizophrenia. And *other* dissociative disorders."

The muscle relaxant really kicked in. From this point on, Mum could not feel a thing. She hardly noticed the bit going in between her teeth.

"Bite down, Eva," Dr. Freeman said. He wet her temples and applied the electrodes. "I'll administer the shock on the count of three. One. Two..."

The shock convulsed through Mum's body. A horizontal jig, as her soul fitted its way out of her body.

Dr. Freeman picked up a scalpel from a tray of surgical instruments and sliced into her bump. Blood and gore.

Mum didn't feel a thing. The soul gliding away, an owl in flight.

Both Dr. Freeman's hands were in her belly. He was cutting through the dense muscles of the womb.

Mum floated. *Is this Heaven?*

Dr. Freeman rummaged around to find what he was looking for, and tugged Baby out of the womb, head-first.

Baby did not look human, was a bloody, purplish-blue in colour, and slicked with wax.

Dr. Freeman deftly snipped the freakish, grey, jiggling birth-cord away, and handed Baby over to Lilit.

Mum looked at Lilit wrapping her baby in a blanket. *I want to hold my baby.*

Baby started to breathe, and cried as the air hurt those tiny lungs.

"Sssssssh," Lilit said, rocking Baby. "My little Babygirl, sssssssssh."

Babygirl?

A girl?

How? Everything was in flux. Mum could not keep up.

DEDICATION

A rt's red slippers. His old favourites, the seams frayed, but still classic. Timeless. By John Lobb of Northampton, and Paris. Motto: 'The Bare Maximum For a Man'.

Her eyelids fluttered fully open, and she realised she was down on the floor, by his slippers, and that there were no feet in the slippers. "Art?"

Art was gone from his armchair.

She pushed herself to her hands and knees. God, but was she groggy. *Must have passed out...?* She sat up on her knees.

Art's dressing gown was all over the chair. *Why had he taken his robe off?* She heard him say: *I blow hot and cold.* Her reply was: *You'll catch your death roaming around the house in your PJs.*

He really was incorrigible. She snatched up the slippers and slung the dressing gown over her forearm. He would put back them on whether he liked it or not. She went directly to the downstairs toilet. Thanks to his enlarged prostate, that was where he spent a goodly portion of his time these days. Sitting. Squatting. *Like a woman,* he would complain.

"Are you on the loo, Art?" she called through the door.

No reply. She opened the door, unlocked. The throne was empty. He was not there.

Perhaps he had ventured upstairs. To their study. At the top room of the house. To write. That was an ambitious ascent, the North face of the Eiger, given that he was so unsteady on his feet. *Ever the alpinist. Daft old bugger.* Altogether stupid to attempt that summit solo, without her for support.

"Art, Art. Wherefore Art thou, Art?" Like Juliet looking for her Romeo, Echo looking for her Narcissus, she went about her search for the beloved. Would she find him hanging off a balcony? Staring into a forest pool, unable to look away, forever fascinated by his own reflection?

She climbed the first flight of stairs. Stopped on the second-floor landing. Strangely tired, out of puff. Drew a breath or two in. Continued upwards, as if sleepwalking. *Yes, it was like she was in a trance.*

The Sleepwalkers. Art's terribly controversial, utterly counter-cultural book on '*Science*'. Subtitled: *A History of Man's Changing Vision of the Universe.* In which he postulated that all of humankind's break-through scientific discoveries had happened in a kind of dream state.

Sonambulistic discovery. It occurred to the Dreamer right there, on the stairs, that she had died. Was dead. The memory of their joint suicide registering, diminished in resonance, as if their right to die with dignity ought somehow to matter, but didn't. *At all really, did it?*

Not if she was here, afterwards. Alive in spirit, and embodied. On her way to check their bedroom, on the third floor. Just in case he had decided to curl up under the bedclothes and have a nap. He was fond of post-prandial naps. Of course, he refused to call them *siestas* because Spanish words returned him to prison. To await his execution.

Their study was on the fourth floor. Art was not the first author to use the murderously draughty, converted attic as his study. Robert Hitchens, friend and lover of Oscar Wilde and Alfred Douglas, had apparently written *The Garden of Allah* up there, romance amongst shifting Saharan dunes of the imagination. She had watched the film, starring Marlene Dietrich, and that brooding actor who played Sherlock

Holmes... *Basil Rathbone, yes!* She'd always found that thrilling. To be part of the rich Literary history of the house, of Knightsbridge, of London, of the Empire. Cultivating the culture of the cultivated.

The door to the study was open. She went in.Art was sitting behind his desk. He had stubbed out a cigarette, on hearing her approach, but his head was wreathed in smoke. "I literally had two puffs."

"Liar-liar, bum's on fire."

He didn't even smile. He was looking at the Lilith Firestone. Directly in front of him, on the desk. This voice from beyond, this muse that spoke to him. He picked it up. "Better get on with it, eh?" he said.

"Are you sure you have the energy?"

"I can. I will. And I must, if we're ever to finish this."

She sat down, opposite him. Picked up her notepad and pencil. Ready to take shorthand. "I'm ready."

"Where were we?"

She looked at her last sentence, decoded her scrawl. "*Lilith's Baby* is more than a novel. It is a manifesto. Proof there is life beyond death."

Art turned the Lilith Firestone in his hands. He cleared his throat. "Death only seems the end if Time is viewed as chronological. When life is viewed holarchically—life never ends, we holons go on and on, interconnected parts of the greater whole. Eternally, if not infinitely."

CAESAREAN

Adamo heard the jingle-jangle jiggle of keys in the lock. Wakening up... On the couch. Lights on.

The door creaked open to reveal: *Eva—home, from the night shift.* "Hey, Lover," he said.

"Hey." She took off her coat to reveal her everyday clothes, *not* scrubs.

The clock read four. Graveyard shift ended at six. "You're home... early," he said.

She smiled. Thinly. Her face, so pale.

He went over and hugged her, tighter than ever. After the Dragon, the whole nightmare of squatting 8 Blackcross Crescent, he needed a hug, like he'd never needed the touch of a woman before. He kissed her neck, breathed her in.

"Somebody missed somebody," Eva said, breaking the hug.

"Couldn't wait to see my pod and the pea in it."

She laughed, a sort of strange bark he'd never heard her use before. "How was your night-in with David Lynch?"

"Intense. I fell asleep on the couch. Had crazy-horse dreams. Forget nightmares, this was nightstallions. In fact, I'm not sure if I'm really awake or it's still rolling."

She blew out her cheeks, *pffffffftt*. "Yeah. I hear ya on that."

"Ah. Shit. Bad night on the ward...?"

"—Not good."

"Jesus. I'm sorry. You want to talk about it?"

"Not really, no. I just want to crash. I'm totally knackered."

"I'll put you to bed then. *Tuck* you in."

"There'll be no *tucking* tonight," she said.

There was something about the way that she dismissed him that sowed a seed of doubt in his mind: *Is this really my Eva?*

But that was crazy-talk. "I did mean *tuck*," he said.

"Sex-pest." She went into the bathroom.

He headed into the bedroom and laid himself down on top of the duvet. He didn't undress. Just lay there. Staring up at the ceiling. His mind, empty, but on full alert. It was as if he was waiting to hear her screech, *primed*, when it happened—

She screeched from inside the bathroom.

He ran to the door; the meat of a fist pounding on the door. "Eva. Are you all right?"

She was crying, more like wailing.

He nearly pulled the doorknob off, and stepped in. "I'm coming in, Eva."

"No, don't." She was sitting on the toilet, scrubs round her ankles. Her hands were bloody, her face was red, puffed with tears.

He realised: *She has lost the baby. She has miscarried.* The shock of it! The dream of being a good dad stolen away. *Dad. Daddy.* His mouth would not work properly to form words.

"I lost her," she said, into his cheek.

Her...? Everything he did have he gave—the language of arms, hugs and kisses, to try to comfort her, to console himself. He held her hands, until he had blood all over his hands.

Blood. The lifeblood of their baby.

The copper tang of it filled the air. There seemed to be a whole lot of blood. *Is there meant to be this much blood?*

It was him who noticed that the blood was not coming from between her legs, but from somewhere else. "What's that?"

He was pointing at the stapled wound. "What—is—it?"

Eva stared at her belly, pulling the skin-tight to examine the wound, a couple of the staples on the left side had come loose. "It's a C-Section incision."

"What do you mean?"

"I've had a *caesarean*."

"A caesarean...? How can you...? You are only one-month pregnant?"

"I've given birth."

"That's impossible."

Her eyes widened. "Lilit..."

Lilit. The very mention of that name caused him to shudder.

"She took our baby."

He remembered Otto's warning: *She wants the child. She will seize it when your wife gives birth.*

Eva declared: "She stole our baby. We have to do something. I'm going to call the police."

"The police?" *What are they going to do—arrest a nightmare?*

Eva had switched to Sister-Eva-Kadmon-mode: "I'm going to tell them this is a case of infant abduction."

Infant abduction? Two words, which when used together could not be more nightmarish. He had never felt so freaking powerless.

"I'll give them her address," Eva said. "They can go around to that house, and see if they can find Gabriella."

Gabriella? She'd named the baby Gabriella. Gabriella...? He looked at Eva phoning the police, couldn't stop Eva phoning the police, but he already knew what was going to happen, like he had licked his finger and held it up to see what way the hurricane was blowing. *Who would believe any of this? I don't.*

The investigation of 'the crime' would happen like this: the police were very sympathetic, at first. At least the W.P.C. on-scene was, anyway, when she saw Eva's wound: 'psychic triage', her job as she saw it.

The gruff sergeant, name of Evans, requested an ambulance to take Eva and Adamo to A 'n' E, but he was very suspicious of the Kadmons' little ghost story.

Sergeant Evans became more skeptical as he took notes for a formal statement from them, even though they tried to avoid the words 'ghost' or 'demon'. Because nobody these days believed in ghosts or *demons*, just aliens. "Have you been drinking tonight, sir, or eh, taking any other substances?"

"No. I have not." Indignant. *Adamant*. He sat with Eva, behind the white curtains, as she underwent treatment.

They both overheard Sergeant Evan's disembodied voice nearby, saying in low tones: "Satanic child sacrifices? She's a nut-job. He's a nut-job. Tenner it's a straight-up self-harm case, attention seeking, Munchausen's-by-proxy, ennit."

"I heard that," Eva yelled.

"We both heard that, Sergeant," he stated.

It was another 10 minutes before the doctor confirmed that Eva had been, but was no longer, pregnant. "No doubt about it, I'm afraid."

"I told you so," Eva said to Sergeant Evans, feeling fully vindicated, and only then, totally bereft.

"That being the case," Sergeant Evans countered, "What did you do with the baby, Mr. and Mrs. Kadmon?"

This accusation was the first of many to come. Interrogations followed, both of them visiting the police station, giving separate accounts, with the same solicitor present.

Detectives interviewed his Double-Mums, and were starstruck, then mildly terrified, when they meet The Great Nadine Nadiri. Detectives interviewed the couple's landlord. They searched the Kilburn Park flat. No trace of a squatter.

Detectives checked out 8 Blackcross Crescent, where the alleged trespass took place, but found nothing out of the ordinary there. All the doors and windows to the mansion were locked, and the alarm activated.

The same detectives interviewed the owner, Gabriel Samael Belial, a Venetian investment banker, by Skype, much to his irritation. No, he did not want to press charges, he did not want any publicity, *zero* spin connecting him to occult goings-on, no more haunted house stories or he would not be able to sell the property, and heads would roll, the Commissioner will hear of it, *capisce?*

Time passed. Weeks degraded into months. The caesarean scar healed, totally, not a trace on Eva's body. Suspicions grew. Rumours seethed like maggots in the wound. In the eyes of the Law, the parents of the missing child were viewed as the prime suspects in its disappearance (*and murder*), but the Crown Prosecution Service did not find enough evidence to charge them. The sense of injustice rankled with Sergeant Evans, and he sold a sensationalised version of the story to pet hacks on *The Mirror*. The headline: *Real-life Rosemary's Baby.*

The Daily Fear put the couple on trial publicly. Like they did the McCanns over poor Madeleine. Except worse, maybe because Eva was Jewish...? This formerly Nazi-owned rag ran with the front-page headline: *EVIL EVA. Did she sell her baby to Satan?*

The Kadmons became the new McCanns for the British tabloid media to crucify daily, and weekendly. This fuelled rampant speculation on Conspiritualist websites, *David Icke.com* and Alex Jone's *Info-Wars.com*, about the involvement of Arcon, reptilian pedophile rings. Illuminati in utero grooming of a 'moonchild'.

New Right rumours of Sabbataen-Frankist, *Donmeh*-crypto-Jew-Jesuit world takeover on 4chan, 8chan image-boards. Q drops for QAnon followers, accused Neo-Liberal spin-doctors of trying to hush-up any dissenting mainstream media journalists with a D.S.M.A. Notice: news black-out, elite cover-up.

Accusations of membership of Crowley's *Ordo Templi Orientis*. Babylonian rituals to raise demons. Human sacrifice. Cannibalism. International internet infamy was beckoning, until *The Sunday Express* linked the couple to the Great Nadine Nadiri, and the promotion of her latest show: 'Black Moon'. The Kadmons' claims that their 'moon child' was abducted from the womb were thenceforth dismissed as the disgusting publicity stunt of a has-been.

Exoneration in the court of public opinion was what the Kadmons desperately needed, but trial-by-media was tough, and Eva began to lose it. Mainly because she took the accusations to heart, literally shouldered all the blame.

Largely because men live in a state of emotional detachment, a dismissive avoidance of fear, and guilt, and shame, Adamo was okay as a pariah. Relatively okay. In comparison.

Eva however, slipped into the madness defined as P.T.S.D., the severe trauma of losing her child. The public shame, and then the ridicule, had an incredibly detrimental effect on her overall mental health. She was prescribed anti-depressants by the G.P., and referred to a psychiatrist.

Neither lifted her spirits. It was decided that she was at an extremely high risk of taking her own life. To save her from herself, he and her mother agreed to have her be sectioned.

Meantime, to help clear their names, he contacted the Koestler Parapsychology Unit (K.P.U.). He'd heard about the K.P.U. from watching *Sea of Souls* on T.V.

The history of the real Unit began rather darkly, in 1983, with the deaths of the terminally ill, world-famous author, Arthur Koestler C.B.E., and his healthy, much younger wife, Cynthia, in a highly controversial, not to mention illegal, joint suicide pact, involving the barbiturate Tuinal, and alcohol.

The first part of Koestler's suicide note was written in June 1982, and read like this:

To whom it may concern.

The purpose of this note is to make it unmistakably clear that I intend to commit suicide by taking an overdose of drugs without the knowledge or aid of any other person. The drugs have been legally obtained and hoarded over a considerable period.

Trying to commit suicide is a gamble the outcome of which will be known to the gambler only if the attempt fails, but not if it succeeds. Should this attempt fail and I survive it in a physically or mentally impaired state, in which I can no longer control what is done to me, or communicate my wishes, I hereby request that I be allowed to die in my own home and not be resuscitated or kept alive by artificial means. I further request that my wife, or a physician, or any friend present, should invoke habeas corpus against any attempt to remove me forcibly from my house to hospital.

My reasons for deciding to put an end to my life are simple and compelling: Parkinson's Disease and the slow-killing variety of leukaemia (CCI). I kept the latter a secret even from intimate friends to save them distress. After a more or less steady physical decline over the last years, the process has now reached an acute state with added complications which make it advisable to seek self-deliverance now, before I become incapable of making the necessary arrangements.

I wish my friends to know that I am leaving their company in a peaceful frame of mind, with some timid hopes for a de-personalised after-life beyond due confines of space, time and matter and beyond the limits of our comprehension. This "oceanic feeling" has often sustained me at difficult moments, and does so now, while I am writing this.

What makes it nevertheless hard to take this final step is the reflection of the pain it is bound to inflict on my surviving friends, above all my wife Cynthia. It is to her that I owe the relative peace and happiness that I enjoyed in the last period of my life—and never before.

Below it, appeared the following addendum:

Since the above was written in June 1982, my wife decided that after thirty-four years of working together she could not face life after my death.

Further down the page appeared Cynthia's own farewell note:

I fear both death and the act of dying that lies ahead of us. I should have liked to finish my account of working for Arthur—a story which began when our paths happened to cross in 1949. However, I cannot live without Arthur, despite certain inner resources.

Double suicide has never appealed to me, but now Arthur's incurable diseases have reached a stage where there is nothing else to do.

Outraged Feminists argued this was a classic case of Narcissism-and-Echoism, but the Koestlers believed their joint suicide pact was both an act of love, and a radical political act. Arthur was the Vice President of the Voluntary Euthanasia Society, later renamed EXIT. Neither of the two believed that death was the end of life.

After life, the couple's bodies were buried in Mortlake Crematorium in South London. In line with their views on the significance of consciousness, they bequeathed £1,000,000 to any University which would set up a Chair in Parapsychology and attempt to find hard, scientific evidence of what Koestler termed 'The Ghost in the Machine' in his book of the same name.

What with Empiricism and the Materialist Atheism being the core belief system of modern-day scientific academia, there were no takers. Oxford. Cambridge, Kings College, U.C.L and Imperial, all refused to pick up the gauntlet.

The challenge was finally, reluctantly, accepted by Edinburgh University, which hired an American, Dr. Robert Moore, to be the first Chair of Parapsychology in the United Kingdom. He had been drawn to the field by strange personal experiences, involving consciousness-in-time: precognition, *déjà vu*, synchronicity, that 'oceanic feeling' of oneness, which his benefactor Arthur Koestler would have thoroughly approved of.

Under Moore's 20-year-long tenure the unit concentrated on the scientific study of paranormal experiences, E.S.P. and P.S.I. powers, with particular focus on *ganzfeld* tests on telepathic communication between senders and receivers.

When what was left of Adamo Kadmon got in touch with the K.P.U., Professor Moore had passed-on, been succeeded by the *second* 'Koestler Chair', Professor Janice Geburah, a highly sensitive Canuck psychic, whose research focused on N.D.E.s, altered states of consciousness encountered by humans when dying.

Final Dissolution

The dictator, Koestler. Cynthia, his amanuensis. It will take the partnership of Art and Cynth a decade, the last decade of their lives, to write *Lilith's Baby*. Up in the draughty attic study of 8 Blackcross Crescent, haunting the house.

Prof. Geburah was largely Cynth's creation. It was fitting to Art that a psychic woman should characterise a psychic woman. And thus, Janice Geburah came to life. Becoming as meta-conscious as a real human being at the exact point when she met herself on paper.

How spooky was that? For Prof. Geburah, to discover she was both reader and character being read. Dream, dreamer and dreamed. In a phantasmagorical ghost-world of full-spectrum weirdness. *This trippy-as-fuck book.*

What she will read in *Lilith's Baby* will compel her to act. She is their character. The Law of One. Doomed to do what she must do, she has absolutely no choice in the matter. The Law of One. It has been pre-ordained. The Law of One. Plot is character. Character is plot. We are all One. In this fallen world, this shard, this husk, it is imperative she take possession of the blue crystal.

The Lilith Firestone.

Before anyone else could lay a pinky on it. Especially the Atlantean,

Belial. That would be disastrous. If it were to fall into the hands of his cloned automatons, it would be used as a weapon against humanity.

So, it will take Prof. Geburah a drive through the night from Edinburgh to London. Sleep-driving behind the wheel. Dreaming up the empty, dark lanes of M1 motorway, zapping past the Watford Gap at 120 mph. A phantasm on a night-journey, into the heart of darkness. The egregore of London. The district of Knightsbridge. Driving onto Blackcross Crescent. And parking-up in front of No. 8.

It was Cynthia whose force of mind, whose drive, what used to be called 'P.S.I.-power' back in the day, telekinetically propelling the thought-form of Prof. Geburah up the path to knock on the front door.On the threshold of *olam ha-ba*, a total paradigm shift for her tribe, *am nahallah*, and the other races that make up the human species, Prof. Geburah will stare at the angels warring on the door. Ataxia. Her whole life flashing before Koestler's eyes, Cynthia's eyes, her eyes. Everything. All Time. In an instant.

How fortunate had she been to be at Esalen in 1989 when Terence McKenna was lecturing about D.M.T. To have been part of the psychedelic experiments at the Institute, escape Time, meet the machine-elves in a haze of that bitter smoke and receive her eldritch reprogramming instructions.

After she was awarded her doctorate for her thesis, 'The Final Frontier: Going Beyond Death on D.M.T.', how lucky to have been recruited to a 'Black' government program to map the D.M.T. Near Death Realm. Mainlining Dark D.M.T., blood-red crystals extracted from the Mimosa root-bark. Serum flowing straight into the bloodstream, via an I.V.

Staying out-of-time in what she deemed 'the Dome of Eyes' for a day at a time. Laughing in slow-mo, everything frame by flicker-frame, with the neon-blue archangels. Four 'Teals', sitting on four thrones in their chasm of a throne room. Without words, they will let her know telepathically to accept the chair at the Koestler Parapsychology Unit in Edinburgh. This appointment had already been approved, so there was no point in refusing it. She would be Professor Janice Geburah. A historical figure.

A *literary* figure. These Old Ones, with their fearsome Olmec features, did not share why that role, that title, that identity, would become so important, only imparting that her ego, the character that Cynthia Koestler had given her, was of crucial importance to the future of mankind on this timeline, in her reality, 'The New Age'.

A small *click* in the lock of History, and the door of 8 Blackcross Crescent swung open, and there stood a beautiful little girl, smiling serenely. Five maybe. Black hair plaited into cute pigtails. Green-eyed, bright with life. Perfect, in every respect. "Hello," the girl said. "I'm Gaby."

Gabriella, no less. Prof. Geburah nodded. "Is your mom home?"

"She's in the kitchen. Come in."

God, grant me strength, Prof. Geburah thought, and stepped over the threshold. For 'strength' is what Geburah, or *gevurah* means.

Cynthia was proud of that nice touch, even if Art thought it a tad literal, and it made the final edit because this heroine had to be strong enough, much stronger than her creator, to face down death in the form of the 'Mother of All Demons'. To seize the Lilith Firestone. To win, save humanity. THE END.

The holarchy of dictator, amanuensis, and character, were therefore shocked when the whole world they wanted so desperately to save, shrank to the size of the little girl's mouth. "Would you care for some jam? I love jam."

Her house sinks down into death
And her course leads to the shades.
All who go to her cannot return
And find again the paths of life.

THE BOOK OF PROVERBS, 2 v 18

The seventh sphere of consciousness is the spiritual consciousness
[since called intuition], the very highest, when man has a
universal consciousness, when he will see not only what proceeds
on his own planet, but in the whole of the cosmos around him.

RUDOLF STEINER, *Human Consciousness in the Seven*
Planetary Spheres

THE ZIONIST

Recolonisation. It would happen. Because it was inevitable. Palestine was 'The Promised Land'. The Zion of the Lord God's Chosen People. The Jews. The Judahites. The Israelites.

The Romans might have destroyed Judea, razing Jerusalem in 3830, or as the Christians would say 70 A.D., and finally, driven out the Israelites in 132 A.D., but they did not drive Israel out of them, in this 'the Edom Exile'. Home, it remained. A spiritual home. Their Historical home.

1924, and like many middle-class European Jews, Arturo Koestler became a Zionist with a certain degree of reluctance, because he was *secular,* not at all *religious.* Which was not *really* Jewish.

If you cannot quote The Zohar, The Talmud, The Sefir Yetzirah, what sort of Jew is that?

If you do not speak Yiddish, what sort of Jew is that?

If one does not observe the Law, what sort of Jew is that?

If I refer to Jesus Christ by name, instead of oto ha'ish, 'that man' in Hebrew, what sort of Jew is that, really?

Some might say: an *erev rav,* one of those dogs who do not, cannot, and will never truly, know *HaShem.* His only viable answer to this fundamental question of identity was: 'the *new* kind of Jew', 'the worldly Jew'.

At 20, he knew very little about the Jew he was supposed to be, what others saw him as. The plain truth was that he knew so very little about the world outside of *Wien*, who ruled it, and the outrages of their power.

He lived in a boarding house with his parents. He was immersed in his studies in Engineering at the Polytechnic, and his social activities in the *Burschenschaften* and Unitas fraternities. *Wein, weis und gesang.* The stuff of youth. Setting the world to rights over *ein kaffe*. Reading books very publicly in the enchanted *Volksgarten*. Picnics on the Danube. The ballet. The theatre. Opera. Learning to fence with sabres. A lot of drinking and brawling in beer halls with the Pan-Germanians.

It was the violent anti-Semitism of Austrians, like the infamous duellist, Otto Skorzeny—who argued there was only dishonour in fighting duels with Jewish scum—which sharpened the edges of his newfound identity, and galvanised Arturo Koestler to run for Chairman of all 12 Zionist *Burschenschaften* in Austria.

He won, by a landslide. Became recognised as a leader of young Jews. Still, he had no faith. It took a great man to convert him, inspire him to act. A messiah. A political shaman from Odessa, Russia. *Like Trotsky, but notsky.*

Vladimir Jabotinsky.

Jabotinsky was a man of letters, using the *nom de plume*, Altalena; meaning 'swing' in Italian, one of the eight languages he spoke. A poet, translator, brilliant journalist and lecturer,

Jabotinsky had made his name campaigning against anti-Semitism in Russia. *Jewish Youth, learn to shoot!* was one of his slogans and he organised the Jewish Self-Defence Organisation against the pogroms. He was anti-Marxist, staunchly anti-Socialist, violently anti-Bolshevik, advocating an urbane Liberalism modelled on the traditions of the West.

To the Tsar's *Okhrana*, the scum who wrote *The Protocols of the Elders of Zion,* he was a marked man, and was forced to leave his Motherland. Homeless, the patriarch Herzl recruited him to the wider Zionist cause. With the promise of a new Homeland. *Eretz Yisrael*. In this war, he took a new name, Ze'ev, meaning 'wolf' in Hebrew.

'Jabo' was a Modernist. A Revisionist. He rejected the turbid mysticism of the Elders of Zionism. He rejected their visualisations of a glorified ghetto in Palestine. To him 'Young Israel' meant Westernisation, parliamentary democracy, modelled on Great Britain. Education: modelled on the French lay-schools. A national army. Latinisation of the obsolete, and obscurantist, Hebrew alphabet. All of this 'Progressiveness' saw him denounced in different quarters as a heretic, an anti-Semite, a militarist, a British Intelligence agent, and even, a Fascist.

During the Great War, Jabo achieved the impossible: patiently, and persistently, persuading the British Government to agree to the creation of a 'Judaean Regiment': the first Jewish fighting force in modern times. They fought under Field Marshal Allenby in Transjordan. Jabo captained his men to successfully defend Jaffa, and Jerusalem, and was awarded an M.B.E. for his services to the Empire.

Post-war action in Jerusalem. Riots and atrocities committed by the Arabs provoked Jabo to form an illegal defence organisation and exact harsh retaliations. A bloodbath, point-of-fact. The horrified British took Police Action: arresting Amin Al-Husayni, the instigator of the riots and former Captain Jabotinsky M.B.E., both of whom were summarily tried and sentenced to 15 years hard labour.

The fix was in, however, and amnesty was granted to Jabo a few months later. He left the fortress-prison of Acco a notional-national hero. His new fame saw him elected to the Zionist Executive in 1921, but he could not accept their whittling down of his idea of an independent 'Jewish State' to a 'National Home', forever dependent on British goodwill, and resigned.

In 1924, the great man formed his own movement 'the Zionist Activists' whose name was later revised to 'the Zionist Revisionists'. This movement grew into the freedom fighter groups, Irgun and Stern, who played such a decisive part in the struggle for Israel in the '40s.

Jabo did not live to see the final victory, he died of a heart attack in 1940. Nor was he present at the ceremony, when one of the main arteries of Tel Aviv was named after him. Nor was he present when civil war nearly broke out between Irgun, and the Israeli Defence Force— known as 'The Altalena Incident', because the ship running French guns into Begin's forces was named Altalena, after his swinging alter-ego.

In 1924, Jabo steamed into Lundenburg, the frontier train station where Arturo Koestler, and his fraternity-brother, the Goliath Puttl, had been instructed to greet him. Arturo noted his hero was carrying a book, which turns out to be Dante's *Divine Comedy*, and commented on it. "I am attempting to translate it into Modern Hebrew," Jabo said.

They talked Dante, while Puttl tried to pin a badge on Jabo's lapel, and truss him up in their colours—a violet, white, and gold sash. "Forgive me, Puttl," Jabo said, taking the sash and putting it in his trouser pocket. "I do not want to scare off the waiters in the dining car while we have lunch, which we must do precisely now, because the Wolf is ravenous."

That night, Jabo's speech in the Kursaal, the largest concert hall in *Wien*, was a remarkable event. *Talk about personal magnetism.* The demagogue held his audience rapt for three hours without ever resorting to cheap oratory. Avoiding repetition. Not a single cliché. The power of his speech rested in its transparent lucidity and logical beauty. *Zion will happen in our lifetime.* It cast a spell on all there. *Have faith. Believe.*

Arturo Koestler was so entranced that he and some brothers started up the Austrian branch of the Zionist Activists. Their stated aims:

That the aim of Zionism is to establish a Jewish State on both sides of the Jordan.

That the prerequisite of a Jewish State is the establishment of a Jewish majority in Palestine.

That a majority can only be established by mass-immigration, facilitated by an international loan instead of by international beggary.

That instead of costly and diminutive Utopian experiments, the Zionist organisation should concentrate its efforts on attracting the capital of Jewish industrialists and financiers and the masses of the Jewish middle classes.

That to facilitate the development of industries in Palestine, temporary protective tariffs should be established.

That a Jewish militia should be legalised under British command for the purposes of self-defence, to end the humiliating situation of the Jews in their own country having to rely on the protection of British soldiers, at the cost of British taxpayers.

That to break the hostility of the British Colonial Office and the Palestine local administration, a mass petition should be organised in which world Jewry laid the facts, and its aspirations, before the people of Britain and its Government.

That after a Jewish State is established, it should be incorporated as the seventh dominion in the British Commonwealth of Nations.

Most of their points, Jabo's programme, were taken up by Orthodox Zionism in later years, but in 1924 the official line was that this 'Mephistophelean manifesto' was an extremist viewpoint, from a tiny minority of un-Orthodox Zionists.

The Zionist leadership of Dr. Weizmann publicly scolded and chided Jabo and his naughty boys. Dr. Weizmann had to tread a very thin line in order not to offend the Doges of the British Empire. Off the record, Dr. Weizmann could say: "A Jewish State. Always to think of it. Never to speak of it." In his wise old heart, Dr. Weizmann was probably very relieved that the cavaliers in the movement could go up to the front door and batter it in, whilst he practiced a more Machiavellian 'back door' diplomacy to gain entry. *Young Man, Old Man. In the long run, both approaches would be necessary to win.*

Weltanschauslich. So it was, the seeds of a revolutionary Zionism were planted in Arturo Koestler. He was talking the talk, but far from walking the walk. Further still, from shooting the gun, hurling the bomb. It took a series of personal tragedies before the activist came to actively envisage himself emigrating to Palestine, making *Aliyah*.

The first was the fall of his family. The swindlings of a friend, precipitated bankruptcy, the utter ruin of his father in the courts. The loss of any sense of a stable home, shelter, protection in a time when Austria was also in economic ruins. His father and mother journeyed to London to seek investments. The Rothschilds were friends of his mother's family, the Jeiteles. Jewish capital would reverse his father's misfortunes.

Meanwhile, he was left *alone* for the first time. With a beggar's allowance. He did not handle his independence well. His daily routine fell apart without his mother's scoldings. He lazed around in bed for half the day.

Perhaps it was lack of food, the price of a loaf of bread reached a thousand *Kronen*, but when he got up, he had little or no inclination to study Engineering in the library. Instead, he read up on psychology of Freud, Adler.

Kant informed him that Reason was absurd, abdicating itself before the problems that really mattered, like infinity, eternity, the possibility of immortality. Einstein reinforced this relativity. Chaos. The aftermath of the Great War. Entropy. Fatigue. Depression. *How is a man to reconcile with chaos? Where can order be found, relevance realised? Civilisation actualised?*

In the contemplation of action, the mechanics of humanity. And so— he specialised in social engineering. And, Zionism. This spiral continued for several months on the trivial plane of routine. Until, the hungry Hungarian in him has almost starved to death, and destitution beckoned; the ultimate fate of many of poor, hungry Hungarians who could not sell their labour, their possessions, or indeed, their bodies.

One night in October, he was discussing free will and determinism over tea, with his friend, Orchov; ugly, warm-hearted, tormented, and sincere, Orchov, who believed in God, and fate, determinism. He would defend free will against Orchov, arguing that within certain limits, man had the freedom of decision, and mastery of his fate, and convinced himself so utterly, that the walk home, through the cold rain, felt like a rebirth. *Exaltation. Irreligious fervour. An oceanic feeling.*

By the time he got to the boarding house, he was manic with what the Germans call *'fernweh'*: the aching desire to freely explore the far-flung world. He fetched out his Index, the matriculation book for the Polytechnic, and burned it in the fireplace. Without this record of all examination marks, a student could not pass, could not graduate. The act of book-burning was unpremeditated. It erupted from his unconscious. Total rebellion against the predetermined *professional* fate his parents had created for him.

The night after the book burning, he had a dream. A vivid dream of buying a spade. An echo of a childhood daydream. Five-years-old, before he went to school. Angry. Lonely. Wishing he could run away from home, his mother and his governess, he saw men digging up the tram tracks in the street. *If you can buy a spade, you can work in this gang, earn a living from the streets. Be free. Be a man. Call a spade a spade.*

It was a sign—Back to the land!

Into that dream, he read a new life as a *Khaluts*. The life of an honest labourer, tilling the earth of the Promised Land.

Making Aliyah

Cynth Koestler, the Zionist-come-lately who had once been know as 'Eva Kadmon' was out, trekking in Northern Israel. Taking her regular hike up and down the afforested slopes of Mount Gilboa.

Meditating at the summit, Transcendental Meditation. Sitting in the Lotus, staring down reality like a Buddhist monk staring at a rotting corpse, chanting:

"*Nam myoho range kyo.*"

"*Nam myoho range kyo.*"

"*Nam myoho range kyo.*"

An hour of clearing the mind was enough every day. There was a dry zing in the back of her throat. She spat it out and rose to her feet. The marine tinge of ozone in the air, promised thunder and lightning. *Soon.* Dark clouds blowing in from the Med'. The first blusterings of the storm riffling into the branches of the cypress oaks.

She picked up her yoga mat, shook it out, rolled and packed it in her rucksack. Then, she got going. Back downhill. Passing the stacks of new cut logs racked up by both sides of the path: resin perfume, pure alkali.

Where the path forked, she turned right, the track fell away steeply.

Her heels rubbed in the boots, painful on the hard skin there. *Should have worn two pairs of socks, inner one thin and outer one thick.*

What brought her to Zion, the making of her *Aliyah,* all of it seemed impossible now. The abduction. The trial-by-media. Being sectioned. A six-month-long course of E.C.T., flashing in and out of existence. Followed by treatment with 'heroic doses' of psilocybin.

The miracle of her recovery of sanity and her *teshuva,* her reconnection with *HaShem,* was like a surprise party that she kept being brought to, over and over, *Surprise-surprise!* and had to pretend she didn't know what was coming, every time. There was a strange feeling of gratitude that accompanied this enforced taken-abackness.

Creaking trees sheltered her from the gathering wind but, climbing over the rickety fence dropped her into a grassy pasture, and the force of nature was lying in wait here, rushing at her, taking her by surprise, rocking her back on her heels. She leaned into it, but it was already changing direction, rippling off right, through the grass.

Crossing the pasture—a few raggedy goats huddled for shelter under a lone, skeletal myrtle in the far corner—she came to a gate. Beyond that, lay the Japanese Garden. Built by Japanese Christians: the *Makuya,* who believed that the Jews return to the Holy Land was a fulfilment of Biblical prophecy, that the state of Israel meant something in the great scheme of things and should be supported at all costs.

Entering this highly cultivated Eden after the wild forest of the craggy mountain was peculiar. *The Far East transplanted here. The Japanese reordering of Nature. That Oriental attention to detail which so satisfies the eye.* She followed the stone path snaking down the slope to the pool, and onwards. There was no temptation to leave the path, even in a breaking storm. *One doesn't walk on the grass in a promenade garden.* The walk represented life's journey, all its different stages, and vistas over the Valley of Yezreel were a wondrous part of this, her life. Lake Kinneret, the Sea of Galilee, glimmered in the distance.

Their oasis in the desert. The Promised Land. Home away from home. Nestled amongst the cypresses at the foot of the mountain, lay *Heftzibah kibbutz.* A detached two-storey concrete farmhouse. Basic, but the perfect off-grid hideaway for two international pariahs, two refugees, two fugitives.

The Great Nadine Nadiri had lived on the *kibbutz* in the '70s. Nadine said they could disappear here, and they had, almost totally. Thanks to a sizeable donation from her, they had assumed two new identities as dippy-hippy-trippy-hipster Trustafarian sorts.

Adamo became Arthur Costler, 'Art' for short—in a conceit almost as conceited as the great author himself. And she, Eva Kadmon, became his wife, Cynthia Jeffries, or 'Cynth' as she preferred. 'The Cynth', when he was drunk.

They acted out this role-reversal in their afterlife to fulfil their destiny. They were the anti-heroes that got away, away from the madding crowd. Into a self-imposed exile.

It was not ostracism, not banishment, but the effect was the same. Israel was erasure. This was a renewed nation-state, 12 tribes reborn from their Armageddon, the *Shoah*.

No one cared about their past here. The two politically incorrect characters Adamo and Eva Kadmon had in effect suicided like the Koestlers.

She walked up to the glass door, opened it and entered.

He was spilling out of a small armchair by the old stone hearth, reading. Always reading by the fire, all winter, spy novels, twentieth century spooks. "*Erev Tov*," he said.

"I just missed being blown away, and no more." She slipped off the straps of her rucksack and set it down by the door.

"I heard it on the radio—if this is the Wind of God, and it can blow for 50 days and nights."

"Yeah." She unzipped the coat, slid her arms out of it, and hung it over the head of the banister. "February blows."

"Let's pray to God it isn't His wind," he said. "Would you take a drink?"

"Mmm." She went over to the battered brown armchair by the fire.

He got up. "Jack D. do?"

"Yup."

He went into the kitchen. Cupboards opening and banging closed.

Or is that distant thunder...? she thought. *Who cares. We can weather any storm.* She settled back into the chair with a sigh.

The cold sweat on her back, the T-shirt sticking to it like cling-film, was uncomfortable, but oh man it was so good to be sitting down, in front of a log-fire.

He came back and handed her a D.I.Y.-stained glass, nursery red and green triangles, half full of J.D.

'Ta. Liver-killer,' she said.

He laughed. Clinked her glass with a matching one. 'Here's to the Alternative Lifestyle.'

'*L'chaim.*' She downed a gulp. She should not be drinking but screw it, the liquid heat felt good on the tongue, and the bourbon-burn continued the whole way down. She stretched out, tired legs toward the fire.

To think—*We're here. Away from the maddening Goy. Sheltered from their judgment. Practically H-bomb-proof in a country made up of refugees, persecuted pariahs, exactly like her.*

The wind was dunting off the roof.

"Would you like a smoke?" he said.

"I'll have a puff." They had really taken to the role of hippies.

"You roll better than me." He pulled out a pouch from his shirt pocket, tossed it and the Rizlas over.

She was now an expert in rolling, having always avoided it.

"A tray or book, or something?"

"Yup." He got up and went back into the kitchen.

She plucked out two skins, licked the tacky edge of one and then stuck the membranes together.

He came back, handed over a tray. "There you go."

"Ta." She got another skin out, folded it up, and affixed it to the middle for extra support.

"I'll put on some music." He went over to the C.D. player, which was wedged in the crawlspace under the open stairs.

She pulled some green out of the pouch and spread a hairy caterpillar of it out on the skin. Ripping off a piece of the Rizla pack, rolling it up into a filter, and inserting it in the end. Rolling and folding the joint into shape. Licking the length of it.

He selected an album. "Massive Attack coming up," he said. "*Unfinished Sympathy?*"

"HEY, HEY-HEY *HEY*." she laughed. "Lighter?"

He went over to the hearth. Picked up an imitation silver Zippo, handed it over.

The divine ritual of sparking-up. That pungent spiciness rising like incense, filling the room. Eyes closed, inhaling deeply. When she'd had her fill, she snorted the smoke from her nose.

"Give it here, Dragon-lady," he said.

She passed him the joint, settled into the cushions of the chair like a fat cat.

Thunder, distant, lost in the mountains, raging.

The fire catching, a shovelling of coals on the wood, red heat.

Passing the joint back and forth, smoking it away.

The long silences of a marriage that had stood the test. When the Massive Attack *Blue Lines* was finished, she said: "I don't know about you, but I've got the munchies."

He looked up from the dance of imps in a world of the fire. "Yeah, me too."

The flames were the only light in the room; the day a dwindling grey fuzz outside the windows."What about a fish curry? I bought some St. Peter's Fish yesterday."

"Sounds good."

She slapped her thighs and got up. "You can be commis chef."

"Yes, chef."

She went into the kitchen and turned on the light. "I'll cook up the fish and rice, you can cut up the vegetables." She pointed at the chopping board and the knife block by it.

He drew a steak knife. "Where are my victims?"

"In the fridge, here," she said, opening the fridge door. *It smelt of feet, overripe Brie.* "Get the pepper out, the chillies, and the lotus stems..."

"Lotus?"

She spilled a packet of brown rice into her saucepan. "Yeah, lotus stems."

"I love lotus."

"This I know. Crush two cloves of garlic, and finely chop one onion, right?"

'OK. Can I have another Jack D.?"

"Afterwards."

He sighed, and took the condensation-dewed bags of veg out of the cracked tray at the bottom of the fridge. "You're such a slave-driver."

She lifted a blackened wok off a wall-hook.

He grabbed the red pepper out of the bag and picked up the knife. Slicing around the green stalk of the pepper, removing the top and the seed-core, then cutting the pepper into lip-like strips.

"Cheffy. *Veeeee* Cheffy."

THE WOMAN OF
ARMAGEDDON

Resettlement. The pioneer settlement he was allocated to was called *Kvutsa Heftseba*.

Deep in Arab territory. At the foot of Mount Gilboa. In the far east of the Valley of Yesreel, sometimes called 'the Plain of Megiddo', which swept down in a broad arc from the Mediterranean to the River Jordan. Here, in this wasteland, General Allenby and Lawrence of Arabia had fought and won 'The Battle of Armageddon' against the Turks and the Germans, a mere 11 years before, in 1918.

Hard to believe that a millennium ago, the Valley of Yesreel had been the most fertile plain in Israel, but having not seen a plough in that long, it had declined into a stony desert. Land reclamation efforts were hampered largely due to the topography—300 feet below sea level—and the effects that had on the local climate.

From spring into summer, the *Khamsin* blew off the sea; an Easterly, full of blinding sand, gusting up to 80 mph. Temperatures would rise from plain stifling, to an unbearable 113 degrees Fahrenheit, and humidity would drop to below 5%. Legends stated the *djinn* ride this wind, or that it is a demon-in-itself. In ancient Turkish law if a murder was committed during the *Meltemi*, which blew for 50 days, that was considered a mitigating circumstance. The husband would be acquitted.

Nobody informed Arturo Koestler about the *ruah kadim,* the 'Wind of God' as it was known in *The Bible,* before he got to where it so maddened men. Nobody informed him about the dismal settlement in the wilderness either. Wooden shacks, surrounded by dreary vegetable plots. There were two concrete buildings. The cowshed, and the house of the children. It was certainly not the oasis surrounded by date palm trees he had pictured, the Orient of his over-fertile imagination.

Nobody informed him about the people who lived out here. They were nearly all lawyers, architects, Doctors of Philosophy from Vienna and Prague. Aged 20 to 30. Like him, they had no previous experience in agriculture or hard manual labour before settling. They found it exhausting. It aged them prematurely.

When he arrived from Haifa, it was dinner-time, and his first encounter with the collective was in the communal dining hall. He was greeted with nods, but no one talked to him. He was fed, yes. Onion soup. Bread. Goat's cheese and olives. Basic, but tasty. The rules of desert hospitality: a wayfarer must be given food, and a bed. Without payment. No questions asked.

Everyone ate in the mechanical manner of those in a constant struggle to keep their strength up. *Who he is, that is seemingly irrelevant. What he wants, well, who cares.* He felt hurt by this. His ego, pricked.

He would ask for Guetig, one of the leaders of the commune, a one-time member of Unitas, and his point of contact. The man to his right, Dr. Loebl told him: "Guetig is down with malaria."

This made him very wary of the mosquitoes. And the yellow complexions of some of the women sitting nearby. The feverish sweat on their brows. He explained to Dr. Loebl: "I've come to join the commune."

"For good?"

"I was hoping to spend a year here and then go to Tel Aviv, find a job or go into politics."

"Ah, so you are a tourist."

"No. I came here to work. *Hard.* To rebuild Zion."

"What *are* your politics?"

"I am a Revisionist. Jabotinsky inspired me to come."

Dr. Loebl stared at him, weighing, measuring. "Many come here. Because of the economic depression in Europe. Few are suitable for the life. Fewer are chosen. Forgive me, I do not think this will be right for you."

"I see." Crushing disappointment. *There is no Plan B*. He had no money and was relying on the collective to support him, for they did not use money here. "I have nowhere else to go."

"I'll talk to the Secretary. See if they will put you on probation for a few weeks. You can try."

Dr. Loebl gave him a bed for the night. A *hard* bed. Sleep deprivation by whining, biting mosquitoes.

When he did fall asleep, he was awakened by the shrieks of the *Khamsin* blowing in. Woman-like shrieks. *Hell hath no fury like Hell herself.* It seemed all of King Solomon's demons were clawing and battering the ramshackle hut.

He closed his eyes, pulled the sheet over his head. Sleep was a long time coming, and full of dreams of a naked, black-haired woman, an otherworldly beauty, in a huge bed. Under the covers, she took him in her mouth. Pumped his manhood. Her finger entered him as he was gasping in ecstasy. And, she was not done when he was, wanted more. And somehow, he had more to offer, right away. There was nothing this woman did not know, nothing she would not do to feed upon his seed.

In the blast furnace of morning, the sun barely risen, his trial began in earnest. Dr. Loebl assigned him to work in a staked-out plot of arid earth: "Clear the stones first. Hoe the earth into ridges."

It was back-breaking work. After an hour or two, his thumbs and fingers were not simply blistered, but holed. Tears, weeping tears. His thoughts swimming in the heat-shimmer of wind and sun. *Every joint doth protest.* Still, he did the job without complaint. When it looked like he would collapse, Dr. Loebl told him: "Fall out, rest in the shade, drink some water."

The second and third days were no better. At the end of the first week, he started to develop the same rhythm as the others, a natural economy of movement. The physical strain eased. He acclimatised somewhat. What he could not adapt to, was the sense that no job was ever finished, it went on and on, and there was little in the way of personal satisfaction because it was a collective effort. Truth be told, by the second week, he began to hate the hoe, the spade, the earth itself, and he could not hide his aversion from the others, because everyone saw right through him.

The oddest thing. They could read his mind, and his body. The commune. Because he was being watched. Everyone was watching everyone else. It was impossible to hide any trait of character, a mood, discontent. Any sparks of friendship, or animosity or sexual attraction were immediately known to all. As if they were one consciousness. X-ray transparency. Group-mind. There was nowhere to hide. No privacy. No individuality. Nowhere for the ego to go, except into the group mind. Not even in the night. On guard duty. Alone. His watch, until 02.00. *Halt! Who goes there?*

Arturo Koestler: lone sentry standing, smoking in the moon-shadow of Mount Goreb. An Enfield .303 slung over his shoulder. Lone but, not alone.

Who is this sentinel? A communal vessel, part of the commune, communing with oneness, is this Communism? Even in the deep darkness, he felt them all, the collective, watching. *Judging, like Mother. It was infuriating.* He felt like he was losing his sanity. *Three and a half weeks. You are completely unfit for this collective life. It is not for you.* He read later that this sense of collectivisation, this *psychological communism,* led to a psychological crisis in one in every two *khaluts* in two to three years.

Out there, out on the edge of the settlement, he stood, the lone sentry in the dark heat of the night, breathing in hot darkness. He wished a Bedouin would appear. To fight. To kill. So he would be hailed the conquering hero.

"This is where Saul fell to the Philistines..."

He nearly leapt out of his skin. Fumbled the rifle. It hit the sand.

Dr. Loebl emerged from scrub behind him, pistol in hand. "If I had been a Bedouin you would be spit like a kebab now."

He nodded, ashamed. That was what he felt here. *Naked. Ashamed of himself. Like Adamo in Eden, after eating of the fruit of the Tree of the Knowledge of Good and Evil.*

"I came up here to say that the Members' Assembly have given preference to other candidates. But you already knew that, yes?"

And he did. He knew he had failed the test, and he did not like to fail. *He* had failed, himself. It was not his right-wing political affiliations that swayed the collective. Jabo's paramilitary spectre. He would not make excuses. This was personal.

"Do not be disappointed in yourself, Arturo. You came here to ask yourself some hard questions. Take the answers, and move on into the kind of life you need. Learn. More."

"Thank you for giving me a chance, Dr. Loebl." Along with this sense of dejection, there was a strange kind of relief that he would never toil with a spade again.

There followed months of gnawing hunger, a diet of cigarette smoke. A parade of odd jobs, dismissals. P.R. Agent for the Revisionists. Lemonade vendor. Architect. Down-and-out in Haifa.

The idea formed slowly. Over many a tea in The Garden of Eden, his favourite Arab café. *How to turn life's failures into success—Writing.*

He wrote about his experiences in the form of a *feuilleton*, a travelogue, entitled 'Arrival in Palestine' and sent this to newspapers in Europe.

No news for several months. It had disappeared into a black hole. Then he was on a beach in Haifa, thin as a rake, with an old friend from schooldays, Reich. "I never thought you would become such a famous man, Arturo," Reich said.

"*Famous*—for what?"

"A man who is printed on the front page of the *Neue Freie Presse* is a famous man."

"Show me."

Reich took him back to his apartment. "There. It says Arturo Koestler."

He read the article in a state of sweaty disbelief. The realisation: *Neue Freie Presse is like The Times of Central Europe. This is a major breakthrough. No more trying to sell articles into the Zionist papers, ha. This is the ticket. The start of a career as a journalist.*

There was a glaring error though, in the second phrase of the third paragraph: *the water in Haifa harbour was still like green grass.*

"Glass. Not *grass!*" He was mortified. Much to Reich's astonishment. "The editor should be shot," he cried.

And, it was not the only disappointment connected to his breakthrough. He discovered several weeks later that it was his mother who pulled strings to get him published. *Infuriating woman! Like Lilith, haunting him. Why couldn't she let him find his own two feet? Make his stand. Be a man.*

STRANGERS OF GALILEE

Delta-9-tetrahydrocannabinol.

'Art'—and Adamo *did* think of himself now as 'Art' if not 'Arthur'—was in the habit of smoking a joint first thing every morning.

Light it up and, altered state. The world as hallucination. He could forget Adamo Kadmon. That persona had well and truly died. Reflecting on his previous life was like reading the biography of a historical figure. Most times, that is.

This morning though, the drugs won't work. His mind was still churning. Sitting up on the bed, in the half-lotus position, he tried desperately to still the mind. *No good.* There was no escaping the fact. *We. Lost. Our. Baby.*

Mostly, he preferred to believe it was a simple miscarriage. *Random. An act of Mother Nature.* It was sometimes easier that way. Or to tell himself: *Little Gabriella was too good for this world, so she went to a better place.*

Sometimes though, when his intellect failed, and imagination ran away with him, it was the demon-woman— he never used her name— who spirited Gabriella away. This myth served to give his suffering as a man *meaning*. His grief became cosmic. His struggle to save his family, legendary. History took the form of any number of hackneyed metaphors to express this terrible, hollowing loss.

To believe.

In demons. To truly believe, when you were so conflicted. Mourning in real-time, could be so overwhelming. When to remember. When to forget. How to forgive. Who to forgive. These choices can drain the very life out of you. But for now, here in Israel, he was recovering, they were healing. Slowly. Here. *We are.*

No doubt.

This place was helping them get stronger; transcend their past. Being *Other*, living other peoples' lives *really* helped. Especially for...Cynth. *Nearly said Eva, dummy!*

The Cynth, his Cynth, was miraculously better. Full of life. The light, the fire of a new faith in her old religion. Raring to go. Already downstairs, listening to the Red Hot Chilli Peppers' *Californication*, and doing the dishes: clattering the crockery, jingling the cutlery together.

Time to get up. Face the day. He stubbed out the joint on the rim of the mug of water he'd brought up last night as a quencher. The ash mizzled into the empty base, and he dropped the butt in, to drown.

Raising himself up, he blundered his way into the kitchen for breakfast.

Ether. The peeled banana reeked of the stuff. *Heady enough to get flies high.* He bit off the pointy top of the unripe fruit; stripped the banana-skin right down, floppy, and wolfed it in two bites.

"The wind has died down. It's not a bad day. Do you want to go for a hike to the Lake?" he said.

"Surely you mean the Sea, Goy-boy?"

He smiled. Like everything in the Holy Land, Lake Kinneret had at least three names: Jewish, Christian, and Muslim. "We can stop in and see Estraya on the way. She's always got good gear."

"I'll make us a pack lunch."

Supping at his tea silently, he watched her in the kitchenette: slapping some mayo onto thick white bread, adding Brie and salad, to make doorstep sarnes. She was somehow oblivious to his voyeurism, humming along out of time to the tune of the Chilli's *Around the*

World, cling-filming the sandwiches. *That's my lovely wife.* He got that squiggly-eel feeling in the back of his head, a sort of pleasurable pins and needles of the brain.

She fetched a packet of coffee out of the cupboard, poured it into a *cafetière* and added some water from the kettle.

As she decanted the coffee into a thermos flask, he ran his fingers back through his hair; electric ripples through the follicles. Looking at her, he never wanted his entrancement to end.

She packed the lunch into the small rucksack lying by the door; fetched a blanket from upstairs.

They set off. 25 degrees centigrade in February. Breezy; the tops of the cypresses nodding in agreement with the wind's direction. He adjusted the straps on the rucksack to fit tight round his chest. The pack was stuffed with food, the picnic blanket, their coats, the towel, and it was bulky, if not that heavy.

A half-mile into the hike, in the middle of a massive date plantation, a tractor *phut-phut-phuted* down the road towards them, blue body and white cab, dragging a tall trailer.

She moved to the left verge and stood as far in as she could without slipping down into the irrigation ditch.

He followed her lead, standing on the very edge.

The tractor, a Fendt, slowed down as it approached them; side-to-side rocking of the suspension, blue smoke snorts from the exhaust column.

He waved up at the *kibbutznik*, a Thai guy. Practically every worker was Thai. The mass immigration of Jews had slowed to a dead-stop. No *olim* worked the communes of the Holy Land. No Arabs. No Palestinians either. The *kibbutzim* had become plantations staffed by East Asians.

The Thai guy waved back, smiled, and stepped on the gas.

A cloud of acrid blue smoke hazed up the whole road. He held his breath as the tractor-trailer chugged away, but still, burnt oil. In the mouth. He coughed, hacked up some tar, and spat onto the road ahead.

The wind blew the blue haze away, and the view of the sea, clear and sparkling in the sun, was so bright it slashed at his heart, too beautiful to be true.

The roads down to the sea were easy. In spite of the rising heat. The land melted away, sinking down to an impossible 700 feet below sea level.

Set waaaaaay down on this underworld shore, Estraya's cottage was part French-style villa, part ramshackle-pioneer. The outbuildings were topped with rusty corrugated iron rooves. A tin-whistle-flue trailed white smoke onto the wind.

An olive tree shaded the gate. There was a chain looped over the nub of the gate."Hello in there, Estraya!"

The clatter of a screen door being opened, out back, and Estraya came around the gable, past the Land-cruiser parked in the driveway. She was dark-haired, swarthy-skinned: a Sephardic Jew, the Spanish offshoot of the Chosen People, the Anussim who were called 'conversos' because they were forced to convert to Catholicism or die. To defend herself, and her belief in HaShem, in this day and age, this 'Soldier of God' had an M4 carbine slung over her shoulder. "Hey, Guys."

"Hey," he replied.

Estraya was wearing a big grin on her face. "You going for a swim?"

"Yeah," Cynth said.

"Come on in."

"Okay." He unchained the gate from the post, and they went up to the back door. A dead cactus lolled over the edge of a shattered crock by the door. It was impossible to avoid all the bits of blue and white delft triangles laid out like pieces of some 3-D Chinese jigsaw puzzle; they crunched their way in.

Estraya hung the M4 up on a rack beside an old Uzi submachine-gun.

He took a seat on a stool in the adjoining living room. "Layla not at school today?"

"We're keeping her off. There's been another rocket strike."

"*Hezbollah*?" Cynth had to ask.

Estraya nodded. "Landed near Safed. Iron Dome, my ass. Anyway, Layla's loving it. Hours on the Play Station."

He laughed. "And doing *kung fu* on you, no doubt?"

"*Krav maga*," Estraya corrected. "Kicking the shit out of me."

"Girls these days," he said.

Estraya pulled out a joint. "You want a puff, Art?"

"Thought you'd never ask," he said.

Estraya lit up, took a few drags, handed it over.

He took a long-deep breath, zing of zinc, passed it on. Sweet amnesia.

"Fuckballs-high," Cynth said.

"Total fuckballs." He giggled. She was so in-and-out of focus, she had two, four, six faces, twelve, legion. *Concentrate.*

Cynth puffed, and blowed, puffed and blowed, like a bellows. "Mega —fuck—balls."

Estraya brewed up mint tea in a battered copper pot. Gas rings *hiss-firing.* Rattle of metal boiling-roiling on metal. The wraith of steam pirouetting up from the spout.

Cynth sidled off into Layla's bedroom. Truant laughter.

Estraya flicked on the sound system; the *zhum* of an amp in a Bose base speaker behind the stove. Sibilating stereo from the two treble speakers set up on shelves in the corners of the room: dusty Pioneers. Track selection. Floyd's *Dark Side of the Moon.*

"Here." Estraya passed a mug.

"Ta." He took his tea, supped at it.

"We're having a barbeque later. Soph's back from her watch. With something special. You have to try it."

"Count us in." He nodded. Estraya's wife was a character. A fiercely proud Nazarene, she worked as a crystallographer at a Top Secret base, bunkered somewhere in the valley. Sasers were her thing. Zapping missiles out of the sky with sounds. Project: Melchizedek, she called it. Her off-duty mission was: "To change this fucked-up world one trip at a time—because inter-dimensional travel broadens the mind".

Cynth sighed. "If I get any higher my head will float off."

"Don't worry. It's very mellow. The Ancient Egyptians called it 'The Flower of Dreams'."

"What is it?" he asked.

"Combo-entheogen. The sticky buds and petals of *nymphaea caerulea*—'The Blue Lotus'. Tiny pieces of *amanita muscaria*, 'Fly Agaric'. And a pinch of *Mandragora Officinarum*, 'Mandrake'."

"Wow. That sounds kind of heavy-duty-trippy," Cynth said.

"Take it from me—it's the lucid dream of all time. And I do mean —*all* time. All people, too."

"Plant medicine," he said. "Just what the doctor ordered."

Layla leapt into the room to show off her high kick, a roundhouse kick.

Cynth looked suitably impressed by the display of girl power.

"Ninjas call this 'The Touch of Death'," Layla said. She demonstrated this pressure point on the neck of Cynth.

"Ow!"

"Sorry," Layla said.

Cynth pulled away, was suddenly crying a lot, gushing.

"I didn't mean to hurt you."

His mouth flattened into a line. He saw through the tears. To the loss. How sneaky it was.

"Layla," Estraya yelled. "Leave Auntie Cynth alone."

The Jerusalem
Sadness

avah. No 29. Street of the Prophets. Jerusalem.

It profited the famous prophet Arturo Koestler to take up residence in No. 29 in 1929. Right in the heart of the city. Two minutes from the Mosque of Omar, where for a shilling, a traveler could be shown the Angel Jibril's fingerprints on the rock that wanted to ascend to heaven with the Prophet Mohammed.

Jibril. Gabriel. The Messenger. Arturo Koestler was given a new title to correspond to his new position in the Ullstein Newspaper Group: 'Our Correspondent in Jerusalem'. His prophecies took written form in *feuilletons*, mainly. He wrote about the Orient for Occidental readers, Gog and Magog travelogues:

'The Café of the Arabian Nights'

'The Vices of Beirut'

'Gay Tel Aviv'.

His task was to transport people to The Holy Land without all the hot bother, and expense, of foreign travel. To bring Zion into the parlour.

Ironically, Zionism as a movement, had come to a standstill. Fact: the British ruled Palestine. They had slowed immigration to a trickle. Arturo Koestler, Zionist Activist, was now just another European journalist out here. He was not exactly proud of what he did for a living but, it paid the bills, his own, and those of his mother and father, whom he now had to support.

1000-Marks-a-month was nothing to be sniffed at. Certainly not bad for a 23-year-old. The *feuilleton* took him places. His beat extended to Damascus, Beruit, Amman, Cairo and Baghdad. Thus, he got to leave Jerusalem and meet the great men of the Middle East.

Arturo Koestler—his full name and title featured above every article —should be grateful to the *feuilleton*. He would be—if he could be. But deep down the *littérateur* recognised bad writing when he saw it. This mystical blend of travelogue, essay, and short story. Always written in the first person singular. In a knowing, whimsical, subjective style. Literally oozing authority, dripping with the Liberal or Socialist Germanic philosophy—*Weltanschauung* again—of the newspaper, and the opinions of the correspondent.

Facts, *nein*. Tracts, *ja*. *Facts, a famous German editor wrote, are not fit for the reader when served raw; they had to be cooked chewed and presented in the correspondent's saliva.*

The *feuilleton* was the diet of an infantilised Continental, and especially German, readership. Just because everyone else was sticking their head in the fire, did not mean a thinking man should indulge this kind of authoritarianism. He wanted to write differently. Seriously. About the real social issues of the day. Objectively.

So, when the editor of the *Vossische Zeitung*—the champion of serialising Erica von Remarque's brilliant anti-war novel, *Im Westen nicht Neues*—commissioned him to interview King Feisal of Baghdad, he set out to be much more empirical in his approach, report *the* news.

The train to Iraq. First class. It felt good to get out of Jerusalem. The unholiness of the inhabitants of the Holy City was driving him mad, the bad-sad-mad of tragedy without catharsis. He called his melancholic condition 'the Jerusalem Sadness'.

Joseph Flavius, a priest who also suffered from the Jerusalem Sadness wrote: *The union of what is divine and what is mortal is disagreeable*. It was the hypocrisy that did it. The hypocrisy of all the different clergies in particular. Moslem. Christian. *Jewish*. Their petty sectarianism was sickening. The preaching of murderous lies. The mongering of hate. Incitement to riot. Justification of murder. Rewards in the afterlife for martyrs to bathe in the blood of the unbelievers.

The destructive power of faith. Us versus them. The Other. Death cults. *Where was the celebration of Life?* It all served to highlight man's abject failure to come to terms with God here, of all places.

To cap it all, there were no cafés or night clubs, no night life of any kind. People kept to themselves. Church. Clan. Sect. Party. It was an austere, pharisaic town. He could not mix socially with the Arabs because he was a Jew. He could not mix with the Jews because he was a Revisionist. He could not mix with the British *sahibs*, here called *hawadjas*, because his politics were not at all correct. Club. Clique.

Ostracism, and the resultant social desert simply would not do for Arturo Koestler. At all. He came here for adventure. He worked damned hard by day. He wanted to have a good time off-the-clock. He loved his drink. His women.

Horseback rides in the desert were but a temporary cure. Trips to the Sea of Galilee helped. Visits to friends' houses in much more cosmopolitan Haifa; that, he loved. Getting away. Anywhere. Helped to cope. But the Jerusalem Sadness always returned when he did.

Fact. The British rule Iraq. Therefore, upon arriving in Baghdad, as more than a matter of professional courtesy, he visited with Lieutenant-Colonel, Sir Francis Humphrys, the British High Commissioner of Mandatory Iraq.

"Thank you for coming to us first, young fellow," said Humphrys.

"I felt you would be most able to provide some background on the escalating conflict between the Arabs?"

"I'm sure you'll understand, but we could not possibly comment on that at this juncture."

"Would you say the British rule of Iraq and Transjordan— the fact of a standing British Army in the region—the only thing that is preventing all-out war between the Arabs?"

"No comment."

"What, in your opinion, is the likelihood of Ibn Saud's army of Wahhabis chasing the Sherif out of Mecca after this declaration that he is 'Caliph of all Arabs'?"

"I am sure His Majesty will give you His opinions. We wouldn't want to prejudice His Majesty's remarks. Although, in light of recent developments, His Majesty ought to be cautious in his statements."

King Feisal received him in the Baghdad Palace. In a dazzling white room, octagonal in shape with a high ceiling supported by eight pillars. The great hero of the Arab Revolt against the Ottoman Empire was seated somewhat incongruously on a settee, when his guest was announced by the Private Secretary: "Arturo Koestler, Your Majesty."

It felt strange to bow, but he did, deeply, for he had read *The Seven Pillars of Wisdom* and had a good deal of respect for Lawrence of Arabia's great ally. The King 'Aurens' made had often declared himself a friend of the Jews and the Zionist cause.

King Feisal nodded back. He was wearing a black linen suit, and a black *iraquiya*. He looked ill, tall and too thin. *Frail. Frail, at 40. And the light of hope had gone out of his face, his eyes. Dishonour could do that. Humiliation could do that. The Baghdad Sadness. The British would do that, in spades.*

He had arranged that interview should be in French because he spoke French and the King spoke French.

The Private Secretary showed them to two armchairs and remained by His Majesty's side as pleasantries were exchanged. Arturo made much mention of Colonel T. E. Lawrence—his memoirs, which he kept losing on trains. "Do you keep in contact?"

King Feisal smiled, like a man not a king. "Aurens has never left the desert. He is one of us."

The ice well and truly broken, he asked his first official question, in slow, clear French: "Now that the Arabs have won their freedom from the Ottoman Empire, what is Your Majesty's opinion on the possibilities of unity in Arabia these days?"

"The unity of Arabia, the rebirth of the once so mighty empire is every Arab's wish." King Feisal spoke as if tasting each word. "But progress is slow, hampered by the present *peculiar* circumstances."

An indirect reference to the British. "Peculiar, Your Majesty?"

"The foreign influence is not favourable to this development."

Shorthand. Scribbling down every word in code. "You mean the British Empire?"

The Private Secretary coughed a warning.

King Feisal sighed. "History will take its course, and in the end our idea will triumph. Sooner or later the rebirth of Arabia will become a fact."

"I have travelled through Palestine, Syria, and Transjordan and seen the beginnings of a Pan-Arab movement, a Pan-Arab renaissance, but it seems to be lacking a co-ordinating centre?"

"A co-ordinating centre. This may exist—even if it is not easily visible from the outside."

"Might one infer that the centre is Baghdad?"

The Private Secretary shook his head. "Absolutely not. The Sherif of Mecca is the Caliph of All Arabs."

"Understood." He smiled, conceded. He steered the conversation towards even greater controversy. *The very secret war. He must avoid mentioning the word 'war'.* "How significant are the reported border skirmishes between the Wahhabi Kingdom in Central Arabia and Your Majesty's troops?"

The Private Secretary intervened: "Border clashes between tribes are entirely normal at this time of year. Reports of skirmishes. Rumours of war. These are the exaggerations of newspapers to sell copies. If only reporters would report the news, tensions would not be inflamed. All would be well."

He had to avoid mentioning Ibn Saud by name. Expressly. "Is what is going on in Central Arabia a concern for His Majesty?"

King Feisal pursed his lips. "Developments in Central Arabia do not affect the Arab Renaissance one way or another. Never, not even at the peak of the Caliphate, did the peninsula share in the high civilisation of the Arab Empires. It would be too much to hope that this would be different in future. Central Arabia is today, more than ever, a country of ignorant savages."

The Private Secretary nearly swooned. "We would appreciate it if you would not quote His Majesty's last sentence."

King Feisal barked something in Arabic at the Private Secretary, and then smiled. A kingly smile. "Quote it, as you will. It is the truth."

"Thank you, Your Majesty." The interview was over, he had the substance of the article. He left that dazzling white room, noting: *Eight pillars—not Lawrence's seven pillars of wisdom.*

Eight.

Back at the Baghdad Hotel, he wrote up his notes in the bar and then began what he hoped would be a highly *objective* front-page *news* article. For context, he included a great deal of research on King Feisal's part in the Arab Revolt, British assurances about the creation of an Arab Caliphate after the partitioning of the Ottoman Empire. The unfairness of the Sykes-Picot Agreement (1916). And the Balfour Declaration (1917), which promised the creation of a Jewish state in Palestine, a further block to Arab unity.

The article was heavily edited in Berlin, stripped of History, to fit sensationally back into the *feuilleton* form with a Liberal helping of *Weltanshauung*. It was given the title: 'Shadow Caesar on the throne of Shadow Caliphate'. Which may as well read: Man of the Past. And that —did—it. *The straw that broke the camel's back.* The Jerusalem Sadness felt like slow death, being stuck in the past, spiritual suicide.

This was not what he wanted to be doing.

This was not his place.

This was not his calling.

This is not—it. What—is—it? Why, he wanted to report real news. History was a dialogic between the Present and the Past about the Future. The Wall Street Crash of 29th October 1929 was real news. As real as life gets—because the world would never be the same after it. He wanted to be where the Future was happening, to write about it, help shape it.

MOTHERLOVE

Cynth picked up a flat stone with sharp edges and hurled it out onto the lake; skimming ring after ring after ring into being, nine in all.

"Estraya was saying she is thinking of selling this place," he said. "A global hotel chain want to buy it. $450,000."

"Wowaweewa."

"Yeah. Primo waterfront real estate. But she'll never sell out. Soph would divorce her. Layla would kill her, death of a thousand chops."

Layla, Warrior Princess. She laughed. She could laugh through the hurt, the loss, because there—was—hope. *Where there is life, there is hope.*

She saw her daughter in dreams. Repetitive dreams of Gabriella, living another life, an impossibly rich life in a house of many mansions. She could only watch her Gaby in the luxury of these dreams, unseen, unheard, but when she awoke, back in the *kibbutz,* she felt lucid, more connected than ever to her child. And that helped her recovery. *Hear O Israel, the Lord is our God, the Lord is One.*

A duck quackled away, lost somewhere up ahead in a host of rushes. They walked along the stoney shore hand-in-hand.

They walked in step. Synched, effortlessly. They had become really close here. West of the Jordan. They knew each other in a way that they didn't before their persecution, their loss, their struggle to come back stronger. As individuals. As husband and wife. *Israel is this truly spiritual place. Rough 'n' ready, but beautiful.* To be out in Creation. God's Creation. The Temple of Nature. The House of the Sanctum rebuilt.

Staring across the lake, squinting really. *So bright. Light from above. Light from below.* She shielded her eyes with her hand. Out there, in the centre, a single shaft of light, a sword of light, moved across surface of the waters of the lake; brilliant as a laser, completely dazzling. Like an E.C.T. white-out. *This is where you lose yourself.*

She squeezed his fingers hard. *It seemed so unlikely. That she would or could ever recover. Hour by hour. Day by day. Week by week. Resilient, almost against her own will.*

"I've got the major munchies," he said. "We can have a paddle after lunch, if you like?"

"You're not supposed to swim on a full stomach, are you."

He slid off his backpack and lowered it onto the ground. He unzipped it, pulled their lunch out. "Let's eat."

"I could eat." She sat down, using a rock for a backrest. She ripped out her laces, yanked off her boots and socks, so her feet could breathe.

He handed over two sandwiches. "Dig in."

She half-unwrapped one, bit in. The Brie had gone warm and squishy in the bread, just the way she liked it. "Yum."

"Yes, Chef." He nodded, spread out the blue blanket on the grass, and sat down in the half-lotus position. He ate a sandwich. "Num-num. What about that coffee?"

She fetched out the flask and decanted the black stuff into the plastic cup. She had a quick sip and then handed the cup over.

They passed it back and forth, quickly draining it. Savouring the bitterness.

She wanted to tell him her news here, now. It seemed like the right time. *We are pregnant. Again. You are going to be a dad.* But, she only imagined saying it. *Will not tempt fate. Must not.* Did not want to add to the trauma. The request—*I want our family to live here*—seemed too much to ask, but when her baby grew into a bump, she would pluck up the courage to say what must be said.

"Do this." He picked a ball of cling-film.

"What?"

"This," he said, and spread the transparent plastic out, like a used hanky. He scrunched the four corners together, trapping a balloon of air, with a few crumbs in the middle.

"I know what you're doing." She picked up a wrapper, dumped the crusts out, twisted the straggles, tighter and tighter.

"One, two, three." He clapped his hands together same time as her: *pop!* Flushing a heron out of the rushes, two *kreeches* of protest, flapping low along the waterline.

She laughed. "I haven't done that since I was a kid."

There was a post-digestive lull, in which he rolled a joint, and sucked up some smoke.

She stripped off her t-shirt, lay back on the blanket in her bikini top, stretching her legs out to soak up some sun. Neon-red flared, trapped behind her eyelids.

He pointed at the nick on her calf. "Nasty."

"Almost fatal. Just as well I'm a nurse, huh. Or, was."

She lay there, trying to relax, but it wasn't happening. "Swim?"

"*Never.*" He got up, dusted dirt off his arse. He ripped out the laces, wrenched off the boots, and stripped off socks, T-shirt, shorts, blue boxers, leaving everything in a heap.

"Skinny-dipping eh?" She laughed.

The water's edge. He plonked a foot into the clear water.

"What are you waiting for?"

Baby-steps out from the shore, waters up to the waist. "Just trying to plot a course of least resistance through the rocks."

"Big baby." She pulled her T-shirt over her head, unclipped the bikini. Stripping off jeans and pants next. Stepping in, gingerly, feet stirring dirt off the stones. Her lower half looked brown and stunted in the fresh water. Bubbles winked up from the bottom.

"So warm, isn't it?" he said, swimming out, cutting a V in the waves.

She pushed off, into a bobbling breaststroke. Then flipped over to float still on her back, to relax, gaze up at the clouds in the blue sky.

He swam over, took her in his arms. "I am going to have you, right here, Woman."

She kissed him. "Not if I have you first, ya filthy animal."

THE HIGH PRIESTESS

"I have never been to a brothel," Bebe said. "I am 21. That seems absurd to me."

He laughed. "*Quel catastrophe.*"

"If I was a man, this chasm, this Grand Canyon in my education would not have happened." She downed her glass of Alsatian red in one go, and stood up. "Let's go to *Les Halles.*"

He was forced to down his wine and follow her to the 'Houses of Paris'. His body was fatigued after the late shift in the *Salle des Journalistes*, where he worked in smoke-filled rooms as the Chief's *negre*, rewriting French newspapers stories into German newspaper stories, until 11.00pm. *But, a brothel, with Bebe!* This prospect reinvigorated his filthy mind.

"We will both write about this adventure." She skipped across the terrace of the Dôme to the exit, like a girl.

Baby-faced Bebe is seriously fun. He had been seeing her for nearly three months now. Ever since he transferred from the Ullstein's Jerusalem office to 23 *Rue Pasquier*, Paris, there was a spark between them.

Work together. Play together. It had happened quite naturally. An office romance. They were happy. She made him happy, even in the Great Depression. 'The Paris Happiness', he called it.

Going to a brothel together will be fun. He was young, showing his youth. He did not realise that this was another test. Like her test on the Marne, when she deliberately capsized their rowing boat to assess how he would perform as a life-saver, with absolutely no regard for the cost of his new suit and favourite suede shoes.

She took him by the hand and led him. Somehow, she knew the way to 'Sodom on the Seine' as it was known. Over on the Left Bank. Or was at least following directions she had been given to the *Maisons de Tolerance*.

She had a place in mind. *Aux Belles Poules*. The Beautiful Hens. 32 Rue Blondel. This particular 'closed house' prided itself that it was *open* to men, and their mistresses, or indeed wives, as the case may be. Respectable females were not viewed as competition by *Les Sérieuses*; professionals do not suffer from the jealousy of amateurs.

"I want to see the *tableaux vivant*," she said. Inside the parlour of *Aux Belles Poules,* with lewd, rude, downright obscene mock-Roman frescoes splashed over every wall, she was not disappointed.

Ironic columns, jutting erect in a pastoral background, silvan glades of watery willows. On stage, there were six nude, voluptuous girls. Temple prostitutes, worshipping Inanna, led by a High Priestess here in Nature, her element.

The happy couple were shown to a table and sat down.

"How many times have you been to a brothel, Arturo?'" she asked.

Close to the mark. As always. She should be a journalist, not the Chief's secretary. He frowned. Decided: *mild indignation is the correct response, no words.*

"Oh, come on. You're a man of the world. It's 1929. Tell me."

"Once or twice." That was of course a lie. He had visited several of the more *serieuse* houses since his arrival in Paris. He had sampled the house speciality in *Le Chabanais*: a champagne bath with two *putes, à la* Edward VII. Troilisms were his cure for the Jerusalem Sadness, almost as much as falling in love with Bebe was.

"Liar."

"*Et tu?*" He smiled. "You seem to know the way here like the back of your hand."

"Yes. I bring all my men here. I tell them all it is my first time. Men love the idea of taking a virgin to a whorehouse. Actually, I work on commission for the house. This is how I supplement my income."

"I see. How entrepreneurial of you."

"So. Who are you most drawn to?"

He looked around, making a point of looking closely, lecherously—to see how she might react.

She snickered. "Pervert."

He pointed out a blonde. *Any blonde would do, to provoke her.* The choice of girl would not be his anyway. "She is attractive."

"I like her." She pointed to the dark-haired beauty centre-stage in the Temple *tableaux vivant*. The High Priestess herself. "Can we talk to her? See if she is fun."

It stirred him. *To think in a short space of time if things went well, he might be sharing a bed with Bebe and the High Priestess.*

He waved over a waitress.

The waitress came over. "What would sir like to drink?"

"Two glasses of champagne."

"Is it possible to speak to her?" She stood, and pointed.

"You have exquisite taste, *Mademoiselle*." The waitress laughed. "I will ask the High Priestess if she would care to join you. Then, I will bring your drinks over."

She winked. "I *do* have exquisite taste."

"In men. For certain." He leaned across and kissed her on the lips, playfully.

They both watched the waitress relay the request to the High Priestess, who looked over, a long, languorous stare, followed by a nod over in their direction.

The way the High Priestess sashayed to their table, the jiggle of her breasts, the sway of her hips was sexually mesmeric to him. It was no less than the Goddess descending to Earth. He felt it. That falling into love. That swoon he so craved.

Bebe was watching his response, intensely.

He did not see. Did not care. *Bebe has been erased. Bebe is just that. A baby. Whereas. This. This is a goddess.*

"Ahem." Bebe turned scarlet.

The High Priestess stopped, looked down at him, held out the back of her hand...

He bowed his head, to kiss it like a gentleman, but before his lips met skin, she pulled her hand away. "I believe *Mademoiselle* requested my presence. Not Monsieur." She sat down—beside Bebe.

They all laughed.

"Call me Lilit, *ma Cherie*." She took Bebe's hand and kissed it.

They laughed some more.

"Call me—Bebe."

A scream. A comedy sketch in the making. He laughingly desired them to be more than friends. *To force Bebe's head down, to lap at Lilit's nipples.*

"And does he have a name?" Lilit asked. "Your slave?"

"Yes. But it's not important."

The waitress returned with the champagne on a tray.

"I'll have a *crème de menthe*, Slave," Lilit said, smiling.

He tried to avoid staring at those perfect breasts. *Impossible.*

Bebe loved how Slave was being put in his place. "You do not like *les alcools*, Lilit?"

"Ah, no, Bebe," Lilit said. "They give me terrible indigestion."

"Yes. They do, don't they."

And so was launched a conversation of ingestions, digestions, congestions. Of diets. Of livers. Of stomach complaints. Bloating on champagne. It was incredibly intimate. The sort of confessional female chatter that he found irritating, entirely tedious, but he could-not-must-not show that if sex was to be forthcoming. "I have no problem with wine, beer or spirits," he quipped. "I'm an alcoholic."

They ignored him.

How very dare they!

Switched their conversation to the weather, then *haute couture*, then the exorbitant cost of living in Paris these days. 10 minutes slipped away in an intensity of throbbing want. He waved the waitress over and ordered a Remy Martin, a large one. "Am I drinking solo?"

"I haven't touched my drink, Arturo," Bebe said, and lifted her glass. "A sign of good company. *Santé*."

"*Santé*." Lilit raised her glass to her lips and sipped.

The redness of her lipstick flared, until it took over his vision and everything was blood. He sighed. "*Santé*."

Lilit switched the conversation: "What is it that you two *do*?"

"Journalism," Bebe stated. "I love it."

"It's not *real* journalism,' he said, all man-of-the-world. "We don't leave the office. We don't interview people in person. We don't report the news. We basically translate French news stories into German news stories."

"It is *real* journalism. We get to tell the truth," Bebe said. "I love writing the truth. I want to be a great novelist someday."

"I'm sure you will be." Lilit nodded. "And you, Arturo. You also have ambitions to be a great novelist?"

A shiver of delight, tingled all over his scalp. It was the first time Lilit had *directly* addressed him. "*Non. Ne rien.*" He shook his head. "Novelists write about the past. I am a journalist because I want to write about the Future with a capital F."

Lilit laughed scornfully. "So, you will be a *novel* kind of novelist? Yes. I can tell you will be. I can *read* your future."

Psychic as well. The waitress delivered the huge bulb of brandy and he gulped it down. His heart quickened to a sickening speed.

"Did you foresee that I am going write an article about meeting you Lilit?" asked Bebe.

"I did," Lilit replied. "That is why now we must talk about what I *do*."

And so—that was what they *did*.

They talked about having sex. As a profession. Arousal as a job. Orgasms as cash-in-hand. On the record. Bebe actually took her notebook out of her bag and scribbled Lilit's words down: *To make a man come quickly, finger his asshole.*

It hardened him, listening to Bebe being corrupted. To the point where he could not bear it any longer. He downed his remaining brandy in two hot gulps. "Now, beautiful ladies. I'd like to go to bed now." He tried to accompany this declaration with a roguish twinkle in his eyes.

They both turned to look at him. Bebe, staring daggers. But it was Lilit who spoke for them: "Ah, for that act, you should go home, Arturo —much happier than in this place."

"Yes, we should go home," Bebe said. "It's been a long day in the office, and he has a very early start tomorrow."

His humiliation was *not* complete. There was a long night ahead with Bebe. Back at his place. Circuitous questions about his intentions. Their sex was angry, if filthy, fingers-in-the-ass. *The attempt to repossess him, fucking like a whore. To make him hers again.* But she had lost him, and knew it, and it was horrible.

He however, did not realise what *he* had lost. When Bebe left in the morning, that was the end of them. They remained colleagues, but that was the end of the Paris Happiness. And there was no replacing it. Running on empty.

Substituting a fantasy for reality, he tried to find Lilit, exercise his lust. But was duly informed that the High Priestess no longer works at *Aux Belles Poules*. That news frankly broke his heart. He had to make do with some girls that *did* work there, for relief.

Desire returned. Daily, but it was subsumed into *being* a Newspaperman, confabulating the news—making up stories to distract the masses from their desires. Nightly, the search became a compulsion, the search for her. Every night, after his shift ended, he tried to find her in different Houses and, did not.

He took his fury out on the girls who were *not* her. Rough sex. Sadistic sex. Degrading *les putes*. Rapine misogyny, grown of one abject loss.

It did not matter what *he* wanted—they would *not* meet again, until, firestone-in-hand, he summoned her forth, and she took full possession of 8 Blackcross Crescent.

Burnt Offerings

"I'm not killing them," said Art. "We Brits aren't cold-blooded killers."

"I'll kill them, City-boy." Soph didn't bat an eyelid.

The Holy Land was a strange land; harsh, brash, violent, bloody. Israel disturbed him, because he was not used to living in the real world. Is-real. His inexperience of this reality made him feel small, stupid. Like a boy, all over again. Man, could he use an antidote: Is-Fantasy. The Flower of Dreams. The lucid dream of all-time, amen.

"Let's make chicken, people," Soph said.

Everyone headed out the back door. The coop was across the yard, right beside a poly-tunnel crammed full of tomato and weed plants. The hoppy reek wrinkled his nose; contrasting sharply with the ammonia reek of bird-shit.

Soph lifted the lid off a bin by the gate. Scooped a rush of yellow meal into her palm.

"I'll fire up the baby," said Estraya.

"If there is no fear, the cock won't get his dander up." Soph scattered the corn through the mesh fence into the coop.

The birds ran for the kernels.

Soph shook up a hemp sack. "I'll grab them."

"What do you want me to do?" he said.

"What men do—chase birds."

He shrugged. "I resemble that remark."

Soph lifted the latch. "Just be ready, they're quick."

He stood, ready. To chase.

Soph went in. "Here, chick-chick."

The red rooster, with long yellow legs, black glossy feathers in the chest and tail, raked the ground with its claws, pecking at the dirt.

He followed. Closed the gate behind him.

"Here chick-chick."

Hungry, brown hens came clucking out of the arched hole in the rickety hen-shed; the sides patched with the coloured lids of biscuit tins.

"Here chick-chick."

Warbling away, the hens swarmed over each other to get at the corn. Only the cock was watchful.

Soph pointed out her victim, on the edge of the flock, plump body, white flecked wing-tips. In one fell-swoop, she bagged it.

Small squawks of protest.

He did his best to chase birds, and they fluttered away, feathers ruffled.

With her back to the hens, Soph's hands closed round the rumpling body in the sack, fingers seeking out and stretching the neck, long and thin. Muffled distress.

A twist of fabric, a stretch of flesh, and it was over. As easy as that. One less beak to feed, and the birds were none the wiser, because they were at their pecking again.

"Two more, and we'll dine like kings," Soph said, pulling the corpse out of the sack, and handing it over.

He took a hold of the hen's spindly legs, slimy-black. "Yuck!"

"Take it to the kitchen," Soph said.

So, he backed out of the coop. Closed the gate. Ferried the dead bird into the kitchen. Laying it down on the table, the scrape of quills on rough wood.

Layla picked up the hen by the legs, and started ripping feathers out of the breast.

"Pluck-time. Auntie Cynth I need your help.'

Plucking, ewww! He washed his hands in the boxy Belfast sink, rolling the muciferous remains of a bar of soap through his fingers, slippery, suds spiralling down the plughole. "Tell me you don't want help, ladies?"

"Go be manly with the barby."

So, he went out, helped Estraya fire-up the gas barbecue.

It would heat up quickly. When the temperature hit 220 Fahrenheit, she laid some cobs of corn on the griddle to brown, fingers cautious of the hot metal. The juices dripped into the coals, hissing and evaporating.

Less than five minutes later, it was cooked, and everybody sat down to devour their barbecued, buttered corn. Wordlessly. It was that fucking good.

Soph only had to smile and Layla and Cynth would return to the kitchen, and feathers would fly.

"Dream-time."

Soph had a unique way of smoking: 'The Space Helmet'. It was constructed from an ancient album cover, U2's War, with blu-tack moulded around the hole in the corner. The pre-rolled joint was sealed into the hole with the blu-tack. "You ready for the trip of your life, psychonaut?"

"Hell-yeah." He put on the Space Helmet.

"Launch in T-minus-10, nine, eight, seven." Soph lit him up.

He drew a deep breath.

Four, three, two, one, blast-off: along a dark tunnel, into the brilliant white light of a hospital ward, with her waiting by his bedside, waiting ever-so-patiently, for the coma to end, his resurrection from the car crash. "My baby. My big baby, the biggest baby."

That was *her* pet-name for him!

Not Eva's.

Never Eva's.

Always, Lilit's.

Acknowledgments

If you enjoyed *Lilith's Baby*, it would be very kind of you to post a review on Amazon.

Pregnancy is a very weird, fevered, dreamlike experience. Especially, when looking back on it. Lilith came to almost embody my terror that I would lose my son, Gabriel, before he was born. He is eight years old now, past infancy, the time when Lilith seizes children, but my terror of her has not gone away, will never leave me, it seems. Living with Lilith is a daily part of me being a parent.

Thank you to all those who helped me wrestle Lilith 'Mother of All Demons' onto the page. It only took fifteen years. You know who you all are.

This novel has been adapted into a weekly, multi-voice Spotify podcast, *The Lilith Codex*, which will expand the cosmos, slow-burn, adding agents of darkness as we go.

My next novel, *The Dao of The Witch*, is available on Amazon.

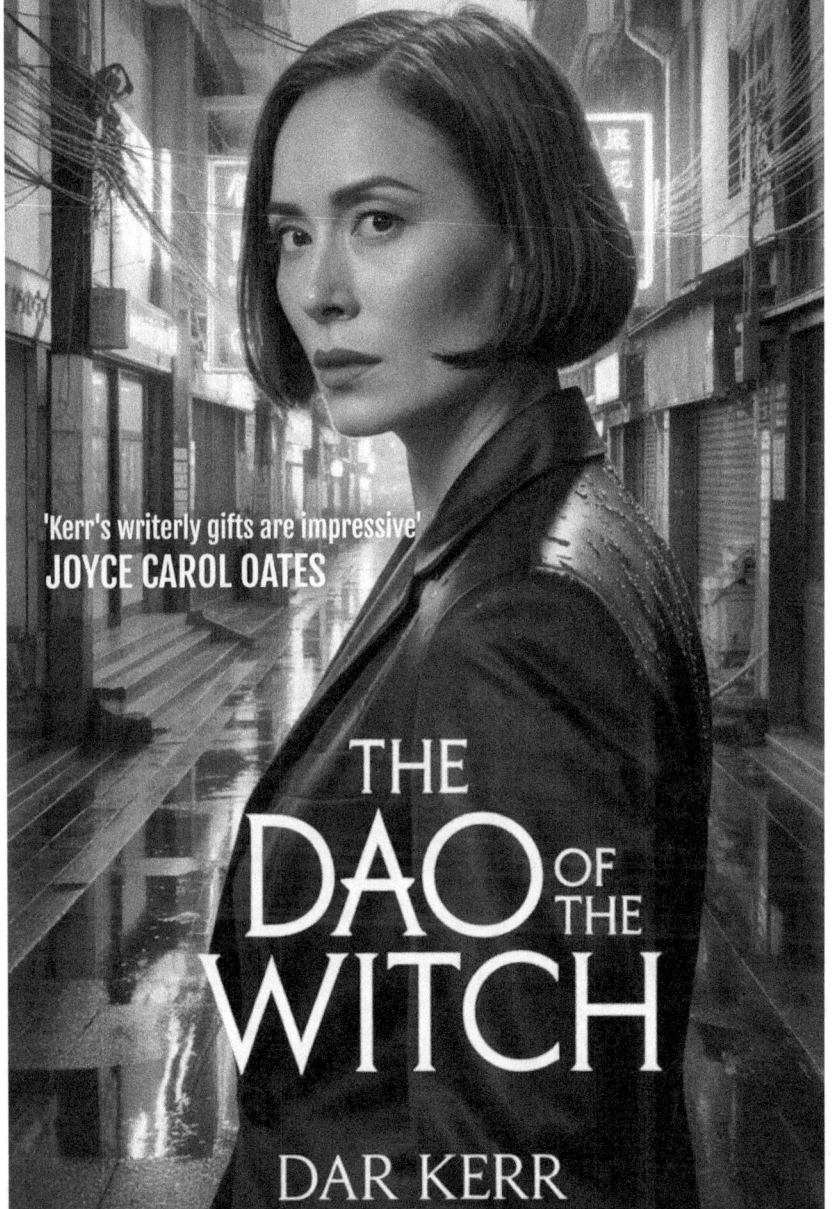

'Kerr's writerly gifts are impressive'
JOYCE CAROL OATES

THE
DAO OF THE
WITCH

DAR KERR

www.ingramcontent.com/pod-product-compliance
Lightning Source LLC
Chambersburg PA
CBHW070851260626
47170CB00007B/2578